• BALDWIN'S LEGACY BOOK THREE •

CULMINATION

NATHAN HYSTAD

Cover art: Tom Edwards Design

Edited by: Scarlett R Algee

Proofed and Formatted by: BZ Hercules

ISBN-13: 9798617716155

Also By Nathan Hystad

The Survivors Series
The Event
New Threat
New World
The Ancients
The Theos
Old Enemy
New Alliance
The Gatekeepers
New Horizon
The Academy
Old World
New Discovery
Old Secrets

The Resistance
Rift
Return
Revenge

Baldwin's Legacy
Confrontation
Unification
Culmination

The Manuscript
Red Creek
Return to Red Creek
Lights Over Cloud Lake

PROLOGUE

The breeze against Ina's face was refreshing. She closed her eyes, the hot sun beating down on her cheeks, the rays comforting rather than invasive. Ina spent most of her life underground, but was grateful to have been on surface duty for the last few weeks.

Others dreaded the endless chores, but she appreciated the time working here more than most. Living below had never felt right to her, as if it went in objection to her basic needs. Not many agreed with her on the subject, so she kept her thoughts to herself.

Her hair was trimmed short; choppy thick strands stuck up at all angles, and she ran a dirty hand through it as she soaked up the sunlight.

"Break isn't for another two hours, Ina. You better hope they don't catch you slacking like this," Carl said, bumping her as he walked by with an armful of moss.

"I was just feeling the wind," she said softly, crouching to pick up her latest load of the soft green substance. It was damp along her forearms, and she smiled to herself at the stolen moment of peace that was now over.

"I don't care what you were doing. If you don't want to feel the whip, you'd better cut it out," Carl said, glancing at her as he moved toward the gathering pile. Their task was nearly completed, which meant they'd be leaving the surface, not to return for months.

Over the years, she'd made it her mission to steal bits

of time where she could, fractions of minutes here and there. Ina worked hard, perhaps harder than most, and she thought this allowed her the ability to enjoy herself on occasion. No one cared. The Adepts never bothered her about it; only the other people in her Group complained.

They all knew she was favored over them, and they sought to knock her down where they could. Ina didn't care. None of this was the way it should be. Humans shouldn't live below the ground, nor should any of the other races in her Group.

She walked to the stack of moss, dropping her load at the edge. She wiped her hands on her pants and watched as the other hundred people finished their task.

"Good work, Group," Nadin said, her yellow eyes enhanced in the sunlight. "Since we have finished early, we can head below. Once we have the carts loaded." Nadin was a small woman, her nose pinched, her mouth always tight-lipped, making her appear angry – which she often was.

Carl stood beside Ina, and she watched as his gaze drifted to the fields far beyond their Group. She followed along, seeing the huge metal object rising into the sky. It was hideous, yet beautiful. Arms stretched wide, at least ten of them, jutting from the center of the ship. It was rare to catch a glimpse of the Adepts' vessels, and she almost felt special today. What were they doing? Where did they go while the Groups remained below ground?

She'd never been on one, but she'd heard the old stories, as most of the Group had at one point in their lives. Ina was third generation, but she held her mother's spirit close to her heart. As Ina watched the vessel roar into the air, continuing as it lifted through the atmosphere, she thought about her mother's whispered words late at night.

This isn't our way. You're human, Ina. Your grandfather was from Earon, a lieutenant in the War, the same War that ended with him captured. We are slaves. Don't forget it. Never forget it.

Ina had been so young, confused by the hushed ranting, but she'd promised she'd defy them, to fight where she could, and that was why Ina took her little breaks. Tiny infractions to let the Adepts realize not everyone could be indoctrinated by their lies. Her mother had been taken a week later, along with fifty others. That was the way of the Adepts.

Most of her Group had forgotten the old ways. Few remained from the second generation, with the exception of the elders like Nadin, and they showed no signs of passing on lessons from the first generation: the ones that had been taken in the War so long ago.

Carl grunted as he closed the cages around the collection of moss, and Ina helped him power up the controller. He passed it to her, and she used the lever to direct the cart toward the opening in the ground. A lift arrived, and Nadin motioned her to drive the load to its destination.

Soon Ina was heading below the surface, the heat of the sun, the gentle breeze a distant memory that she'd cling to until the next time she was chosen for work duty. She wished she could volunteer to take someone's spot, but they weren't allowed to swap roles. It was forbidden.

A tall thin man met them below, his eyes hollow, his skin pallid. "Leave the cart. You are to head to Five." His voice croaked like he hadn't spoken in days.

Ina's heart raced with an instant flash of fear. Five. That was where her mother had gone so many years ago. That was where they all went, with no hope of returning.

"It's our time," Carl said, a shimmer of indignation across his face.

Ina saw it now. They were slaves, pitiful and beaten. Whatever the Adepts wanted with them, it had something to do with the War. For fifty years, her people had been forced to live here, to feed themselves, to manufacture clothing, to build ships for the Adepts, to procreate, so their population would grow.

Ina could hardly feel a thing as she plodded through the corridor at the front of the line. All one hundred of her Group were moving toward Five, and she nearly turned as they neared the exit for Two. That was their home, the massive city, giving them residence and so much more. It wasn't a bad place to inhabit, but after feeling the sun on her face, painfully aware she wouldn't see it for months on end again, she was almost ready for the next step. Perhaps her mother was still in Five. Maybe this was the start of her new life, one she could finally be happy with.

Judging by the expressions on the rest of the Group's faces, they didn't think so. Whispered rumors claimed it was the end of the line. The people that had served their purpose were moved there, never to be seen again. Once, Ina had heard a man mention a device the Adepts used to wipe the minds of the Groups. Then they were put into armor and transferred to one of the huge ugly vessels.

Was Ina going to suffer the same fate? Was her mother alive on one of the ships, drifting through space with no memory of Ina or her previous life? At least she would discover what it was all about. She wouldn't have to speculate on what her existence meant any longer.

The corridors had always felt homey, bright and tall, but as she strode onwards, past Three, then Four, they were shrinking around her. Her legs were already aching from a hard day's work, and others were protesting as they moved toward Five. The exit was unassuming, the same as the others: a giant metal doorway, this one with dents on the outside. Ina pictured a previous Group fighting back before being pressed through the entrance. She glanced to the floor, half-expecting to see blood stains, but the surface was clean, nearly immaculate.

"What do you think is on the other side?" Carl had found her, and he stared forward, eyes unblinking.

"Our deaths," Ina said softly.

There were none of the Adepts here, only their Group. Nadin led them, taking orders from whoever had left the instructions.

"I'm ready," Carl said.

"I'm not. We don't have to do this," Ina said, her voice rising in volume. "There can be another way. None of the Adepts are here. We can keep going."

"Five is the end of the line," Nadin said, frowning.

Ina's cheeks swelled as she inhaled a lungful of recycled air. "Why do you say that? Because *they* told you so? Look" – Ina pointed down the corridor, where the path continued – "there's more here. Perhaps our salvation lies beyond."

Nadin shook her head. "Wrong, child." She pulled out a weapon tucked into the back of her pants. Ina had never seen the woman armed before, and she stepped away. The door opened, and out came five of the Adepts, their dark exoskeletons ominous and intimidating as they waved weapons around. Their mandibles clicked in anger, and Ina hid among the rest of her people.

Her rush of rebellion was washed away in cold sweat as she watched the Adepts motion her people through the door and into Five. She kept her head down, trying not to lock gazes with any of the Adepts. It worked, and soon she was out of the corridor and into the mysterious section of their underground home.

The space was wide open, a massive courtyard with hundred-foot-tall ceilings, and she peered up to see dozens of the Adepts leaning over balconies, wearing dark robes, and they chanted as the people were urged into the area.

The door labeled "Five" slammed shut, sealing them in. The sound might as well have been the snapping of a rope around her neck. The rest of her people – some Tekol, Callalay, Zilph'i, and human – stood frozen, gawking at the Adepts chanting around them.

"This can't be good," Carl said from beside Ina.

She only shook her head, unable to find words. The lights dimmed, and her captors grew quiet as one of the Adepts walked from the far end of the room toward the one hundred newly-arrived people.

His robes were long; two young Adepts trailed behind him, struggling to keep the fringes of cloth off the floor. He was tall, wider than most of the others, and Ina guessed he was older. His eyes were rheumy, his mandibles a lighter shade of gray than his counterparts'.

Ina heard Carl's shallow breathing as the entire gathered courtyard waited for the man to speak. His mandibles clicked together, chattering in their language, which Ina and the others all understood after so long in their presence.

"Welcome, children. You have been selected for a great honor. We're thrust into another war and expect our enemies to arrive soon. We aren't positive when, but we will be ready for them. The Concord has long been a stain on the canvas of our universe. We're instructed to destroy them, and once we do, enlightenment will finally be upon us," he said, and the chanting began in earnest. He lifted a hand, the harmonized tones ceasing. "You one hundred have the honor no other of your kind will attain."

Ina waited for it, leaning forward slightly. How many of them had passed through these doors before her? She suspected thousands.

"War is coming, my children. And you are going to help us win once and for all."

The Adept stared directly at Ina, and the last shred of hope vanished within her as his dark deadly eyes remained unblinking.

ONE

Tom ran as fast as he could, swinging his racket right on time. The glowing ball buzzed as it raced away from him, and he jammed his shoulder into the wall, unable to avoid it at the last minute. He stayed there panting as he watched Brax fail to return the volley. The big Tekol leaned over as the score changed along the wall.

They were tied up. "Captain, I know I agreed to take it easy on you, but the least you could have done was tell me you were this good." Brax's words came out in between gasping breaths and pants.

Tom straightened, testing his shoulder. Not injured. That was a relief. "Brax, if I told everyone I was trained by a four-time Vulti champion, no one would play with me."

Brax stared at him, shaking his head. "You were trained by Bull Hendle? You have to be kidding me. It must have been nice growing up with unlimited resources."

Tom shrugged and waited for Brax to pass the glowing ball over to him. The game was quite simple. There was a barrier in the center of the court; the walls were fair game. All you had to do was hit the three surfaces before the ball was returned, and you gained a point. It didn't matter whether you bounced it from ceiling to rear wall to floor, as long as all three were on your opponent's side of the court.

"In case you haven't noticed, we're tied up, Brax. It seems his lessons only went so far," Tom said, bouncing the ball on his racket. Blue beams of energy stretched over the square paddle.

"I got lucky a few times. Remind me to invite Tarlen next time instead," Brax told him.

"I've given the boy a few lessons. I think he'll be pretty good."

"Of course he will be," Brax muttered.

It was common knowledge that Brax considered himself a slow learner, someone that had to work twice as hard to attain his position, but after knowing the Tekol chief of security for a few months, Tom didn't doubt the man's intelligence and perseverance one bit.

Tom was about to serve when *Constantine*'s AI appeared at the center of the court. "Captain, your presence has been requested by one of the prisoners. Again."

"Tell him I'm busy," Tom said, trying to not let himself be goaded by the bastard.

"You misunderstand, sir. It's Seda Keen that wants a word with you," Constantine said.

Seda Keen. The surname attached to her made Tom grip the racket tighter. "She's asked for me before?"

"Several times, but I didn't think you were interested in speaking with the prisoners."

"Why's that?" Tom asked him.

"Because you specifically told me you weren't interested in talking with any of the prisoners," Constantine said, a slight wry grin on his face.

"Fine. Tell her I'll be there in a while. I have a match to win first." Tom watched as Constantine gave a curt nod and vanished.

"What's that about? Think she's going to try to offer

you something for her freedom?" Brax asked.

Tom hadn't told the others about his previous relationship with Seda. It had been ages prior, not much more than an innocent tryst that had ended with her running away with Lark Keen, his best friend. Tom hated the Assembly and all they stood for.

"I have no idea. I guess I'll find out," he said. "Ready to lose?"

Brax seemed to consider this, but he shook his head, beads of sweat dripping off his forehead. "I don't think so, Captain."

"Good." Tom served, and Brax returned a high shot, hitting the top right corner behind Tom. He lunged, knocking the ball off the side wall directly at Brax, who narrowly stepped away from it, returning it with a weak backhand.

Tom's knees protested as he darted toward center court, taking a long backswing. It worked. Brax was moving in reverse, preparing for a hard shot, and Tom tapped the ball upwards. It hit the ceiling and then the wall as the ball spun, landing precisely on the right side of the hip-high energy barrier that separated the two players.

Brax groaned as Tom's score changed and flashed bright yellow. Victory was his.

"Next time, I won't take it so easy on you. I don't care if you're my captain or not." Brax headed to the side of the court, setting his racket down.

Tom picked up a towel, hanging it over his damp hair. "You did well, Brax. A worthy adversary. You realize what this means, though, right?"

Brax wiped his face with a towel and shook his head. "No."

"It means we now have a standing weekly match. It's invigorating that I have some competition on this ship."

Tom patted Brax on the shoulder as they walked out of the facility and towards the change room. He'd been thrilled to learn they'd added a Vulti court on *Constantine,* and he was glad to make use of it finally. The old man had loved the sport when he'd been younger and had continued to play in his advanced years, albeit not often with Tom.

Tom recalled beating his grandfather for the first time, Constantine angrily tossing his racket as the last point settled on the scoreboard. He'd refused to play Tom again, always making an excuse, but never admitting Tom was the better player.

"I'll be glad to have a chance at redemption." Brax moved into the change room and sat on the bench. "Captain, have you been sent the location for Keen's future home?"

"Not yet. Admiral Benitor decided it would be best to wait until we've offloaded the prisoners and his wife before we're sent the coordinates." Tom headed into the steamer, kicking his shorts off once behind the barrier. The nozzles hissed, sending warm steam over him, soothing his muscles and cleaning him at the same time.

"I wonder how many of these covert prisons there are around the Concord."

"Probably more than we'd like to be aware of. Keen is going somewhere no one will ever find him," Tom said with confidence.

"Let's hope. Do you think we'll see the Assembly again?" They'd been over this before, but he didn't blame Brax for inquiring. The man felt solely responsible for letting Zare and Yur Shen walk freely onboard *Constantine.* He'd run far more diligent screening since the coronation, and with Tom's blessing, had removed ten members from the crew. There was no way to confirm if they were undercover Assembly, but their files each held something in them that made his chief of security wary. Tom figured it was better to be safe than sorry.

"I doubt we've seen the last of the Assembly. Remember when we thought the Statu were done with? Things have a way of returning when you least expect them," Tom said, reminding him of his upcoming meeting with Seda. He'd purposely avoided talking with her since all of this had transpired, but it would be good for him to get it over with so he could move on.

"Sir, you have that look on your face. Is everything okay?" Brax asked.

Tom dried off, dressing as he assured his lieutenant commander that he was fine.

"If you say so. Have you had a chance to speak with Ven yet?" Brax dressed and nodded to two other crew members changing for their turn at a match of Vulti.

Tom waited until the two men were out of the change room, and lowered his voice. "Not really. I've only seen him on the bridge and haven't made time to check in on him. How about you?"

Brax led the way into the corridor, and Tom noticed how good it felt to challenge himself like that. He was tired, but in the best sense of the word.

Brax stopped when there was no one else around and leaned in. "I haven't spoken to him, either. He's…"

"Different?" Tom asked. He knew exactly what Brax meant.

"He was always different, but now he's reclusive. Have you seen his eyes?"

"They're darker."

"So's his skin. I swear it. What do you think it's all about?" Brax asked, worry etched on his forehead.

"It's hard to say. The Ugna maintain complete discretion, even more so than we'd thought. I'll make sure I speak with him, confirm he's in good health and sound mind. Does that take some weight off your shoulders?" Tom asked.

Brax breathed deeply, letting out a sigh as they continued toward the courtyard. "He did save my life out there."

"Indeed. He's a good officer. He helped me solidify our relationship with the Ugna. I doubt we'd have them as partners now if it wasn't for Ven," Tom told him.

They entered the courtyard, Tom admiring the sight of his crew mingling inside. The plants were lush and thick, the air humid and comforting in the center of the cruise ship. He hadn't spent enough time here and wanted to remedy that. Even when he was off shift, he was continuously disrupted, dealing with the issues and needs of the new teams.

Ven was the chief of crew, but because of circumstances, Tom had let him slack in the role. It was time the Ugna man took the reins, mostly because Tom didn't want to deal with the subordinates any longer.

"I'm going to grab a water and check on my staff," Brax said.

"Have you had a chance to name your second?" Tom asked.

Brax grunted: a clear indication he hadn't. "Not quite, but I will soon. I'm sorry I haven't done it yet."

"You've hardly been on board." Tom gave him a smile.

"And that's why you need someone capable to fill my shoes while I'm on a mission... or kidnapped." Brax grinned at him. "I'll see you on the bridge in a few hours?"

"See you then, Lieutenant Commander."

Brax turned, walking away and leaving Tom alone in the courtyard. Seda wasn't on *Constantine*. He didn't want Lark Keen's wife and child on the same ship as the terrorist, for many reasons, so he'd have to make the trek to *Andron*.

They'd moved out of hyperlight several hours ago as they were nearing their first stop. Zovlip was gone, destroyed by all reports, but it wasn't up to *Constantine* to be the first responder. Admiral Jalin Benitor had assured Tom that they were sending another cruise ship, along with three Ugna vessels to investigate the annihilation of the distant world.

Zovlip had been sparsely populated, but it was on the list of potential planets for the Ugna to colonize. Regardless, an entire planet being destroyed was a rare occurrence, and they needed to uncover what had caused it before it was duplicated. Next time, it might be a major world, teeming with people.

Tom glanced out the viewer along the side of the courtyard and imagined they were only an hour from their destination. Bolux Nine was as large a prison as the Concord had. It was infamous among their ranks, and even now, there were a couple of high-ranking admirals behind the bars as news of corruption had come to fruition months ago. He didn't love the idea of mixing Assembly zealots with disgruntled former admirals, but he'd been assured the two sides would never speak on the planet. An entire world of prisoners. It made Tom's skin itch.

Tom stared at space, the stars distant, an assortment of hazy blue and burnt yellow. The entire system they headed to was inhospitable. What better place to detain the Concord's worst? He almost forgot of his impending meeting with Seda as he watched the stars.

He started for the elevator and remembered how

much Seda had loved fruity drinks. He suspected she still did, and he stopped at the bar along the far wall, a Servo-Bot whirring over to him. Tom placed an order for three blended Zilph'i drinks and carried them toward the hangar on a tray. He wasn't looking forward to the interaction, but maybe she'd be more forthright if he bribed her and Luci with something sweet.

---

*T*reena Starling was in charge. When she'd first stepped foot on this bridge a few short months ago, she'd had the very human urge to throw up. Now she was confident in the role, in her new body. Most of the crew were aware she wasn't human any longer, or at least that her vessel wasn't, but no one seemed to treat her differently. After her work with Tarlen to save the day, and their entire ship, they all spoke to her with a respectful deference she hadn't noticed before. She found it refreshing.

Treena stood from her commander's seat and stretched out of habit. They'd been sitting for hours, and their destination was nearly at hand. It had taken five days in hyperlight to access Bolux Nine, and she was happy to finally be here. Once they offloaded the prisoners, they could keep moving, dropping off Keen and finally returning to Earon.

Treena was a little nervous about heading home. Her mother was there, which was great, but she hadn't spent real time on her old home planet for years. Part of her was excited at the prospect of visiting her old town, and Baldwin had promised everyone a few days while they were there. At least eighty of their crew had family on or had once lived on Earon, so it was imperative they had a chance to visit their loved ones. Plus, they'd been through a lot, so the crew needed a brief respite once they'd managed to complete all their tasks, which started with Bolux Nine.

"Zoom on the planet," Treena said, and the acting helmsman obeyed in seconds. The world was small, a cool icy blue hue, matching the feeling of desolation the entire system held. There were dozens of fortifications spread around the world, and the members of the Assembly were to be sprinkled among them.

Tarlen was in Zare's old seat, and Treena smiled as she saw him furrow his brow as his console blinked. She moved behind him and tapped the proper icon. "It's a communication. You press this to reply and place it on the viewer."

He glanced up, clearly embarrassed he didn't know this, and apologized. "Sorry, Commander. I'll do better next time."

She squeezed his shoulder and walked to the center of the bridge. A tiny man faced her from the screen, his hands behind his back. He wore oversized spectacles that appeared far too heavy for his slender head.

"Where is Captain Baldwin?" the man asked with a pinched voice.

"This is Commander Treena Starling. I'm in charge at the moment," she told him. Treena didn't know where Captain Baldwin was, but part of her role was to handle jobs like this one, and she didn't think Thomas needed the headache.

"Very well. I'm Warden Minhaus. Welcome to Bolux Nine. The land of dreams," he said, smiling widely. His yellowed teeth were crooked, and he chuckled as if he'd made the universe's best joke. "I'm sorry. It gets a laugh half of the time."

"How do you want to handle the prisoner transfer?" Treena asked.

"I see you have quite the fleet for a few measly rabble-rousers." The warden squinted behind his spectacles.

Treena didn't like the casual way he referred to their captives. "They've killed a lot of people, Warden Minhaus. They would have destroyed us if they'd been able. Their leader sought control of the Concord. I think you'd do well not to underestimate the Assembly."

"I assure you, Commander, once we have them in our possession, there is nothing to fear. Where are the prisoners now?" he asked.

"They're located on two of the legacy cruise ships, *Persi* and *Remie*."

"And how are they taking it?" he asked, no longer smiling.

"They're locked into the hangars and mess halls, with a dozen guards on each ship," she advised.

"Good. We'll send transports to you, load the prisoners, and bring them to the surface," Warden Minhaus said.

Treena hadn't been expecting that. She'd suspected they'd be responsible for shuttling the lot of them onto the planet. "That will work just fine. I would like to see the facilities first, though." Baldwin had been skeptical of leaving so many of the Assembly in one place, even if it was spread around the world. It was reasonable to ensure peace of mind that they weren't going anywhere before *Constantine* continued their multi-step mission.

The warden appeared confused by the request. "You... want to see my prisons?"

"That's correct. Can you arrange a tour?" Treena tried to get a read on the man. He didn't appear to want their company, but he didn't have a choice. They'd shown up with a Concord flagship, three retired fleet vessels, and an Ugna escort. *Triumph* was a few thousand kilometers behind them, keeping watch. Captain Vat was adamant about escorting them, and Baldwin had accepted with open arms.

"This is unorthodox, but we can give you a tour of my prison. It's the biggest and best in the Concord, I can assure you that," he said, his teeth flashing again. Treena was unsettled by the man's appearance, and she wasn't certain if he was human or something else entirely. It was hard to tell from the viewer image alone.

"We'll be there in a standard hour. Please send coordinates, and prepare for our arrival," Treena told the warden, who only nodded once before the screen went dark, replaced once again by the distant image of the planet and star beyond.

"That was strange," Tarlen said.

Treena didn't want to judge the warden too quickly. "I doubt he gets much company. Tarlen, do you want to see a prison?"

The Bacal's grin was answer enough.

---

*T*he box rose, dipped in the air, and spun as Ven concentrated on it. He was better than ever before. Somehow his death, or near-death, had unlocked closed-off veins of Talent in his body and mind. He eyed the En'or on his nightstand but left it sitting there. He hadn't taken any since he'd been with Elder Fayle on Leria, yet here he was, using his Talent as though he'd recently ingested a fresh vial.

He'd always wondered about the final ritual many of

"Yes. Yes, it's a good thing. Someone has to do it." The gate was unlocked, and the warden opened the door, letting two drones on board. They were fist-sized, and floated through the bus, stopping to scan each of them one at a time. When they departed, the warden stood.

"It's a good thing they didn't find anything illegal on you." The warden stood, exiting the bus.

Treena followed him, asking the logical. "Why's that?"

"Because they would have vaporized you."

Treena turned to glance at Brax, who was carrying a gun. "What about his weapon?"

Minhaus waved a dismissive hand. "There are drones everywhere. They'd kill him before he could fire it." They were inside the walls here, safe from the freezing cold and snow, but she still caught Ven chattering beside her.

"You good?" she asked the mysterious Ugna.

"I am well," he replied.

She hadn't found an opportunity to connect with the man, but since he'd been deemed dead, then returned to *Constantine*, he'd been even more isolated than ever. Treena vowed to change their relationship.

"This way." The warden opened a door, and they entered a well-lit corridor. The walls were the same dark stone, the sheer volume of lights making up for the underground feeling. "As I was saying, Cliffside boasts two hundred and eleven of the most deadly and notorious masterminds the Concord has ever had the displeasure of meeting. They are responsible for at least a combined ten million deaths, and countless other appalling deeds."

The corridor ended, and Minhaus paused, staring into each of their eyes from beyond his oversized spectacles. "Are you ready for this?" he asked.

Treena didn't like the showmanship he was putting

on. Only Tarlen seemed into it, and he nodded vehement-
ly.

Minhaus entered a code onto a keypad, and the door
slid open. "I give you...Cliffside."

———————

Reeve was left alone back on *Constantine* again. She
didn't mind, though. By all accounts, the world below was
a dreadful one, and she had no interest in wandering
around a building full of horrible people any more than
she wanted to fend off the Assembly again.

The bridge was quiet, the second-shift crew surrounding her. She liked them well enough, but she'd been bored
sitting there for the last few hours with nothing to do.
Reeve preferred tinkering away in the boiler room.
Yephion had sent her the latest work-throughs on the
wormhole generators, and Reeve had been toying with
the parameters, content that they were on the right track.

According to Admiral Jalin Benitor, that meant war.
Reeve feared returning to the Statu system and hoped
they had more time before it happened. She'd heard
promises of a bigger Concord fleet, but had yet to see any
more of the newly-designed flagships. Having the Ugna
would be an asset, as long as they obeyed orders. Captain
Wan of *Faithful* hadn't, resulting in his and his crew's
deaths, thanks to Lark Keen and his cronies.

Those people all deserved their sentences; of that
Reeve was sure. "Hurry up," she whispered to herself,
directing the comment at the captain and commander.
Baldwin was escorting Seda and Luci to some unknown
destination, which had really upset Brax and Treena to no
end. He'd assured them he'd be fine, but no one wanted

the captain of the ship to put himself at risk. Still, it had been the Prime's mandate, so they didn't object too hard.

Lieutenant Darl was whistling as he sat at ready from his helm posting in Ven's usual seat, and it took all Reeve's energy to not throw something at the man. "Darl," she said, needing to distract him and herself, "any signs of incoming traffic?"

Darl tapped the screen a few times and shook his head. "Nothing, ma'am."

Ma'am. She'd always hated being called that. "Are there any objects nearby that would be large enough to hide behind?" Reeve stood, stretching her legs. She'd been spending too many hours at a desk. She needed to get some exercise, maybe play a Vulti match with her brother. He always beat her, but at least she sweated like hell when they played.

"Hide behind?"

"Yeah. Hide behind. A rock, a planetoid, a moon."

"Are you planning on hiding us?" Darl asked.

She bit her tongue. *Be nice, Reeve. He's not asking you anything stupid.* "Just check, Lieutenant."

He ran a few scans, and the viewer showed his results. "There are at least three objects within fifty thousand kilometers that could house a vessel cruiser-sized or smaller."

Reeve considered this. Since she had nothing else to do, she kept going. "Okay, send probes to all three." She stared at the zoomed images of the debris. One appeared to be a piece of an old vessel, floating lifelessly in space. One was a below-average moon orbiting the ice world. It was the closest to them. The last was a misshapen hunk of rock, and it was drifting away from them quite slowly.

"Probes dispatched." Darl turned and grinned at her. "Anything else you'd like me to do, ma'am?"

She glowered at him. She really wished someone else was in charge of the bridge.

THREE

*T*om didn't expect a lot of resistance from Seda, but even if she didn't have a weapon, he assumed she was trained to fight in some manner or another. She was still in shape, and he'd placed energy tethers on her arms to detain her as he piloted *Cleo* toward his destination.

Luci sat beside him, staring through the viewer. "Where are we going?" she asked in a tiny voice.

"To your new home," Tom told her.

"What do you mean?"

"You and your mommy are going to live here for a while," Tom said. He almost wished he'd tied her up and left her out back too.

"I miss Daddy," she whined.

"I know you do."

"Where is he?"

Tom didn't have the heart to lie to the small child. "Your father did some bad things. He tried to hurt people, so he's been sent away."

"Did I do something bad too?" Luci asked.

Tom just wanted to get this over with and return to his ship. "No, honey. You didn't."

"Then why am I being sent away?"

He chose not to answer any more of her queries, and directed *Cleo* through the falling snow. The lights were on below, a blinking beacon on top of the home prepared for Seda's arrival. No one knew who was visiting the remote building, and bots had been dispatched to prepare it a couple days ago, rather than the warden's people.

Cleo landed, Tom parking as close to the metal structure as he could. It looked as miserable as he felt outside. He powered the ship down, unclipped the PL-30 at his hip, and told Luci to follow him. He passed her a cloak and waited as she wrapped it over her shoulders.

"Seda, we're here," he said, heading to the cargo hold. She glared at him with hard eyes, and he deactivated her tethers. "Keep this cordial, and you and your daughter can be with each other a long time. Who knows when the Prime will offer you a bargain?"

"I don't imagine that's happening any time soon," she said with a cutting edge. "I don't blame you for this, Tom, but that doesn't mean I have to be happy about it."

"I know," was all he said in reply.

Tom lowered the ramp and passed a crate of supplies to Seda. "Take this. Something a little extra." It was full of games they could play together, and some old Zilph'i texts, but he didn't tell her the contents. She finally gave him a faint smile and took the offered crate.

Luci stretched her arms out, wanting to help, but Tom only patted her head. "Off we go."

The wind blew in snow, and soon the lower half of the ramp was covered in white fluffy cold stuff. Tom had never liked the snow. On Nolix, it was a rare sight, but he'd visited enough places with freezing seasons to develop a distaste for it. Earon had lots of regions where they frequently saw inclement weather like this, and he was glad he hadn't grown up there.

The building they were heading to was squat; a flashing light on the top shut off as he reached the front door. Tom pressed the keypad, not needing a code for admittance, and he waited for the two captives to enter before him. He didn't see any windows from inside, but the lights slowly rose in brightness at their arrival.

It appeared like any house. There was seating, a table on the right edge, and all the cooking equipment Seda would need to survive. Tom guessed there was a bathroom down the hall and bedrooms beyond.

He took them on a brief tour, his gun in his hand as he swept the rooms, ensuring there weren't any Assembly surprises waiting for him. When he was confident they were alone in the remote dwelling, he moved for the doorway.

Seda was already searching through the cabinets, and Tom saw they were stocked with various food products, and there was clothing in the closets. Luci watched it all with the enthusiasm of a small child, and she'd seemed to forget that they were separated from her father.

"What am I supposed to do here, Tom?" Seda asked softly.

"Live your life," he said.

"In here? It's a prison."

"Yes, it is. And you deserve worse." Things would have ended a lot differently if Tarlen hadn't come upon his little hostage.

"I do deserve it. I've done awful things for the cause, but think of the child. Take her," Seda said calmly.

"Take her? I can't do that." He glanced at Luci, her big eyes staring up at him.

"Yes, you can. Bring her, Tom. She's not evil. She's a little girl. You can teach her to hate me, I don't care; just give her the chance to grow up in a better place," Seda said. "You can't let my little girl rot away here."

Luci was crying now, as if she understood the complexities of what her mother was begging Tom to do.

Seda grabbed the girl, pulling her close. She stroked her blonde hair, telling her how much she loved her. Tom couldn't watch.

He considered the options and hated each possible outcome.

He turned to leave and felt the tiny hand grip his.

———

*T*arlen had never been more exhilarated yet terrified in his life. Sure, he'd been scared a lot since the Tubers had lowered to Malin, destroying his home city and altering the course of his life forever, but this was a new kind of lingering fear.

Behind the thick walls and energy bars were dozens of angry prisoners, who wouldn't think twice about ending his life. They walked down the hall, the warden stopping every few cells to discuss the occupant behind the bars.

The floors were dark stone here, and Tarlen thought that he saw bloodstains all around it. Some of them were probably soaked in it years before he was born. From the outside, he'd thought it would be fun to tour, but once the doors shut on them, sealing them inside, he hadn't been able to stop shaking.

"What do you think, Tarlen?" Brax asked him, nodding to the blob in the room they faced. The lights were on, but dim, and he could hardly make out the creature in the shadows. A pool of water separated the bars and the being, the light reflecting off the rippling surface.

"It's interesting, I suppose," Tarlen lied.

"Interesting? This is horrible," the Tekol said. "I don't know about you, but I've wanted to leave since I arrived. I've heard the stories about these prisoners. I was obsessed with saving the universe when I was bright-eyed and about your age. Can you believe I read about this guy in here?"

"No. What did he do?" Tarlen asked, his curiosity piqued.

"He's a Wrooplan, from over near Inprinx. They're water beings. Mostly a civil bunch. Live partly on land, mainly underwater. This sadistic one poisoned an entire village. Nothing even remotely like it had happened among the Wrooplan in their history, and here he was, killing ten thousand or so of his people." Brax and Tarlen were trailing behind the group, the sound of the warden's voice shrinking as they moved farther away.

Tarlen could see the outline of the Wrooplan now, and it began moving from the shadows.

"When he was asked why he did it, he told them it was to hear their spirits drowning," Brax said, and Tarlen felt the goosebumps rise on his arms.

The creature was husky. Fat layers covered its bare torso; the arms were short and chubby, its face a pale gray. Clumpy whiskers shot from the top of his head, and his eyes were black as midnight and menacing as he stared at Tarlen before slipping into the water.

"Let's get out of here." Tarlen tugged Brax's arm and led him away.

"I don't blame you. He made my skin crawl too," Brax said.

Tarlen stopped peering into the cells as they went, and the warden eventually guided them into the center of the prison. The ceiling was clear glass, snow melting as it hit the surface. Tarlen gawked up at the perfect view of the cliff wall of smooth ice. It was beautiful, in an ominous sort of way. He thought Belna would have appreciated it.

He missed her already, and he'd only left her side a few hours ago. Ever since Doctor Nee had managed to get her talking, Tarlen had been in a better mood. She could move around a bit, mostly on instinct, and she swore the bodily functions weren't under her control. She communicated through a speaker, the same technology as Treena's real body had, but Nee was confident he'd find a way to merge her neural pathways with her motor controls and return some of the real Belna to the surface.

Tarlen could only hope so, but Belna seemed in better a state of mind than he would have been if their roles were reversed. She was trapped in her own body. They'd considered whether she could control an artificial body like Treena's, but Captain Baldwin had been told there weren't enough resources to give a random Bacal girl such a valuable asset.

"Welcome to Cliffside's central command," the warden said, his small eyes glinting as he waved his arm in the air. His entire demeanor was far more theatrical than Tarlen had been expecting, and Treena appeared to be growing tired of it.

"Can you show us the plan? Where are our captives going, and who is staying at this facility?" Treena asked.

"We will be placing the acting Assembly captains from *Remie* and *Persi* here. The rest are being spread out among the other prisons." Warden Minhaus walked to a long desk near the left edge of the room.

Tarlen peered around, seeing various guards and workers in the room with them. He recognized a few of the races, but there were others he'd never seen among the Tekol and humans. They were all going about their business, watching video feeds. The room was built of the same rock, the blinking and beeping computer consoles almost looking out of place in the rustic setting.

"These are very far apart," Ven said, pointing at the screen on the desk. Tarlen's gaze followed his finger, and saw the various glowing icons indicating the other prisons.

"That's right. No one can make it between the prisons on foot. Some have tried, and we always let them go," the warden said.

Ven appeared perplexed. "You let them walk away?"

The warden smiled widely, his yellowed teeth flashing as he spoke. "Sure. We send a drone to escort them. They usually don't even realize it. They think they're safe, and they probably are… for a few hours. But after a while, they freeze up, their blood too cold to pump any longer. It's a horrible death. On a night like today, a big man like you would only make it twenty minutes or so." He tapped a finger at Brax's chest.

"Good to know."

Treena glanced around the room. "Thank you for the tour, and your time, Warden. We'd be happy for you to unload the prisoners and take over their charge."

"Glad to hear it. Not that I presumed anything different. Most aren't equipped to manage the hateful and murderous." The warden stood up taller, fixing his crooked glasses.

"I suppose you're right. Then it's a good thing we have people like you to do it for us," Treena told the man, who beamed at the comment.

Tarlen was anxious to leave, and he could tell the others were too. They left the command center, Tarlen taking one last glance at the enormous wall of ice directly behind the prison.

"Ma'am, you're going to want to see this," Lieutenant Darl said, waking Reeve as she dozed off. Her eyes remained open, but using her brother's famous meditating trick, she'd managed to catch a few minutes of rest while sitting up.

Reeve snapped to, turning her attention to the viewer. "The third probe shows something interesting," Darl said.

Reeve stood, walking toward the image. "How interesting?"

"I think there's a ship behind it," Darl said.

Her heart raced at his words. "What?" She'd only had him use the probes because she'd been bored, and she'd wanted him to stop his annoying whistling. "Are you sure? You said it yourself, that's an old chunk of a vessel. Maybe there's still some active power source altering your readings."

He shook his head. "I don't think so. See..." Data streamed over the right side of the viewer. "They did a decent job of hiding it, but I'll be sent to the Vastness if that isn't a corvette of some kind. See the way the..."

Reeve hardly heard him as he droned on. She could see it now too. The energy waves: the first three bars were maintaining life support, the next four keeping the impulse engines primed, while only giving off enough of a read to make others think it was residual power from the section of damaged ship they hid behind.

"Damn it." She rubbed her palms together. "Bridge to Commander Starling."

Nothing.

"Bridge to Lieutenant Commander Daak," she said, registering silence. "What's the issue?" she asked.

The JOT in the seat beside Darl was using the console to check, and she gulped and tapped the screen. "Ma'am, it appears as though the storm below is blocking our communications."

"All the technology in the Concord, and we can't talk because of some snowflakes? You have to be kidding me," she said. Reeve added it to her list of things to research more. If they were going to be running around Concord space, doing on-planet missions every month, they'd have to ensure errors like this weren't overlooked any longer.

"Constantine, where are we with the prisoner transport?" she asked.

His handsome AI projection appeared beside her. "They just picked up the last load. All ships are now devoid of our Assembly captives."

The image on the viewer changed to show the huge, bulky transport vessel provided by the Bolux prisons. She watched as it moved away from *Constantine* and toward the blue ice planet. *What in the Vastness is that ship doing hiding out there?*

"Darl, send a communication. Tell them we're aware of their position, and they are in no way allowed to interfere with our delivery," Reeve said.

"Yes, ma'am." His fingers flew across the keypad, and he smiled back at her, indicating it was done. They waited a few moments, the prisoner transport shrinking in the viewer as it neared Bolux.

Darl paled, and Reeve leaned over him. "What is it?"

"It's a Lobrelion. They claim they want nothing to do with our business. They suggest we don't interfere, as they're acting in accordance with their own bylaws," Darl said.

"And what does that mean?" Reeve scanned her internal filing system, trying to recall anything about the Lobrelion.

Darl was already on it, accessing a file about the Concord partner. "Lobrelions are from the planet Tesserus and joined the Concord three hundred and seventeen years ago…" He made a clicking sound with his tongue as he ran a finger over the screen, searching for pertinent details. "Here we go: 'The Lobrelions brought with them a medical technology previously unheard of. They were able to cure the Duonucleiton disease that plagued over ten partner worlds for decades'."

Reeve remembered it now. "It was rumored they were the ones who'd released the pathogens onto the planets, using trader ships."

Darl nodded. "There's nothing about that in the database, but I believe you're correct."

"So what? Why do they think they can order us to stand down and not interfere?" Reeve asked, reading over his shoulder.

His finger tapped the screen. "Because of the cure, they were granted some liberties. They're allowed to practice their customs outside of Tesserus."

"Meaning?" the JOT beside Darl asked.

Reeve answered, "Meaning they're about to do something that falls within the legal parameters on their home world."

"We can't stop them?" Darl asked.

"Not if they aren't harming our crew members," Reeve said. "I need to reach Starling and the captain."

She tried again, but the communications failed once more. The prisoner transport was too far to see from the viewer now, leaving nothing but *Constantine* and the hidden Lobrelion spacecraft.

FOUR

The storm was brutal, and Tom slipped on the ice, nearly dropping the bundle in his arms. He was foolish for buying into it all. What was he thinking? He peered down at the tiny face, Luci's head wrapped in blankets. He was basically leaving Seda to die out here, and he knew it, but she'd brought this on herself. He had no choice with the Concord law, and everyone knew the appeal process was lengthy, and a pit darker than a black hole.

The child, on the other hand, hadn't been given a choice. She was only four or five years old, and Tom was confident she'd thrive in the care of another family. It was the only thing he could do in this situation, but he would never be able to tell Admiral Benitor about his indiscretion.

Cleo was close, but he could hardly see her through the heavy snowfall, and he got turned around twice on the short trip. By the time he found her, his toes were numb, his fingers aching. The ramp opened, sending warm air over them, and he hurried up the metal incline, setting Luci down.

He could almost make out the lights of Seda's new home in the distance, and wished her the best, despite all she'd done to him and with the Assembly. He imagined her decisions were more based on her father's brainwashing than her own aspirations, but it was too late for her.

Her fate was sealed.

"When can I see Mommy again?" Luci asked. Standing there bundled in blankets, she looked like an alien to him. Come to think of it, any child was alien to Tom. He'd spent his entire adult life on cruise ships, where children were rarely found.

"I can't promise anything, but I'll make sure to let her know how you're doing," Tom said, positive the little girl had some idea what was happening. She took it all with resignation, and Tom left her behind as he kicked the snow off his boots and moved for the pilot's seat.

The ship powered up with ease, and he attempted to communicate with the bridge. It failed. "Starling, come in."

"Captain Baldwin, is it done?" Treena's voice was strong and professional.

Tom glanced at Luci, who was climbing up onto the seat beside him. She fumbled with the strapping, and he took a deep breath before replying. "It's done. I'm heading to *Constantine*."

"The transports are finished with their tasks. The prisoners have been brought to the central prison for processing, where they'll be sent off to various bases in the morning," Treena informed him.

"Very well. See you up there," Tom told her.

"Yes, sir." The communication ended, and Tom pressed the thrusters, lifting from the ground.

---

*V*en sensed the shift in mood around him and waved Commander Starling over.

"What is it?" she asked.

"It's… I don't know, exactly, but the staff is in a panic." Since Ven's heart had stopped, and Fayle had brought him from the brink of the Vastness, his senses had adapted, grown.

"How do you mean? They look fine to me," Starling told him. She was right. On the surface, the white-uniformed staff members were calm, but Ven took a closer look and saw Warden Minhaus' right eye twitch as he leaned over a guard's console.

Ven strode across the room, anxious to be leaving. Their duty was complete, and that meant *Constantine* waited for their return. "What's the matter, Warden?"

Minhaus looked up, sweat beading on his forehead, the skin paper-thin. "We've been sent a message. It's the Lobrelions. They want us to release a prisoner."

Commander Starling came to stand beside Ven, studying the transmission. Ven had never seen one of the Lobrelions before, and he was glad. They were squat; foot-long tentacles emerged from the lower half of their heads, wriggling about their chest and shoulders. They spoke through a slotted mouth, and their eyes were on the sides of their head, each eye moving independently of the other.

"Why would they demand this?" Ven asked.

Minhaus rubbed his temples nervously, and Ven could feel the pressure building in the man's mind. "We have one of their leaders."

Ven could tell there was more. "What else?"

Minhaus met his gaze, his eyes fearful. "You see, we get funding from the Concord, but it's not enough. Sometimes we take a cut."

Lieutenant Commander Brax Daak spoke up from across the room, breaking the silence. "You're saying you barter with bounty hunters and house their catches, is that it?"

The warden nodded. "That's correct."

"Why don't the hunters just kill their targets?" Commander Starling asked.

Brax answered before the warden could. "Believe it or not, some bounty hunters think of themselves as saints, doing the work of the universe. They don't kill objectives, so they have someone like the warden here keep them locked up for the rest of their lives, letting the hunters sleep at night."

"Don't come into my prison and judge me," the warden said, puffing up his concave chest. He stood near Brax, half the man's size, and Brax just stared back at Minhaus.

"What are you going to do?" Commander Starling asked him.

Ven glanced at the screen, where the video of the Lobrelion speaking was on a loop. "We are unable to reach our crew. We could warn Reeve and seek their assistance."

Treena shook her head. "It wouldn't do any good."

"Why?" Tarlen spoke for the first time. Ven had almost forgotten the Bacal was with their group.

"Because they're beyond our Concord laws, at least where they interfere with their own. I encountered them once, years ago. Felix was so angry when we had to let them destroy a transport ship with goods from their system," the commander said.

Ven guessed she would have emitted some emotion at the statement, but was unable to read off her artificial body.

"That doesn't seem fair," Tarlen said.

"It isn't, but it's the law, and we're here to ensure it's met with accordance. Minhaus, you have to free their leader. Who brought him to you?" Brax Daak asked.

Minhaus frowned, playing with his glasses. "I can't tell you that. Confidentiality. Let's just say that enough worlds have been taken advantage of because of the Lobrelions' special rules, and someone grew tired of it. *She's* not leaving my prison."

"Then what? You're going to let them attack?" the commander asked.

"That's right. If they think they can beat my suborbital defenses, then let them try!" He was getting agitated, and Ven wasn't sure if he believed the man's posturing.

"Fine, but we're leaving first," the commander said, and she started for the control room exit. She pulled on the handle, but the door was sealed shut. Brax came to her aid and attempted to open it. Nothing.

"Minhaus, what are you doing?" Brax asked.

He grinned, his yellowed teeth flashing in the bright room. "The prison is officially on lockdown. No one in, no one out, until the Lobrelions are dealt with."

Ven stepped aside as Brax rushed to the warden, grabbing the man by the collar and lifting him from the ground.

---

*C*onstantine was right where Tom had left her, and he smiled as he directed *Cleo* to her perch above the bridge. This ship was spectacular, the best space vessel he'd ever set foot on, and he was excited to see the other flagship once it was completed. He hated how circumspect the admiral had been about its production, like she was purposely withholding secrets from him, but he could wait and see it with his own eyes soon enough.

"Is this my new home?" Luci asked, her bright blue eyes staring at the curves of the cruise ship.

"For now it is," Tom told her. He had no idea what he was supposed to do with a kid. If there were any Assembly members on board, this could be a dangerous move. His best bet was to fly her to Earon and put her into someone's care. Someone who'd never heard of the Assembly and who would raise her to be a strong Concord-loving woman.

He lowered, using the computerized landing software, and removed his hands from the controls, letting the automation take over.

"Come on, let's get you settled," Tom told her, and she nodded.

So far, Luci was taking this really well, but he imagined that when she finally clued in that she was never going to see her mother and father again, she'd have a meltdown. And he wouldn't blame her. Tom had gone through the same thing when he'd learned his parents had been killed.

She could have a good life, still. A fresh start.

Tom helped her down the rungs and into the elevator that led to the bridge. He had half a mind to hide her, to keep her from the crew, but he was done with secrets. He didn't want to follow the ways of his predecessors. He took her hand and stepped onto the bridge.

Reeve was standing in the middle of the area, staring at the viewer. Tom's gaze followed, seeing a boxy ship on the zoomed-in image on the screen. "What's going on?" he asked, and all eyes settled on him, but not before he placed Luci behind the door.

Reeve blinked quickly and shook her head. "I could ask you the same thing, Captain." She paused a moment. "But I won't."

"And the ship, is it a danger?"

"Not to us. Turns out our timing was terrible. This is a Lobrelion vessel, demanding freedom for their leader," Reeve said.

"Why does that name sound familiar?" Tom asked. It was on the tip of his tongue.

"Because we all learned about them in Cultures during the academy. Remember, the one partner with laws beyond the Concord's overall mandate?"

"That's right." Tom recalled his grandfather ranting about the group's special treatment. "What are they doing?"

"Now they're heading for Cliffside, the central prison where the warden's stationed. Their leader is being held there," Reeve said.

"You've communicated with them?" Tom asked.

"Only with the Lobrelions. We can't reach the surface," she said.

He nodded. "So no word from our crew, then?"

"None."

Tom didn't like this. If the Lobrelions were demanding release of the prisoner, the warden would have to abide by their challenge. Otherwise, this could grow violent. They watched in silence as the alien craft moved for the blue ice world.

---

*T*arlen was in a state of panic. He'd been excited at the prospect of visiting the prison world, but after the first few cells, he'd wanted nothing more than to leave and return to *Constantine*. Now they were trapped in the control room, like prisoners themselves.

He wondered if that was how his sister felt, stuck in her own body, her own flesh the penitentiary. If she could deal with that, he could make it through today.

"Why won't they let us go?" he asked Ven, but the Ugna didn't answer.

"I said, let us out of here, Minhaus!" Brax kept shaking the small warden, but it was doing no good. One of the staff was armed, and he held the gun up, his hands trembling as he aimed toward the lieutenant commander.

A moment later, Treena was pointing her PL-30 at the guard. "Lower your weapon. No one needs to be harmed today."

The man glanced nervously at the warden, whose feet still dangled a foot in the air.

"Brax, would you put the man down?" Treena said with an exasperated tone.

"Fine." Brax dropped him, and he fell in a heap.

"You don't understand. If I let them have their way, word will spread. I can't be known as a pushover. The prisons will lose all credibility, and…"

"They'll send someone else to do your job, and then who'll take bribes from the bounty hunters and save for that beach house on Rebuli Maxi?" Brax asked, finishing the man's sentence.

"Precisely… I mean…"

Ven assisted the man to his feet, which was more than Tarlen wanted to do for him.

"Open the doors," Treena urged, and the man relented, bowing his head.

"Leave at your own risk. Once I've powered up our defenses, there's no way to stop the system from attacking you as well," the warden said.

Brax moved for the door, and Tarlen heard it click as the warden used his code to release it. The chief of security turned toward the central desk. The rest of the crew was scrambling about, preparing for the coming attack. "You're saying we might get blasted by you on the way out?"

"That's right." Warden Minhaus stood taller, as if this would persuade them to stay put. Tarlen saw the real reason. He wanted them there to protect him, should the Lobrelions make it past their guns and shields.

"Give me a passcard," Treena told one of the staff. The fearful woman peered at the warden, and Treena pulled the card dangling around the woman's neck, the string lanyard snapping.

"We'll take our chances," Brax said, holding the door wide for their group. Ven went through, then Treena, followed by Tarlen, who ran from the room, nearly bumping into the commander. Brax let the door shut with a slam, and they looked around.

"Anyone remember how we made it here?" Treena asked, and Tarlen took the lead. He'd spent a lot of his youth traversing caves and strange pathways underground back home on Greblok, and he had a system that allowed him to retrace his steps. He was confident he could lead them to the exit.

"This way," he said, jogging down the corridor. The alarms flicked on, the sound gentler than Tarlen expected. They returned to the row of cells they'd encountered earlier, and thick metal bars lowered from the ceiling and rose from the floor, meeting in the middle and locking together.

"I guess they don't trust the power staying on," Brax said as they passed the creature with a pond in its cell. Tarlen peeked at it, seeing menacing eyes poking from the pool, staring at him. He shuddered as they wound their way to another series of corridors. The doors were all locked, and Treena used her passcard to open them. Each corridor had double doors, the first one needing to be sealed before the next would activate.

The alarms grew in volume, and the floor shook. "I think our friends have arrived." Brax peered toward the ceiling, and Tarlen blinked the agitated dust from his eyes as they moved.

"I'm surprised Reeve didn't stop them," Tarlen said.

"She couldn't. According to the Concord law, she could have ended up behind bars for interfering," Treena said, her voice level. Tarlen was beginning to lose his breath, but the commander's body wasn't real; she had no need for breathing.

The hall lights flickered and shut off entirely before a secondary system took hold, illuminating the path enough for them to see. "These guys aren't messing around."

"Think this has anything to do with the Assembly?" Tarlen asked, but Brax shook his head as Treena opened the last door. It beeped loudly as she pressed the card against the reader.

"It's down. They cut the power, and the exits are sealed," Treena said. There was a drone on the ground, its lights deactivated.

"This is the last one. Behind there is the transport we took from our shuttle," Tarlen advised.

"We could try to shoot..." Brax started, and Treena rolled her eyes.

"This is Cliffside. It's supposed to be the number two prison in the Concord. Do you think your blaster will dent this door?" she asked.

Brax slipped the gun onto his hip. "Do you have a better idea?" he asked.

Treena grinned and flexed her hands. "Time to test out this body."

Tarlen stepped back, giving her room, and Ven stood between him and the door in an act of protection that Tarlen appreciated. Treena found a handhold on the right side, and with a swing of her arm, jabbed her fingers through the metal. Brax let out a shout of joy as she pried the door open, her body bent over as she leveraged her strength.

She moved from the exit, the door nearly torn in half. She examined her hand, and Tarlen couldn't see any damage. "I guess they did improve it." Treena grinned at them before stepping through.

They retrieved the local animal-skin jackets and draped them on before heading to the other door, where the bus was waiting.

"Weren't there drones out there ready to kill us if we tried to escape?" Tarlen asked.

"I think they might be powered off," Brax said.

Treena had her passcard held up, and they found this door had been left ajar. Snow blew through the cracks, and already Tarlen could feel the chill from outside reaching for him.

"The door… it's…" Brax spun as they heard a sound from the corner of the mud room.

Three figures emerged from the shadows, and Tarlen gulped as he recognized the wriggling tentacles around their necks. These were the Lobrelions.

They were each armed to the teeth, and over ten different drones hovered above their heads, their screens glowing bright red. Tarlen could almost feel their weapons aiming at his heart, and he placed a hand over it.

Brax lowered his PL-30. "Don't shoot. We're with the Concord cruise ship *Constantine*. We understand why you're here, and we want nothing to do with stopping you. We're only attempting to leave so you can proceed."

One of the Lobrelions stepped forward, his gun aiming toward the ground. His mouth opened, and he spoke in rough Standard. "As it will be. You are free to depart. We will only take what's ours, do not be worried." They turned, crawling through the opening Treena had provided them.

"Guess that's that." Brax shrugged, and Ven was already heading for the waiting hover bus.

"I wouldn't want to be the good old warden," Treena said as Ven powered the bus up. The transport rose from the snow-covered ground, and Tarlen glanced back at the looming ice wall, happy their trip to Bolux Nine was short-lived.

FIVE

"What have you done?"

Treena Starling's arms were crossed, and Tom leaned away from her accusatory glare.

He lifted his hands. "Now hear me out, Commander. I made a judgment call, and I stand by it."

"You can't take the girl away from her mother!"

"I can, and did, and if you'll stop berating me for a moment, I'll tell you why." Tom waited to see if she would relent, and when she finally came to a seat across from his desk, he continued. "That planet is no place for a child."

"It is harsh there."

"That's right. They're isolated, and if this warden doesn't want to send supplies, or if something happens to him…"

"Like the Lobrelions killing him?" she asked.

"Yeah, something like that. By the way, have you heard from the surface?" Tom asked.

"The storms subsided. Apparently, the snow carries miniscule metal elements from the world's mountains, and it blocks communication. Once the snowfall ceased, we were able to reach the warden."

"And?" Tom asked.

"He's alive, and the only thing hurt is his pride. The Lobrelions took what they came for, and he's requesting more funding for the repairs. They may have left everyone alive, but they did decide to make a mess of things while there." Treena actually smiled, and Tom relaxed slightly.

"As I was saying, I couldn't leave Luci there."

"What are you going to do with her?" Treena asked.

Tom set his elbows on the desktop and steepled his fingers. "I'm going to ask the Prime to reconsider."

"What? Seda deserves imprisonment, Tom."

He was glad Treena was finally coming around to using his first name in private settings. It was the way his previous captain had been with him, and he'd always appreciated that about Yin Shu.

"She does deserve it, but the kid doesn't. Look, all I'm going to do is request that Seda is placed somewhere not so… deadly. That shouldn't be too much to ask. And when they agree, we can reunite them. See, problem solved."

"And in the meantime, we have a four-year-old wandering our ship?"

"Only temporarily. We'll bring her to Earon."

Treena's eyes grew wide, and she tapped the arm of her chair with a finger. "I have it. My mother."

"What about her?"

"She's bored out of her mind. She spent a year watching over me after the accident, and she's been stir-crazy ever since. She can care for Luci until we reunite her with Seda."

Treena appeared pleased with the suggestion, but Tom wasn't sold. "You realize that it might be dangerous, right?"

"Does anyone else know you brought her back with you?" she asked.

Tom shook his head. "I managed to keep her presence mostly hidden when I arrived in the hangar. She's in my suite now."

"Good. Leave it that way. If the Assembly is still out there, and they find out we have Keen's kid, they'll want to free her." Treena rose, pacing the office slowly.

"Then it's settled. You can ask your mother to care for Luci temporarily, and we'll have one less problem to deal with," Tom said. He used the screen embedded into the desk to project a star map, showing their next destination. "What do you make of this?"

She leaned toward it; the moon in the image was highlighted. "Is this it?"

Tom nodded, zooming on the 3D image. "Jalin Benitor sent this to me this morning. Coordinates for our next pit stop on the way to Earon."

"How long until we arrive?" she asked.

"A week," he said.

"That's some distance. They really aren't messing around. What's the destination?" Treena asked, and he tapped the icon below it on the screen.

"Wavor. Class Six world. Not inhabited, but it there are suggestions it once was." Tom saw there weren't many details about the planet, but that added up. If the Concord had a secure prison there, they didn't want any red flags surrounding the system.

"And from there we travel to Earon, correct?" she asked.

"That's right."

"Any word on Zovlip?" she asked.

"The Ugna and the cruise ship have been sent to investigate," he said.

"Is that so? Have you heard anything else about the brand-new cruise ship?"

Treena had a smile on her face, and he assumed she knew something about it. "What is it?" he asked.

"Nothing. I just think it's amusing that *Constantine* is so shiny, and yet already old news." She continued to grin at him, and he laughed at her commentary.

"It feels like we've been at this for years, doesn't it?" Tom powered the projection down with the press of a finger.

"We have done a lot in a short time. Do you think we'll really be returning to the Statu?" A look of fear crossed Treena's face, and Tom didn't blame her for feeling that way. He had no desire to traverse another wormhole, and he hadn't exploded inside one like she had.

"I think it's coming. Reeve is confident in the schematics she's been shown, and Yephion insists that with the processed ore from Greblok, they can and will be operational within the month." Tom was suddenly thirsty, his throat dry, his collar too tight. His crew had been through a lot, and he kept telling himself there would be a break after the next thing, but it seemed there was always another immeasurable task to come.

"We'll be prepared," Treena said, not elaborating.

"Let's hope so."

"Is there anything else?" she asked.

"No. You're dismissed."

She left the office, and Tom brought the image of the moon up once again. He would be glad to have Lark Keen off his ship once and for all.

Ven Ittix sat in the courtyard, staring at the vines that snaked along the walls: an intricate balance of life and hope in space. He felt a little like the plant as he observed it. The vines moved toward the lights, designed to promote growth as they simulated sunlight for the topiary surrounding the open room.

He hadn't taken any En'or in days and no longer felt the constant desire for the enhancer. Ven saw a short off-shoot of the plant ten feet above his head, and it had grown twisted, with a larger, more vibrant vine. He concentrated, using his Talent to unwind the smaller one cautiously so it didn't snap. He moved it with his mind, setting it on top of the more established vine, where it would have the opportunity to thrive once again.

Ven couldn't help but feel connected to it, for he felt he had another opportunity to grow.

"That was a kind gesture," someone said from behind him.

Ven slowly turned in his seat, seeing the large form of the Tekol chief of security. "*To be true to oneself, one must be true to every living thing.*"

Brax took a seat on the bench beside Ven and looked toward the vine. "I don't recall that one. From the Code?"

Ven shook his head. "No. It's a saying from my Elder."

"I like it. Look, Ven. I've said it many times, but I want to thank you for what you did out there near the Belt." Brax's hands were fidgeting in his lap.

"Think nothing of it," Ven assured him.

"Nothing of it? You were dead. You saved my life and stopped your own heart. I just want you to know I consider you a true friend, Ven, and if there's ever anything you need from me, all you have to do is ask," Brax said, and Ven felt the rush of sentiment peeling off the Tekol. He tried to close the walls around his Talent, but the man's insistence still sneaked through.

He wasn't used to having such strong Talent, and a

thought came to him. Was this why the Elders were all so powerful? Had they gone through a similar experience as him? Perhaps it was the way of the Ugna to die, only to be reborn stronger than ever. He'd have to meditate on it later, because there was no one around to ask.

"Did you hear me?" Brax asked.

"Yes, Brax Daak, I heard you. As I said, I only wanted to help you in a time of need. I acted as I was taught by my Elder."

"Either way, you're stuck with me now, buddy," Brax said, and Ven sensed his energy shift.

"I am glad. To… have a friend." Ven had never considered anyone a friend, even back home as a child. Sure, there had been other children his age at the village, but they'd rarely had fun, and all they did was train their minds and bodies in the ways of the Ugna. If it didn't relate to the Talent, there was no place for it in their days.

"If you're done playing with the vines, are you ready for our meeting?" Brax asked.

"Meeting?" Ven asked. He didn't recall seeing anything on his schedule.

"Reeve and I have been talking about wanting to have weekly meetings to discuss the ship, the missions, and the crew. You know, the chiefs all in one room for an hour a week." Brax rose from the bench.

"And you would like me to be included?" Ven stood too, stretching his back. He hadn't realized that he'd been sitting here for hours on end already.

"You *are* the chief of crew, aren't you?"

Ven had to pause. Some of his memories were still blurry, but it came to him quickly. "Yes. The captain has reminded me of this role that I haven't fully begun to explore. I would be happy to meet with you and your sister."

"Good. I'll bring her a coffee. You know how she is without a cup," Brax said.

Ven followed the chief of security to the ServoBot at the bar and watched him order the beverages. "Do you want one?" Brax asked.

"I'm unfamiliar with the beverage," Ven admitted.

"Never too late to start." Brax added another to the order, and soon three insulated cups of steaming coffee were placed on the bar top by the robotic hand.

Brax passed one to Ven, and he accepted it, smelling the pleasing aroma. "Beans and hot water."

"Nothing better." Brax led him through the corridor, toward the meeting room on Deck Five.

Reeve smiled as her brother arrived, two cups of coffee in hand. "I love having my own personal ServoBot."

Brax started to pass the beverage over but pulled his arm away. "Take that back, or I'm drinking both."

She grabbed it anyway and motioned for them to have a seat around the table. It was meant for large meetings, but since it was the nicest meeting room on the ship, she'd decided it was as good a place as any for these new gatherings.

"Welcome to the first of many discussions. I'm glad we're doing this," Reeve said before blowing on her coffee. She watched as Ven did the same, awkwardly taking a sip. "As I was saying, if we're going to be a successful crew, we need to be on the same page."

"I agree," Brax said. They both glanced at Ven, and he set his coffee on the table.

"I also think they are a good idea. What would you

like to talk about?" Ven asked, his tone monochromatic as usual.

"I thought we could share the state of our crews, and where we think we could improve ourselves," Reeve said. When no one spoke, she kept speaking. "I'll go first. The boiler room is running smoothly, and after the incident with Yur Shen, I've been working with Brax's team closely to ensure nothing threatens the safety of the ship and our crew again."

"And do you find my team is doing a good job?" Brax asked, his eyes hopeful.

"Yes. We have shifts, with over ten guards taking turns watching each deck below Four," Reeve told him. "On my staff side, I rely on Harry a lot. He's taking on more of the leadership role as I've been spending more time on the bridge, and that won't likely change in the near future."

Reeve divulged more details, perhaps going overboard, but they both listened with rapt attention. When it was Brax's turn, her brother talked about naming a human as his deputy chief, mostly because he didn't want to be looked at as playing favorites by giving the title to one of his top Tekol officers. The man's name was Kurt Trevling, and Reeve had met him on a few occasions. He seemed a great selection, and she said so.

Reeve understood his reasoning, and told him she supported his decision.

When it came to Ven, he sat silently for a minute before saying a word. "I understand the role of chief of crew, and know that it's a traditional role, but I do feel as though it would be better suited to the ship's AI, perhaps."

Reeve snickered, and Ven stared at her. "What is funny?"

"Ven, most of the scheduling and issues are dealt with at another level. The chief of crew has to consider things like who does what in a time of emergency. The captain will have his hands full if we're in a full-blown battle, right?" Brax asked.

"That is accurate."

"So what happens when we're under attack, and half of our ship is shut down, sealed off because it's been compromised? Who commands the crew to different tasks during a crisis?" Brax asked.

"That would be the commander, or you, Lieutenant Commander," Ven told him.

"I'm sorry. Ven, a lot of those decisions will be made by you," Reeve said. "You know from experience that Brax is usually off-ship when disaster strikes."

Brax frowned. "Okay, you have me there, but that won't always be the case."

"Regardless, the chief of crew is there to pick up the pieces when needed. They need a strong and analytic mind that puts the crew's lives ahead of their own. We already know you believe in that, Ven. You proved it when you saved my brother's life," Reeve told him, her face and tone serious.

"And in the meantime? When there is no disaster?" Ven asked.

"Then you get to ensure the scheduling roles and software are running optimally, and talk to the department heads when needed," Brax said.

Reeve remembered something important. "Ven, I forget this is your first posting. Most of us have grown up in the Concord, and Brax and I have been in this since we were teenagers. Baldwin, even longer than most of us. You'll learn it all and do a wonderful job."

Ven nodded. "Thank you. I can only hope that is

true."

Brax shook his cup, and it sounded empty, so he set it on the table. "Since we're all here, why don't we discuss the upcoming and inevitable return to the Statu system?"

Reeve cringed, thinking about the battle they were destined to lead. "We can do that."

Brax had come prepared, and soon they were observing images of the warship they'd brought with them, working over weaknesses, and opportunities they'd have to take once across the wormhole.

Reeve noticed that Ven remained silent for most of this part, but she could tell by his red eyes following along that he was paying close attention.

---

*I*na woke to a beam of sunlight hitting her eyes. Until this week, she'd never slept above the surface, not once in her twenty years. The buildings were made of stone, poorly insulated, and she found herself too cold in the nights, too hot in the daytime.

They'd been put through some testing that first day, and now everything was clearer. She needed to help the Adepts in any way she could. It was in the name of the Adepts that she did everything. The words of her ranting mother repeated in her mind, but she realized that her mother had been sick. The Adepts loved and cared for them, and it showed with every task they set the Group upon.

Carl was rising from the bunk next to hers, and she watched him stretch his arms into the air. "How did you sleep?" she asked the young man.

"Well. And you?" His feet hit the ground, bare soles

slapping on the cold stone.

Ina had already changed; her work overalls were dirty still, but she'd managed to scrub a layer of dust from them. "I'm rested." That was all she said. They'd been told to remain quiet, and with so many of the Adepts nearby, she wasn't here to make waves.

Their first few days had involved receiving tours on one of the Saviors. That was the name the Adepts had for their large space vessels. One hovered outside the building they slept in, its presence adding a constant hum and vibration to the ground and structure. It had taken two nights before Ina had grown accustomed to the strange feeling in her teeth.

Ina loved being onboard the *Savior*. She imagined the rush as they headed to space, prepared for battle to defend their home against the evil invaders. She wondered what the enemy looked like, and she pictured ten-foot-tall eight-legged creatures; more ominous versions of the poisonous insects that lived below ground.

Ina smiled as the rest of the room awoke. One rising member seemed to rouse the next, and so on, until all one hundred of their Group were up and dressed, ready for the day. Soon Ina was following Carl out of their sleeping chamber and into the gray-skied morning.

Light drizzle fell on them, but Ina didn't mind, not one bit. It was a welcome respite for the girl who'd spent over ninety-five percent of her life under artificial lights, doing menial chores.

A few of them whispered softly as they lined up for their morning orders, and Ina's gaze drifted to the flat hovering stage lowering from an extending arm of the ship two hundred meters away. Everyone hushed at the sight, and in a few minutes, five of the Adepts were stepping off the platform, walking toward their Group.

The leader was the same Adept, his robe no longer brushing the ground, so no one scurried behind him, ensuring it didn't dip into the dirt. The four behind him chanted lightly, and he came to approach their Group, as he had with the rise of each day's star.

"We are pleased to see you all again," the Adept said, his gray mandibles clicking as he spoke. "Today we begin with telling you about your enemy."

Someone gasped beside Ina, and the Adept glanced at the boy, his small mouth curling into a smile. "I know you've all read our texts, but they do not explain the magnitude with which we despise our enemy." He stepped closer, walking the long line of their Group. He stopped in front of Ran, a thin Tekol girl Ina often talked with. "The Concord are wraiths. They feed on the souls of justice. They destroy worlds with the tap of a button and zero remorse. They must be stopped. We were once a proud people, filling two planets." His finger lifted as he pointed to the sky. The delicate outline of their neighboring planet hung over the horizon.

"We were fine staying here amongst our own kind, but the Concord, in their never-ending desire to expand their clutches, came and waged war. What you see now are the remnants of this war. You have been spared, your souls cleansed in our underground cities. You are pureborn, no longer tainted by the evil in your predecessors. You will help us in this final call to erase the demons from the universe." The Adept walked along the line, and he stopped at Ina, staring into her eyes once again.

"My father said they were good. He told me the Concord was…" The Adept shot a device aimed at the boy, and the human youth fell to the ground, slumped over. Ina and the others stayed motionless as two of the Adepts came to gather the fallen member of their Group, dragging him onto the platform.

"As I was saying, you will each play a great role of this war. Today we are going to show you how to use our weapons." He broke his gaze with Ina and kept walking. A bead of sweat dripped down her back as she stared toward the unconscious boy.

SIX

"*T*his is good." Luci ate the vegetables; holding the fork like an adult, she pressed more of the legumes into her mouth.

"I'm glad you're enjoying it." People had begun to wonder why Baldwin was spending so much time in his suite eating alone. He was looking forward to arriving at Earon so he could pawn the child off onto Treena's mother.

"Why aren't you eating?" Luci asked. Treena had come by to visit a few times, and Tom could tell she'd taken to the child. She was right about one thing; kids were resilient. This tiny girl was already doing far better. She'd spent the first few nights crying out in her sleep, asking for her mommy, but that had already stopped. She was almost used to her new surroundings.

Tom glanced at his plate, and poked a piece of salad with his fork. "I'm eating. See?" He chewed, and Luci giggled.

"We're going to be visiting a new planet soon. We'll be dropping you off for a while," he added, not wanting it to be a shock.

She kept chewing, her eyebrows rising. "Will I see Daddy and Mommy there?"

Tom took a drink of water and set the cup down, unsure how to answer her delicate queries. She was a smart one, far more intelligent than he'd first suspected. He could see the way she tiptoed around questions, trying to sound like she wasn't worried one way or the other by the answer. He needed to bite his tongue around her. "Maybe. I don't know yet."

"Okay," Luci said, not adding anything else.

A light flashed near his door, and Tom pushed his plate to the side. "Go ahead, Constantine."

The AI appeared, causing Luci to giggle again. She was enamored with the projection of Tom's young grandfather, and Tom was more than thrilled to let the computer program read her stories before bed.

"Story time?" Luci asked, and the AI only smiled politely at her.

"Not yet, sweetie. Captain Baldwin, it's time. We've arrived at our destination," Constantine said.

"Good. Will you watch over Luci? Contact Commander Starling if anything should arise?" Tom asked of him.

"Very well." Constantine crossed his arms, grinning at Luci, who continued to eat her food.

"I'll see you later, Luci," Tom told the girl, and left his suite, careful to ensure that no one was in the hall outside his room.

If they'd arrived at Wavor, then Brax would be bringing the last remaining prisoner to the hangar, where they'd accompany Keen to the surface of the planet's solitary moon. Brax had already moved *Cleo* to the hangar, so they didn't have to walk Keen through the bridge. Tom didn't want the man anywhere near his crew.

He moved with purpose to the hangar and entered right after Brax and his contingency of officers. They flanked a man, his head hanging to his chest, his posture slouched as he shuffled along. Tom noticed that Lark

Keen was bound with chains, as well as energy tethers. Brax really wasn't messing around with the Assembly leader.

"Captain, we have the coordinates for his final stop, but I haven't loaded them into *Cleo*." Brax tapped his temple. They'd been sent the details by encrypted message from the admiral, and they intended to keep the location secret from any potential Assembly members still lurking in the shadows.

"Good work. Keen, I suppose you're as happy as anyone to get this over with?" Tom stepped in front of his once-best friend turned adversary, and the man lifted his chin, his gaze settling on Tom.

"Baldwin. I didn't expect to see you." His words were raspy, his throat raw-sounding.

"And why's that?" Tom asked.

"Because I've been requesting you for two weeks now, and no one's listening to me," he said.

"Keen, the time for talk is over. You're going away for the rest of your life," Tom said firmly. He wished he'd been absent for this, but Benitor had asked him to be the hand of justice, and he would do the honors – with Brax at his side, of course.

"We'll take it from here," Brax told his crew, and they nodded, relinquishing control of the man to their superior. *Cleo* sat on her landing gear near the exit, and Tom took the lead, letting the other two men follow him.

"Baldwin, I can help you. Help the Concord."

Tom stopped outside the vessel and turned to face the prisoner. "You just won't give up, will you? First you try to take over, now you're offering to help the big bad Concord. What would your followers think of you?"

Lark Keen only smirked at this. "You must understand that when your back's against the wall, you need to do what's best for you and your family."

His mention of his family sent warning bells off in Tom's head as he thought about Luci secreted away in his suite. He wondered if Lark somehow knew about that. "I would never sell the Concord out as quickly as you'd betray your Assembly, if that's what you mean."

"Sure you would. What about your grandfather? He sure turned a blind eye after the War, didn't he?" Keen was trying to goad him into something, but Tom was past caring.

"You're a pit stop only, Keen, so if you wouldn't mind shutting up and getting inside." Tom waved to the extended ramp, and Brax shoved the cuffed man up the incline.

"I have no choice entering your fancy little vessel, but I won't keep quiet," Keen warned them, and Tom rubbed his temples when no one could see him. It was going to be a long trip. They settled in to the ship, Brax in the pilot's seat, Tom facing Keen on the rear benches.

"I never meant for her to die," Keen said softly as they pressed into space. The planet was gray with red blotches, the oceans small but plentiful as they surrounded a continent directly ahead of the viewer.

"I don't care," Tom told him. He wasn't even confident who Keen was talking about, but he assumed it was Zare.

"She was a good girl, hardworking student. When Seda convinced her to join us, I was thrilled. We didn't have many Zilph'i in our ranks," Keen said.

It was becoming clear. "Are you trying to atone for your sins, Lark?" Tom asked him.

"Nothing like that. I wanted you to hear it from me. I have a heart. I'm still the person that caused trouble with you when we were boys," Lark replied.

"You know what? Constantine was right. You were a bad influence on me. I'm glad you disappeared, because one of those days, you were going to get me kicked out of the Academy. Then where would I have been?" Tom wished he could have ignored the man, but he did have a half-hour to kill.

"Would that have been so bad? All you ever wanted was this, wasn't it? To captain a cruise ship for the Concord, just like the old bastard. You never thought for a moment that your mother would have wanted you to live a civilian life, maybe on Earon. You could have married, had a job. With a brain like yours, you'd have made a fortune." Lark stretched his arms out as far as the tethers would allow and returned his palms to his thighs.

Tom almost laughed but stopped himself. "Imagine that. Baldwin's Batteries, for all your intergalactic power source needs."

"Has a nice ring to it," Brax said from the front of the ship.

"Maybe we could have been partners. In another timeline," Keen said.

"Right. In another timeline. Until you stole my patents and tried to wage war on my business, right? Because no matter what dimension we're in, there's no happy ending where we're friends, do you understand that?" Tom asked.

Keen nodded slowly, his fingers drumming his knees. He seemed agitated, nervous about something, so Tom decided to just ask. "What is it? You're clearly wanting something."

"Can I see them? One last time?" Keen asked, blinking quickly.

"They're gone, Keen. Dropped off already," Tom lied – or, at the least, gave him a half-truth.

"I see. I don't deserve it, but I'm going to ask one thing of you," Keen said.

"You're right. You don't deserve it." Tom knew what it was going to be, and he sat there, waiting.

"Check on them once in a while. Not physically, but just… make sure they're fine. It's my fault, not theirs," he said.

"Your fault you were caught, you mean?" Tom was tired of the conversation, and he turned to check on their progress. The pocked surface of the moon filled the viewer, and Tom watched as they neared it. Eventually, he spotted the structure. It was almost camouflaged among the gray dust and rocks, but when Brax repositioned the expedition vessel, he could see its shape.

"Welcome to your new home."

---

*B*elna sat quietly as Nee pressed the medispray to her arm. Her eyes were milky white, with no colored iris to be seen. He guessed they were brown like her brother's. Nearly all the Bacal were of the same ilk: dark, thick hair, with dark eyes. The girl was pretty, her features long, also like Tarlen's.

"Are we close?" The voice emerged from the speaker beside her bed.

After Nee had realized that Belna was lingering somewhere inside her brain, he'd moved her to a room in the crew quarters, one close to Tarlen's. She needed constant care, but most of that had been resolved by programming a ServoBot to stay with her.

Nee glanced over at the tablet and smiled. "Yes, my dear. We're close."

Belna's mouth remained closed, but her voice carried through the device, much like the tool Treena had used when she had no artificial body to inhabit. "Good. If this doesn't work… I'd like you to…"

Nee touched her forearm with a gloved hand, shaking his head. "Belna, don't go there. We *will* figure this out." Doctor Nee was confident this technology would be important when they returned to fight the last of the Statu. They would find slaves behind the suits of armor, and he wanted to be able to free them. He'd speculated with Captain Baldwin about how many they might have on their hands, and it could be in the tens of thousands.

So many had been taken during the War, and if the Statu had kept them alive, they might have bred an army.

"Besides, we're almost at Earon, where I'll meet with an old colleague," Nee told her.

"Who's your friend?"

"Vicci DeLarose. She heads the research and development team at R-emergence, which has an office at Aris on Earon. She'll be the one to crack this wide open," Nee said, and though Belna didn't move, he heard a slight muffled cry. He realized his slip of the tongue. "No, dear. Not cracking you open; just the problem. You see, I'm close, but there's something blocking your mind from the central nervous system, and I can't isolate it. Vicci is the best in the business, and I'm confident she'll find a way."

"Will I be staying there?" Belna's voice was small.

"I hope not. The captain has given us five days to ourselves at Earon, and Vicci has already committed her time to your case," Nee advised her.

"Thank you. For everything," Belna said, her voice clear over the speaker.

"You're welcome." Nee stood, slipping the tablet into his lab coat. "I'll make sure Tarlen's told you're free for company."

"Can you ask him to stop by tomorrow? I..."

"What is it?" Nee asked, leaning forward.

"I'd rather he didn't spend all his time worrying about me," she told him.

"I don't think he minds. Tarlen is rather fond of you," Nee said.

"I know, but he has other roles to play. He's just a Bacal teen, but somehow he's on a cruise ship and studying for the Academy. I don't want to mess anything up for him," she said softly.

Nee patted her hand. "I understand. I'll leave the decision to him."

Nee left her on the bed, wishing there was more he could do for the girl. The door closed, and he walked through the hallway. His own suite was in the executive wing, and he decided to call it a day.

The trip only took a few minutes, his pace brisk, and once he was inside the room, he crossed the large space to settle at the built-in viewer along the wall. He activated it, seeing the world they'd stopped at. Keen was being placed somewhere on the planet, he imagined, though it didn't appear to be habitable. None of that was Nee's business. He was only glad they were rid of the last of the Assembly prisoners.

Constantine was once again theirs. Nee sat at his desk, removing his white gloves one at a time. He stretched his fingers, happy to let the air settle on them. With a tug of the drawer, Nee pulled out a vial of lotion and began spreading it over his hands, kneading it into his palms. They warmed, and he melted into his seat as the lotion eased the stiffness.

Kwants weren't common among the Concord, and for good reason. Doctor Nee closed his eyes and recalled the feeling of the Radhas shrieking and sizzling beneath his poisonous touch. He would forever be a danger to others, and here he was, healing their ailments aboard this beautiful vessel.

His parents would be proud, but they were gone. There were times when Nee wondered at his own choices. He'd left his planet twenty years ago, to the chagrin of his friends and family, but he'd never been one to be content with what was laid before him. He'd always sought the stars, ever since he was but a tiny white-haired child. When the Concord had passed a new law, allowing all Concord partners the ability to apply for entrance into the Academy, Nee had jumped at the opportunity.

He opened and closed his fists, happy to be free of the gloves momentarily, and crossed the room, finding a bottle of fermented Linel juice from home. He poured a liberal amount into a clear crystal glass and took a sip.

The taste buds on the front of his tongue danced. Here he was, a single Kwant aboard a crew made up of Founders. It was no wonder he'd taken such a liking to Tarlen. They were outsiders among the clique.

Still, Nee did like the rest of them, and they'd shown him nothing but respect and friendship since he'd joined their ranks. He especially liked the big Tekol, Brax, and he'd never imagined looking up to a man his own age, but Captain Thomas Baldwin somehow had that effect on everyone around him.

Nee settled to his desk once more, bare hands wrapped around the glass, and he brought his tablet out. He brought up Belna's file and continued sorting through the details. There was a way to heal her, and he was going to find it.

Brax lowered the ship through the energy shield. He'd been given a code to gain access, and the light blue field around the structure had flashed three times when he'd entered it into the console, sending it to the moon's server.

"Captain, I'll land as close as I can." Brax didn't wait for Baldwin to reply. It was clear the man was angry and wanted nothing more than to offload Keen and return to his ship. Brax felt the same way.

The building was the size of the Ulia temple: three stories with a utilitarian appearance. Nothing was built for beauty, only function, and it was all bland, the color matching the dusty ground around it. Brax landed *Cleo* near the entrance and used the expedition craft's external sensors to determine that the air was breathable.

"It's an artificial dome keeping the air in and invaders out," Thomas told him. "I wonder how many people work here. I'd hate to be stationed at such a depressing post."

Lark Keen had stayed silent, and Brax stood, crossing the cramped vessel to tug at the man's arm. "Up."

Lark rose, a smile on his face, as if he had a secret Brax wasn't aware of.

"Lieutenant Commander, would you please see him off? I'll remain here on the ship." The captain stared at him, and Brax nodded.

"Of course, sir." Brax had heard their conversation, and he didn't blame Baldwin for not wanting to see the man he'd once called friend any longer. Keen didn't move, and Brax shoved him gently toward the exit.

The Assembly leader paused at the end of the ramp and peered up into the ship. "Baldwin, it was never personal. For what it's worth…"

Brax pushed him again and told the man to keep it quiet.

Keen's new home was even more dismal as Brax neared it. The walls were roughly shaped, and Brax did everything he could to avoid staring up into the dark space above the moon. From here, the planet of Wavor felt so close, he could almost touch it.

There was a series of ten or so steps leading to the front entrance, and Brax was startled when the double doors pressed outward and two robots emerged. They were GuardBots, but clearly more advanced than the ones Brax had seen working on Nolix. These were new models, their exteriors shiny and metallic. Red bands were painted across their arms, legs, and waists, adding a pop of color to their silver bodies.

"Welcome to Wavor Manor," one said without inflection.

"I'm Lieutenant Commander Brax Daak of *Constantine*, here to deliver our prisoner, Lark Keen," Brax told them.

Both of the GuardBots' eyes glowed yellow momentarily, and the other one spoke in reply. "We have been expecting your arrival. Please enter." They stepped to the side as one, and Brax followed Lark through the door. There were lights embedded into the dark walls, but otherwise, the entire foyer was bereft of any charm or furniture.

One of the GuardBots walked forward, removing Keen's energy tether. Before Brax could object, it had snipped the chains around his arms and feet, the metal snaking into a pile at the traitor's shoes.

"You might want…" he began.

"We have no need to fear the prisoner," it said, and

ed.

"Treena…"

"Yes, honey?"

"Can you brush my hair? I don't want it frizzy."

Treena nodded and watched Luci dart across the room, grabbing a brush from the countertop in the bathroom. She thought about the captain ordering a brush to his quarters, and assumed he'd had a few questioning glances from the staff as they delivered the child's doll alongside it.

A few minutes later, Treena sat beside Luci on the makeshift bed, calmly stroking the brush through her thick blonde hair. Treena found herself humming a song her mother used to sing and stopped herself. She was getting too close.

Treena dropped the brush and moved from the bed. This was their enemy's child. Seda and Lark Keen were terrible people, and their allies would kill to retrieve this girl. What was she doing delivering the time bomb into her mother's arms?

"Treena, what's wrong?" The girl's lip trembled again.

Treena backed into the wall, feeling the need to escape the confines of Baldwin's suite. "Nothing," she lied. "I realized I'm late for my shift. You finish brushing your hair and go to sleep, all right?"

"All right."

Treena pressed the door open and heard the tiny voice telling her goodnight as she entered the hall.

She'd have to tell Baldwin she wasn't able to do this any longer. Babysitting wasn't part of her job description, and she'd tell the man that.

Treena paused in the hallway, knowing the girl didn't deserve her cold shoulder. With a heavy heart, she opened Baldwin's door again and poked her head inside.

Luci was actually brushing her hair, her doll tucked under her arm.

"Goodnight, Luci. I'm sorry for rushing out. Have a wonderful sleep." Treena watched as the girl's face morphed into a smile.

Treena left her then and decided to head to the bridge an hour before her shift began.

———————

*T*homas Baldwin watched as they snapped out of hyperlight, entering Earon's vicinity. The world was four hundred thousand kilometers away, but halfway there, they'd find the space station that had housed the three old cruise ships trailing behind *Constantine*. *Persi*, *Remie*, and *Andron* had been modified, and Tom had suggested to the Prime that the vessels were still battle-worthy.

After some deliberation, the admirals had determined they needed to be returned to Earon Station, where they belonged. Anything modified by the Assembly couldn't be trusted, not without a full diagnostic and weeks, if not months, of work on them. Tom was given the impression that the war with the Statu wouldn't wait that long.

"Captain, we're setting course for Earon Station," Ven said. Lieutenant Darl was beside him today, and Tom was pleased with Zare's replacement at the helm. He was smart and quick to action, which were both good qualities in his opinion.

"On the viewer," Tom said, and Treena stepped onto the bridge, casting a weary glance at him before settling into her commander's chair beside his. "Everything good?" he asked, suddenly worried something had happened to his little guest.

She only nodded, staring toward the image of the station. It was far more than the simple name suggested. The main component was made into a half-sphere: a flat panel with thrusters beneath it, covered by a sizable metallic dome. From here, it all seemed insignificant before the expanse of space beyond, but the station was nearly as large as a city on Earon.

Over a hundred thousand people lived there at any given time, with half that many again visiting. Smaller disks spread out from the central section, each connected by what appeared to be tiny rods. Tom had walked through them, and they were actually immense thirty-foot-wide corridors.

From this vantage point, Tom could make out the far left warehousing region, where the three decommissioned vessels had been stored for the last few decades. They weren't entirely sure how the Assembly had come to possess the classic ships, but Tom expected some answers when they were onboard the station.

"How long has it been?" he asked Treena.

She met his gaze. "Since I've seen Earon, or the station?"

"Both."

"I spent some time during my recovery at home, so only a year ago for the planet, but years since I've visited the station. I'm kind of looking forward to it," she told him.

"So am I. I haven't stayed here in a decade or so," he said. The last time had been a quick stop there only a few months after joining the crew under the command of Yin Shu.

There was another cruise ship parked at the outer edge of the station, and Tom squinted toward the zoomed image. "Ven, who is that?"

The Ugna used his mind to tap a few controls on his console, and turned to peer at Tom. "Captain, it's not recognized in our software."

Constantine appeared, walking up to stand near Tom.

"Con, do you know anything about this?" he asked.

The AI shook his head. "Ven, if you would zoom on her, please."

The image of the cruise ship centered and filled the viewer. Tom froze. It was a mirror image of his own. "What have they done?"

"It appears as though the Concord has delivered the other flagship they've been promising," Constantine said.

"Captain, do you understand the significance of this?" Treena asked.

He did. "That we're going to war as soon as our business on Earon is completed." He'd been hoping for longer. His crew had been through so much in a short period of time, and returning to war after a few short months wasn't going to be great for morale.

Ven guided *Constantine* in, the trip taking a long twenty minutes. Tom wanted to reach out to the station administrators to ask about the new craft, but he refrained. There would be time to see it when they arrived, and Tom could be patient about it.

"Captain, they're requesting we bring the legacy ships to the warehouse first. Would you like me to relay the orders to the fleet?" Ven asked.

"Yes."

Tom watched as *Andron* led the other two toward their final resting place, hopefully. He imagined the security out there would be far superior after word spread of Earon Station's massive blunder. There were rumors that the Callalay had requested the decommissioned vessels be transported to their planet instead. So far the Prime hadn't made a final decision, or if Xune had, Tom wasn't privy to it.

Tom noted how Constantine's AI projection's gaze followed *Andron*'s path, as a version of his grandfather watched it head into the bay leading into the side of the warehouse. The building was massive, *Andron* looking like a speck against it as the ship moved through the field and into the immense hangar.

He wanted to ask Constantine how he was feeling about this, but once again thought otherwise.

They waited while the other two – *Persi,* then *Remie* – disappeared into the huge floating structure, and Tom turned his attention to the other end of Earon Station as Ven guided them ever so slowly toward their docking destination.

After a few minutes, *Constantine* came to a halt, and the lights dimmed momentarily as they attached to the station. Reeve would be held up in her boiler room ensuring everything went smoothly, and that there was nothing nefarious from Earon Station entering their system. Tom didn't trust anyone fully any longer, and Reeve would do what she could to maintain their safety.

"Executive Lieutenant Ven and Commander Starling, with me. The rest of you stay on the bridge until your shifts are over, then feel free to explore the station. We'll notify you prior to our departure," Tom said, rising from his seat.

It was time to visit Earon Station. His gaze drifted to the viewer, where a mirror of *Constantine* could be seen docked a kilometer away.

Reeve wanted nothing more than to rush off the ship and find some good food and drink, maybe some live music, but she stayed in her seat long after she'd dismissed Harry and the others. Captain Baldwin had asked her to stay vigilant and confirm the software wasn't hacked or monitored in any way, and that was what she was going to do.

The sound of bootsteps echoed from the boiler room entrance, and she turned around, noticing her brother walking toward her.

"Hey, Reeve. I thought I'd see if you wanted to join me." Brax went beside her, leaning over to see what she was doing.

"I'd love to, but..." The computer program beeped, and she checked the results. Everything looked copacetic, and she intertwined her fingers behind her head as she kicked back in her rolling chair.

"You seem smug about something." Brax laughed as he turned to leave the room.

Reeve rose from the chair, her legs a little wobbly after sitting for the last three hours. The Star Drive was powered down, but the Bentom ball remained floating in the center of it, and she stopped to watch it.

"Do you ever wonder what it was like before all of this?" she asked.

Brax's footsteps ceased. "Before what?"

"This." She pointed to the Star Drive. "What was it like for our people hundreds, even thousands of years ago?"

"I guess it was fine. I mean, they wouldn't have known any different, right?" Brax asked.

"Good point. I just wonder how we would have dealt with being early interstellar crew members," she said, still watching the drive.

"I would have hated every minute of it." Brax came to stand next to her. "And you would have thrived, like you always do."

She leaned her head on his shoulder. "You never give yourself enough credit, brother. I've seen you risk your life over the last few months and return unscathed every time."

"I'd say *unscathed* isn't the proper descriptor."

"You know what I mean. You're a great chief of security, and you would have been even back then."

It was obvious Brax wanted to leave *Constantine*. He kept trying to entice her from the boiler room. "Reeve, you do realize that most of those initial crews either died in space or ended up crippled from exposure to radiation and artificial gravity."

"And yet, there's something enchanting about being one of the first to traverse the universe, isn't there?" Reeve finally took his hint, and exited the room.

"No, there's not. Give me a flagship like this one any day, over the old welded-together clunkers we learned about in history on Nolix," Brax said.

Reeve and her brother entered the elevator, and when it arrived on Deck Four, she noticed how quiet it was in the central corridor. "They're all gone?"

Brax nodded. "If you're not on shift, you're on the station."

"Then what are we waiting for? Let's see Earon Station," Reeve said, getting an eyeroll from Brax.

"What do you think about the new cruise ship?" he asked.

"I've only seen it through the viewer. Have you heard who the captain is yet?" Reeve asked.

"We don't even know the name. I guess Baldwin's

heading over there now," Brax said.

"Why didn't you join him?"

"He was requested to go alone with the commander." Brax acted perturbed by this as they walked.

Reeve passed through the hangar, and she smiled at two of Brax's officers, guarding the exit to the station.

"Stay vigilant," Brax told them, nodding as the siblings walked through the exit, side by side.

"You as well, sir," the armed woman on the right said.

The passage connecting *Constantine* to the station was dimly lit, but wide and tall enough to load and offload skids of supplies. As if on cue, Reeve moved to the side as a forklift beeped its horn, carrying goods onto their ship.

She glanced at Brax. "Don't worry. We inspect each skid of cargo before we allow them in. If anyone is trying to sneak anything unusual on, we'll catch it."

"Sign of the times," Reeve muttered.

"What's that?"

"Sign of the times… I just mean it's too bad we have to go to such extreme lengths to secure a shipment of produce, isn't it?"

"It won't always be like this. We're on alert after the Statu, followed by the Assembly." The corridor ended, opening into a hub. Here it was far brighter, the walls a light gray, smooth with welcoming screens along them.

A friendly human female appeared on the screen, and they stopped to listen to her message. She had dark hair pulled into a ponytail and the kind of face that made her feel like an old friend. "Welcome to Earon Station. For a directory, please use the touchpad. If you know the name of your destination, please say it, and I will create a path for you."

Reeve raised an eyebrow and motioned for her brother to answer. She assumed he had a spot planned. Brax cleared his throat and spoke softly. "Gideon's Grill."

"Gideon's Grill." The woman vanished, and an intricate map appeared. The red line moved down the corridor, through the central dome, and three disks over. "This trip will take forty minutes to walk, or you can tap the screen on the lower right corner to request transport."

"What do you say?" Brax asked.

Reeve grinned. "I could use the walk."

EIGHT

Tom was excited to finally be here. The weeks leading up to it had been stressful, amplified by the fact that he'd been hiding Keen's kid in his suite. They were only stationed for a couple days; then he'd be able to pass Luci on to Treena's mother, granted that the woman was willing to harbor the fugitive's child.

Treena had refused to ask her over the ship's communicators, and Tom had to agree. That could be traced.

"I wonder why they're being so secretive about this whole thing," Treena said.

"I agree. Something feels off, but we'll find out soon enough," Tom replied.

They were down the corridor, taking the walk from *Constantine* to the new vessel, and he stopped at the entrance to the other ship. There were two guards inside, and their expressions were hard as Tom approached.

"Hello. I'm Captain Thomas Baldwin and this is Commander Treena Starling, requesting permission to come aboard," Tom said, and he noticed a crack in the stoic man on the left's face. He let a grin out and motioned for them to come through the entry.

"Captain Baldwin, so glad you made it here in one piece. I half expected you to be thrust into another intergalactic war on the way," a voice said, and Tom squinted at the approaching woman. She wore a matching uniform to his, the collar red, indicating she was the captain of the vessel.

Treena laughed. "How in the Vastness did you end up captaining a ship, Rene?"

Tom's jaw dropped. Rene Bouchard was standing twenty meters away from him. She continued walking until she was right in front of them. A Callalay man stood behind her, hands clasped behind his back. He was younger than Tom might have expected from a commander, but his deep-set eyes held an intelligence Tom instantly recognized.

"Treena Starling." Rene hugged Tom's commander, and they held it for a moment longer than he'd have expected. He had no idea they were such old friends.

"You didn't answer my question," Treena said as they broke the embrace.

"If I told you that, I'd have to kill you," Rene said with a laugh. "Kidding, of course. I was up for a promotion when one came around, and after all the mess your captain here caused after taking down the Prime, positions opened up."

She pressed a finger into Tom's chest, and he almost backed away. "You know none of that was my fault, right?" he asked.

"What are we talking about? The Statu and the Prime, or when you left my suite in the morning and never contacted me again?" Rene wore a big grin, and Tom glanced at Treena, who was watching their interaction with great interest.

"I..." Tom was at a loss for words. It had been so long ago, and they'd both had too much to drink that night.

Rene set a hand on his forearm and shook her head slowly. "Don't worry about it, Tom. We were young, and we both needed to blow off some steam. It's not like I've sat around for the last decade wondering if we'd ever be reunited."

Tom nodded and turned his attention to the Callalay commander. "You know us, but we haven't had the pleasure of meeting your number one."

The man's skin was dark grey, his head bald, and the ridges on his forehead were long, subtle. "Pleased to make your acquaintance, Thomas Baldwin. I've heard a lot about you from my mother."

His mother? And it clicked. "I'm so sorry, Kan. We didn't want… we needed to fend them off."

"Captain Baldwin, it's quite all right. My mother knew what she was getting into when she signed up to captain the *Cecilia*." Kan's eyes misted slightly.

"She was a great woman, Kan. I… I loved her as a…" Tom was about to say *mother*, but that wasn't fair to Yin Shu's memory, or to the memory of his own mother Cleo, so he held back.

"I appreciate that."

Treena appeared confused, and Tom saw the pieces merge together in her mind. "You're Yin Shu's son."

Tom smiled, happy to see the young man again. "You were only a kid when I first met you, Kan. Remember when you came to Ulatross with us?"

"I remember," Kan said.

"Okay, since we've all been reunited, what do you say we discuss a few things?" Rene said. She'd always been a bit of a wild card, even at the Academy. Top of her class, but she hadn't climbed the ranks as fast as others because of her brash personality. It seemed the new admirals thought there was room for her now that their numbers had thinned.

Tom took a look around, seeing an exact spitting image of his own hangar. "How are you liking the ship?"

Rene led them out of the space and down the corridor, toward the meeting room. "We've only been onboard for a week, but so far so good. I managed to keep her from entering a wormhole or anything, so I win top prize on crew care." She patted his chest, spinning on a heel to enter first, leaving Tom in the hallway.

Treena paused from the doorway and leaned back, whispering in his ear. "I remember why I liked her."

Tom sighed and entered. The lights were dim, the computers off, and Rene took a seat at the head of the table, pointing to the chair beside her. He took the offered seat, and Treena sat beside Kan Shu at the other side.

"Care for a beverage?" Rene asked, and Tom glanced at Treena. Did Rene suspect that Starling wasn't human, or at least that this body wasn't?

Rene peered at Treena as if reading his mind, her mouth downturned as she frowned. "Sorry, Treena. Are you okay if we have a drink?"

Treena grinned and nodded. "No problem. I'll join you. This body has some advances. Apparently I can taste too, though I haven't tested it much."

A ServoBot emerged from the far corner of the room, a bottle of Vina in its grip. It settled a tray on the table and poured four glasses before rolling away.

Rene passed them out, and everyone stood after her, raising their glasses. "To new old friendships."

They all tapped one another's cups, and Tom took a sip of the red Vina. It was a great vintage, and he settled to his seat, deciding to throw a curveball at Rene before she fired at him. "Careful, Rene. This is how we started last time," he said quietly.

She winked at him, her pale blue eyes shimmering. "I

remember."

Tom felt the gazes of Treena and Kan on them, and he sat forward, setting his palms on the table. "What would you like to discuss?"

"We have a lot to go over. Most importantly, the Statu. I've read all the files, but I want to hear everything firsthand," Rene said. She took a drink from her glass, and Tom noticed how confident she was in her captain's role. It was nice to see. He could only hope he'd exuded such a level of assuredness his first couple of weeks, but she was doing a good job convincing him she was in charge.

Treena tapped the table with a finger, drawing their attention. "Before we discuss that, I need to know."

"You need to know what?" Rene asked.

"The Link. Who's the AI on this ship? What's her name?" Treena asked the question they'd all been wondering, but Rene's presence had thrown them for a loop.

Rene Bouchard smiled and directed her gaze at her young commander. He fidgeted with his glass, but met Tom's stare. "My mother is the AI. Welcome to *Shu.*"

Tom pictured his previous captain, and then she appeared before them, a younger version of the proud Callalay woman.

"Hello, Thomas."

———

*K*riss grabbed Tarlen's hand as they rounded the corner and picked up her pace.

"Where are we going?" Tarlen asked. Being raised on Greblok, he'd never expected to be on a Concord cruise ship, let alone this massive space station outside the human home world of Earon. It was a little overwhelming.

"You'll want to see this, believe me," Kriss said, and he didn't argue. She'd been here before, having grown up on Earon.

They'd already taken two transports and had walked for nearly an hour. Tarlen had a notion of the approximate distance, but he was shocked to see it continue on, disk after disk, connecting corridors.

So far, they'd stopped for food at what Kriss called a food court, and Tarlen had sampled dishes from around the Concord partners. He was still full as they jogged.

"This is it." Kriss slowed, and Tarlen turned his head. There was nothing left. It looked like the end of the station.

"You brought me all the way here to stare at a wall?" he asked, growing impatient with his guide.

"No, Tarlen. I brought you here to show you this." She pressed a screen to life, and soon the wall began separating, revealing the most picturesque sight Tarlen had ever witnessed.

His breath caught, and he grabbed the viewer frame to hold steady.

"Isn't it…"

"Beautiful." Tarlen stared at Earon. They were some distance, but the viewer zoomed on the planet. The system's star was farther behind it, and she hadn't been wrong. This was the perfect time to come and see the view. No wonder she'd hurried him so much.

A moon reflected the light, and Tarlen couldn't stop staring from their incredible vantage point. "My brother used to come here all the time," Kriss said.

"Brother? I didn't know you had a brother," Tarlen told her.

"That's because I haven't mentioned him."

"Where is he? On Earon?" Tarlen asked.

She nodded, but tears fell down her cheeks, confusing him. "He's dead, Tarlen. My family buried him on Earon at our estate."

Tarlen wasn't sure what to do, but he sidled up beside the girl and set his arm over her shoulder, pulling her in. "I'm sorry."

She wiped her tears away. "It's okay. He died along the Border three years ago."

"Who did it?" Tarlen asked.

"A race called the Kraur, from deep space," she said softly. Tarlen had never heard of them, but they were still studying Concord partners in school and hadn't moved on to the other races outside of Concord space.

"Do you want to talk about it?" he asked.

She shook her head, leaning into him. "No. I just want to watch."

He remained silent, staring at Earon.

They stayed there for another hour, hardly speaking, only existing. He watched the planet change positions slightly over the time and began to think about Belna. Doctor Nee felt he was on the brink of a breakthrough and swore a woman on the planet in front of him would be able to assist the process.

Tarlen hoped so. Even though they hadn't been sent to fight the Statu yet, everyone on *Constantine* was talking about the inevitable mission coming to fruition very soon. Tarlen had been on the ground level while helping rescue the Bacal people during their initial visit, but there were still more of his kind that had been left behind. With Doctor Nee's help, they'd rescue as many Statu slaves as they could, freeing them from the torment they found themselves locked into.

"Want to go see the zoo?" Kriss asked, and Tarlen

grinned.

"They have a zoo here?" He was skeptical.

"You really are gullible, hey, farm boy?" she asked, poking him in the ribs.

"For the one hundredth time, I grew up in a city." She took his hand again, and they started back the way they'd come.

Gideon's Grill was as good as advertised. His old crew member Calin swore by the place, and Brax had been meaning to try it for a long time.

The meat dishes were perfectly spiced, the bread as soft as a pillow. "What did you think?" Brax asked his sister, needing to speak loudly so she could hear him in the packed establishment. Most of Reeve's last course remained untouched, and he used his fork to grab a hunk of meat from her plate.

"It was... a lot." Reeve glanced around, and he felt like her mind was somewhere else.

"What is it?" he asked her, his mouth half full.

"What's what?"

He stopped chewing, tilting his head to the side. "We're twins, remember? I can tell."

"It's this... entire thing we've been doing. When I received the call to work on *Constantine*, I was so thrilled."

"And now?" He drank some water, washing the food down. He flagged the server, a gorgeous human woman with eyes bigger than saucers.

"I can't shake the feeling like I'm never going to have what I'd been expecting," she told him as the server arrived.

"We'd like a couple of your finest Tarponian Foggers." Brax held two fingers up and grinned at his sister's glowering stare.

"Really? It's…" She checked the time. "Okay, I guess it's a reasonable hour for a Fogger."

The server passed Brax a knowing smile, and sauntered away. "Go ahead. You were saying?"

Reeve slapped his arm, diverting his attention from the human woman walking to the bar. "I was saying that I expected this new flagship to be an exploration vessel, like we were told when we signed up. Instead, we've been thrust into an old conflict and are responsible for so many things." Her shoulders slouched.

"We'll get there. There's some unfinished business. Do you think I wanted to join *Constantine* only to find myself kidnapped from Greblok a week later?" The server returned, not only with the Foggers, but with two shot glasses of a mysterious purple liquid.

The drinks he'd ordered misted over the edges of the tall glass, settling on the table before slinking toward the ground. When was the last time the two of them had drunk one of these together?

Reeve pointed at the purple liquor. "We didn't order those."

The server flipped her hair and nodded toward the bar. "That man asked me to send them over."

Brax's gaze wandered to the man, who'd turned to face the twins from across the busy restaurant. "It can't be."

"What? Who is it?" Reeve asked, and Brax waved his hand in a dismissive gesture.

"Never mind. I think it's time to leave," Brax told her.

"Look, you're finally loosening up, and now you want to leave. Forget it." Reeve picked up her Fogger and took a sip. The server cleared the last of the plates and left them alone.

Brax had to move quickly. The bastard was coming their way. "Come on. I said it's time to go." He reached for her arm, but Reeve snaked away.

"Seriously, brother. Calm down. We're not going…"

"*When you realize life is cyclical, you can be at peace with your failures.*" Brax heard the man before he saw him standing a table over. The group next to them had begun to depart noisily, blocking his view of the bar.

Reeve froze at the voice, and Brax slapped a palm to his forehead. This was going to be ugly.

"Cedric, what a surprise," Reeve told the Tekol man. He wasn't wearing a uniform, but Brax would recognize his old Academy nemesis anywhere.

Cedric's eyes softened, and he stuck his thick arms out, as if to embrace Reeve. To Brax's surprise, his sister stood up, her face glowing with affection.

"I'm so grateful you're happy to see me. I never expected this reaction…"

His words were cut off as Reeve decked him squarely on the chin. His head spun to the side, and Brax already saw blood dripping from the man's lips.

Reeve shook her hand and returned to her seat, taking the purple shot with one tilt of her head. "You were expecting something more like that?"

---

*T*he ship was so quiet, and Ven found it refreshing. His shift on the bridge had ended a couple of hours ago, but he'd managed to stay onboard *Constantine*, opting for meditation rather than self-indulging on Earon Station.

With his mantras repeated a thousand times, he blinked his eyes open before commanding the computer to increase his light output to fifty percent. His room was immaculate, and Ven rose from the floor, tucking his meditation pillow safely underneath his bed.

His gaze settled on the end table, where his En'or sat behind a locked box. He reached out with his mind, letting his senses search the nearby vicinity. He felt something, a small presence nearby, and it was afraid. Content, but afraid... not scared, but anxious; confused, perhaps.

Ven thought he was the only one of the executive crew remaining on their vessel at the moment, but he guessed he was wrong. The En'or no longer sang to his blood, and he tested his Talent, using it to bring a glass of water from the edge of his table. It floated toward him with ease, gently stopping in his outstretched hand. He sipped the tepid water and set it on the table.

This was why Elder Fayle hadn't seemed concerned when he'd expressed his addiction, the longing that constantly knocked on the recesses of his mind. She knew he would eventually be changed into... whatever it was he'd become.

Ven closed his eyes and saw something. He'd been seeing it ever since he'd woken with Elder Fayle bent over his face. It was a pattern of lights, a flickering of ambiance stretched just beyond his comprehension. Now it burned on the backs of his eyelids, and he opened them wide, only to see the pattern dancing across his room.

"It is not real." Ven said the words out loud and slammed his lids shut. When he checked again, the lights were gone. What was it? Had Ven truly been sent to the Vastness and returned? Did all Ugna go through this process? He had so many questions but no one to teach him.

Ven saw a blinking light on his desktop console, and

he used his Talent to power the screen on. With a brief press of air, he checked the messages without using his hands. For the first time since joining *Constantine*, Ven had a private communication directed to him.

He sat at the desk, unsure who would have reached out to contact him. He opened it and saw it was written not in Standard, but in an ancient Ugna text only acolytes could decipher. His breath picked up pace as he read the message.

Ven Ittix – Seek me on Earon. Find transport to Zealand. The Temple of Sol is your destination. – Elder Hamesly.

Ven stared at the screen, reading it over a few times to make sure he had the information memorized, and then he deleted the communication.

Elder Hamesly had been on Leria years ago but had left when Ven was still a youth. He'd never heard the man's name again, and the other Elders had only told the acolytes that he'd gone on to bigger ventures.

Instead of leaving his room, Ven pulled the circular pillow from under the bed and settled on it again. He needed to meditate on this.

NINE

Tom found it hard to believe Yin Shu was here with them. He watched her AI projection from the corner of his eye and more than once caught her returning his glimpses. Her son, Kan Shu, seemed at ease with his mother's presence, and Tom understood. It hadn't taken him very long to grow accustomed to his grandfather being on his ship.

"And you kept Tarlen?" Rene asked.

Treena must have noticed his distraction, because she answered the question directed at Tom. "We didn't *keep* him. Captain Baldwin offered him a spot in the Academy, and we asked him to stay with us on *Constantine*."

"Why the special treatment?" Kan asked.

Tom thought the budding commander asking that question spoke volumes, when the young Callalay clearly held his current position because of who his mother was. The same could be said about Tom, and he knew it. Even more so, in his own case.

Tom answered the question lingering in the air. "Doctor Nee is working on his sister."

Rene leaned in, her hands finding her almost empty glass. "The one he rescued from the Statu's clutches?"

"That's right. Nee thinks he can find a way to bring her back, but let's not get into that tonight." They'd been here for three hours, and Tom was growing tired.

"I suppose we should allow you to return to *Constantine*," Rene said, standing. She walked over to Tom and placed her arm inside his, letting him escort her to the exit. With a glance to make sure they were alone, she whispered in his ear, "I don't blame you for leaving when you did. But if you ever want to... see my Bothi coin collection, all you have to do is... knock."

She walked away, her commander following close after, leaving Treena standing beside the table. "What the hell was that?"

Treena seemed to have forgotten that the AI remained in the room with them, and Tom pointed at Yin Shu's projection. "Can we have a moment?"

Treena caught on and nodded, entering the hall. "I'll be in the hangar."

"I'm right behind you." The meeting room door slid shut, and he turned to face Yin Shu. "Hello, Captain."

"I'm no longer a captain, sir. I'm an AI representation of the woman you interpret as Yin Shu." Yin was around thirty years old, a far cry from her sixty or so years when she'd died defending the wormhole against the warships. She stood straight, her arms at her sides, and Tom crept closer.

"Are you in there?" he asked.

Her brow furrowed. "Who?"

"You. The real Shu." Constantine had managed to disable the restrictors around his personality, and Tom suspected Yin might have done the same.

"I assure you, I am a representation..."

Tom raised his hands in front of his chest and backed away. "If you say so. I was hoping to talk to you. I guess it's pointless now."

The AI flickered, and she appeared between him and the door. "Tom, it's me."

He laughed, happy to hear the voice of the woman he'd admired so much. "I knew it! Why are you hiding being this persona?"

"Because I'm not supposed to access these memories. I am…"

Tom finished the sentence for her. "You're only meant to recall tactical and battle procedures, assisting with ship-related issues."

"That's correct," Shu said. "Does this mean…"

He nodded, not needing to tell her that his grandfather's AI had done the same trick. "He's far less ornery as a thirty-year-old, I do have to say."

Yin Shu gave him a rare smile. "You'd be amazed at how little matters once you no longer have a body."

"How much do you remember?" he asked.

"We're updated twice a standard cycle. They stored my memories two months before I brought Admiral Hudson to rendezvous with *Constantine*," she said.

"But you know about that?"

"I did some digging. I… I really sacrificed myself, and *Cecilia*?"

Tom had to tell her the truth. "You did, and you made me take her Link too. I asked Benitor to recreate her in a flagship, but I guess they had other ideas."

"Perhaps they'll rebuild her after all," Shu said.

"You saved us that day, Captain, and I'll always remember your sacrifice," Tom told her.

"And I'm looking forward to returning to finish the job," she replied. "It was a pleasure seeing you. Please keep my indiscretion our little secret."

"Constantine doesn't seem overly concerned about it any longer, but I'll keep your secret for as long as you want it."

"Thank you. We'll be seeing you soon, I take it?" she

asked.

"We're on our way to Earon for a few days, then I anticipate we'll receive the command from the top. I haven't seen our Ugna fleet escorts yet, but the moment we do, we'll be activating the wormhole generator."

"I have a bad feeling about that weapon," she said.

"It's not a weapon. The wormhole device is a tool powered by the Greblok ore," he corrected her.

The AI projection shook her head. "I know what I said." She vanished, leaving him alone in the meeting room, considering her words.

Not long after, Tom found himself opening his suite door, mentally exasperated and ready for bed. He peered to where Luci slept soundly, and then at his couch, where he'd taken up sleeping while he had the small guest.

He still hadn't petitioned Admiral Benitor, but it was time. He sat at the desk, careful to keep the lights dim, and opened a communication with the woman's office on Nolix. He typed the message in, requesting they move Seda and Luci somewhere more hospitable. Tom blinked his tired eyes, reading over the short request a few times before sending it.

Now he simply needed to wait for the reply, which could take a couple of days with her busy itinerary. Tom slid out of his uniform and under the blankets on his couch. As sleep found him, he pictured *Constantine* and *Shu* flying side by side after emerging from a wormhole's mouth, only to find hundreds of Statu warships.

———————

"You still know how to win over a man's heart, don't you, Daak?" Cedric rubbed his jaw.

"Come on, it's been an hour. Surely a big strong Tekol like yourself can take a punch better than that," Reeve goaded him. The first few seconds of seeing her once-partner had sent her into a spiral of self-loathing and hate, but after she'd decked the man, it had all raced out of her, releasing like steam from a pressure relief valve. Brax was eyeing the guy from his seat across the table, but her brother was more bite than bark.

"I can't believe you're on *Shu,*" Reeve told him.

"And I can't believe the ship has Yin Shu on it," Brax said. "We just saw her. I wonder who was bumped?"

Cedric leaned an elbow on the table and took a drink from his Fogger. "I don't know, but she's been great so far. Who would have thought we'd both be executive lieutenants, Reeve?"

"I struggle to believe that too," Brax said under his breath, and Cedric turned to him.

"Okay, I understand why your sister hates my guts, but you? We were tight in school."

Brax laughed, the sound forced and strange in the quieting restaurant. "Tight? You were on me every chance you had. You tried to have me kicked out at least twice!"

"Kicked out! I don't know what in the Vastness you're talking about, but it wasn't me."

"Sure. What about the time you told the Academy I cheated on my Operations final? They grilled me for an hour." Brax's voice was elevated, and Reeve pressed a finger against her lip, cautioning him. A few other patrons were glancing their way.

"You got me there, but I wasn't trying to narc on you. I only thought your score was impossible, and I mentioned it to someone. It turns out you were just better than me," Cedric told him, and Reeve noticed her brother relax.

"You mean that?"

"Of course I do!" Cedric tapped his glass on the table. Reeve guessed he'd partaken in a few too many libations that night, and she slid the beverage from his reach.

"What about my sister?"

Reeve stood, motioning for Brax to do the same. "Okay, I don't need you to fight my battles. As you can see by the bruised ego and chin on Cedric."

Cedric stood tall, stepping toward her brother, and she sensed a long-overdue fight about to take place. She had half a mind to let them duke it out, but they were executive crew members of the Concord's most elite spacecraft, and she didn't want word spreading that Baldwin's crew were troublemakers.

She ran around the table, shoving Brax away from Cedric. "We're not doing this here."

"Listen to your sister. She's right. She always is." Cedric turned and walked away, leaving Reeve thankful.

"Brax, we're going to let him go, then call a transport to bring us to the ship," Reeve said between clenched teeth.

"He treated you like garbage. Don't forget that." Brax shrugged off her hand and headed for the exit.

A while later, Reeve found herself in the boiler room, the same place where she'd started the night hours prior, and was surprised to see Harry sitting there at his desk.

"What are you doing here?" she asked her deputy chief.

He lifted his gaze from the computer screens and gave her a tired smile. "I've never enjoyed space stations. Something about them gives me the creeps."

"You and me both." Reeve sat in her chair and rolled it across the room beside Harry. "What are you working on?"

"Remember the files you were sent from Leria? With the generator simulator?"

"Yes, of course." Reeve watched as Harry activated a simulation, a series of complex equations scrolling across the screen before a 3D projection of the wormhole opened on top of his desk.

"Wait, that looks different." Reeve stared at it, but she was full and had three drinks in her system. She was running a little behind.

"That's because I changed something."

"Is that so? The great Harry has bested me, along with the entire Zilph'i engineering team at Ulia?" Reeve didn't deny the possibility, but she'd already been told the wormhole would work.

"The variance is small, but there was one equation off. If we used their current process, we would have ended..." He used the console to power up an intricate star map, this one spreading across the floor behind them. Different systems were glowing in green light, and she spotted at least twenty star systems from her vantage point.

"What is this?" She stood, walking around the 3D projection.

One of the quadrants flashed yellow, and Harry spun in his chair. "That's where we would have emerged from the wormhole. A system six months in hyperlight from the Statu. And from my projections, the entire thing would have collapsed minutes after we'd traversed it."

"Harry, this is amazing. We need to alert Yephion and the others." Reeve buzzed with excitement, and even though she was exhausted, this was sure to be a long night.

---

*L*ast night was unforgettable for Tarlen, and he woke early, ready for another day of exploration. Kriss had been a great guide, and he hoped her dad would let her join him on Earon Station again today.

The visitor indicator flashed on his door, and Tarlen slid from the comfort of his bed and into a robe before instructing the computer to open it. Constantine stood there, hands crossed over his chest.

"Good morning, Con. We're not doing classes today, are we?" he asked.

"Nothing like that, Tarlen. The captain has asked me to bring you to the hangar."

"Captain Baldwin?" He was dumbfounded. Surely the captain had better things to do than concern himself with a Bacal teen.

"Do you have another captain?" Constantine asked with only a slight hint of amusement.

"When does he want me there?" Tarlen asked, seeing it was roughly an hour before most morning shifts began.

"In ten minutes." Con vanished.

His hopes of spending another day with Kriss outside the classroom disappeared with the AI projection, but the prospect of having time with Baldwin almost superseded Tarlen's young love. Almost.

Tarlen hurried to prepare himself and managed to find a clean and pressed Junior Officer in Training uniform before he ran down the corridors and into the elevator to find the hangar deck.

As promised, Captain Baldwin was present, along with Doctor Nee, Brax, and Commander Starling. Tarlen waved at Treena. Ever since their misadventures, he'd felt a special bond with the woman, and she seemed to return his admiration. He considered her like an aunt or an older sister. They were all in uniform, and Tarlen was glad he'd worn his as well.

"Where's Reeve?" Brax asked, and the captain shrugged.

"I requested her attendance, but she said she was too deep in something and asked to remain undisturbed," the captain said.

Tarlen thought Baldwin looked tired, but so did Brax. The only one that was bright-eyed and cheerful was the doctor, and he set an arm around Tarlen's shoulders. "Hello, my boy. Are you ready for a history lesson?"

"History?" Tarlen was confused, until Constantine appeared near the hangar's exit to Earon Station.

"If you'll join me, we have a transport ready to bring us to the museum and archives," the AI said.

Captain Baldwin waited for everyone to enter, and he gave Tarlen a pat on the back as he entered the snub-nosed vehicle. It had four wheels per side and was built to carry at least twenty passengers. Tarlen sat on one of the benches facing each other at either edge of the transport van.

"How are we bringing Con with us?" Tarlen asked, aware that a Link was required for the projection to leave *Constantine*.

Brax held a device in his hands, and he placed in his pocket. "I'm on Link duty."

"Did you guys see the new ship last night?" Tarlen asked. "I mean... sir..."

Captain Baldwin settled into the seat across from him and nodded. "We met with Captain Rene Bouchard and Commander Kan Shu, aboard *Shu*."

Tarlen was shocked. "You mean... after... your old captain?"

"That's right."

Brax nodded. "I happened to meet one of their executive team last night."

Baldwin craned his head to lean over Nee as the transport began driving through the wide corridors. "Is that so? What did you think?"

Brax grimaced before he spoke. "Reeve punched him."

Baldwin's eyebrows furrowed, and Tarlen watched it all with interest.

"Tell me there was a good reason," the captain said.

"Between us, he had it coming. She and Cedric have a history," Brax said, and Treena laughed.

"So he's the one that made her so skeptical about relationships, is he?" Treena asked.

"The one and the same. He's a good officer, but a real blowhard," Brax said.

"Where's Ven?" Tarlen asked, noticing the Ugna wasn't along for the ride.

"He's requested some alone time," the captain said.

Treena cleared her throat, an indication that they shouldn't be discussing it in front of Tarlen. "Tarlen, you're in for a treat. But today is about more than just a visit in time. We need to learn what we can about the Assembly leak here. Somehow they managed to steal four decommissioned ships without raising a red flag. That means an extensive cover-up was performed."

"That's right, Commander. Brax, you and Treena will interview their team to uncover any information that's suspicious, and I'll bring Tarlen on a little tour to see if we can find anything out of place," the captain said.

"Sounds like a plan. Doctor, would you like to join us?" Brax asked, and the Kwant rubbed his gloved hands together.

"I think I'd rather see the storage facility with the captain, if it's all the same," Nee said.

"Captain, I'll go with Lieutenant Commander Daak and record the conversations," Constantine told them, and the captain slapped his knees and leaned back.

"Then it's resolved," Captain Baldwin remarked.

Tarlen watched out the tinted windows as they drove, seeing various turns and intersections among the intricate system of corridors and disks that made up Earon Station. It was all miraculous and intimidating to the boy from Greblok. He felt the song of adventure coursing through his veins, excited to be along with the cruise ship's executive crew. He wished Belna was here with him.

The trip only took another ten minutes, and when the transport stopped, Tarlen exited, noticing that the vehicle hadn't been piloted by a person. They found themselves in a foyer with huge ceilings and numerous viewers along the sidewalls. Tarlen saw the rest of the station from their vantage point at the far edge of the structure, and found it hard to believe they were many kilometers from where Kriss had shown him the night before.

The floors were shiny and white here, the lights soft and welcoming. Above the massive doorway leading to the storage facility was a string of letters in Standard, and Tarlen read them to himself. *Earon Station: The Concord Archives*. The words were embossed in silver, and Tarlen had a shiver of thrill shoot down his back.

The Concord was so old and powerful, and their history was stored behind these doors.

"How do they keep this place safe?" he whispered to Brax as he watched the captain and Treena stride to the guards at the entrance.

"Earon has some of the best defense systems in the

Concord. If they determine it, no one comes or goes within five thousand kilometers," Brax said.

"Then how did Keen steal those ships?" Tarlen asked.

"That's what I'm here to find out."

TEN

*T*om hadn't been here in years, but he was quite familiar with it. As the guards allowed him and the team entrance, he pictured the first time he'd come along for the tour. Tom had been six years old and visiting the museum section with his parents. When Constantine Baldwin had asked them if they'd like to see the facility, Tom's father had said something about not wanting to subject his son to the horrible realities of the Concord's war machines.

Tom hadn't understood then what his father was implying, but he did recall his mother, Cleo, convincing her husband to let their son join his grandfather on a tour. In the end, Tom had accompanied Constantine alone.

"Do you remember?" Constantine asked from beside him, and Tom nodded, blinking away the memories.

"I do. You held my hand and showed me each ship, explaining the relevance, the history behind them, and what they did to solidify and expand the Concord's reach. It was one of the reasons I wanted to join the Academy. I think I decided that very day, to be honest," Tom said.

"You were so young, I didn't think you'd retain the memory."

"Being aboard the same vessel that Andron Loor had occupied was enough to inspire anyone. He was a genius who paved a path for the entire Concord so long ago. The Tekol should be proud of that," Tom said, and noticed how Brax straightened his posture at the praise of his people.

The entrance was closed off here, the ceilings lower, with five doorways separating them from the rest of the facility. A dour-looking Zilph'i in a beige pantsuit waited behind a desk, and Tom crossed the tile floor to speak with her.

"Hello..." He read her nametag. "Hainy. We advised you we'd be coming, and..."

Her expression remained uninspired as she tapped her tablet to life. "Yes. From *Constantine*." She slowly scanned over their group and returned her stare to the screen. "Curator Johnson will be with you shortly. Please wait over there."

Tom turned to see Treena clenching her fists behind him.

"So much for a welcome party," she whispered to him as they walked toward the designated seating area. There were only four chairs, so they all stood, moving into a circle to face once another.

"I wasn't expecting this kind of treatment. What do you think their problem is?" Tom asked.

"Well, according to Benitor, this place has been under intense scrutiny since we learned of the theft of the retired cruise ships," Brax said.

"Not to mention the old uniforms and weapons, like the Assembly's stolen PL-25s," Treena added.

"I wouldn't be surprised if our good friend Hainy over there wasn't poked and prodded a few times herself," Nee said, getting a laugh from Treena.

"Be that as it may, she should show some respect to the guests," Tom said, still bristling from her reaction.

The door on the far right opened, a sign on it denoting the entrance as "Staff Only." The man was smiling, and his left foot dragged on the floor as he came to stand near them. He was short, wearing a white lab coat, his hair sticking up in thin wisps over his ears.

"Welcome. Welcome. I'm so thrilled you could view the archives at Earon Station. Imagine, the crew of the infamous *Constantine* coming to see me," he said, grinning from ear to ear.

Tom wished Ven was there with them so he could get a read on the man. He had half a mind to send a message to the ship to transport his Ugna officer over here, but he let it be. Ven seemed to be having a difficult time after his resurrection, and Tom didn't know where to begin guiding him after something so traumatic.

"Thank you for hosting us…" Tom searched for a nametag that wasn't there.

"Curator Johnson." His hand darted out in a human greeting, and Tom shook it. "But call me Bob."

"Okay, Bob. Are you in charge here?" Tom asked.

"I am now. I was recently hired after everything that occurred last month. I come from the largest human museum on Earon. You know… historical items from long before Earon," Bob said.

"Wait… what does he mean, before Earon?" Tarlen asked, but Tom didn't want to dive into the long history of his race at that moment.

"We didn't always live here. This is our second home," Tom told Tarlen, and his tone kept the kid quiet as they continued. "Bob, where's the previous curator?"

The man's eyes shrank, his fingers nervously picking at invisible lint on his jacket. "I heard he was sent to Bolux Nine."

Great. "If you'd please take Commander Starling and Lieutenant Commander Daak to the staff area, and give them access to everything?"

"I… I'm not sure…" Bob stuttered.

"We have the admirals' blessing as well as the Prime's in this case, Bob. You wouldn't want us to report that you weren't cooperative, would you?" Tom asked the rattled man, and he smiled again.

"Surely it won't come to that. I'm more than happy to give you access to all our data. We have nothing to hide, and I think you'll find our assessment of what transpired accurate on all counts." Bob led Brax and Treena away, Constantine following behind.

When they were alone in the foyer, Tom directed Nee and Tarlen to the entrance on the left.

A guard stood vigilant, and allowed them passage into the immense structure beyond the doors. Lights snapped on as they walked into the space, and Tom was once again impressed with how grand the station was.

"*Time passes, technology advances, but the heart of the Concord remains through the ages.*" Nee whispered the Code saying as they walked toward the first waiting vessel.

The warehouse housed over one hundred decommissioned crafts from the entire history of the Concord. Each of the Founders' initial concept demos was present, along with various cruisers, warships, transport shuttles, and suborbital dropships. Tom wondered if the ceiling heights would be able to accommodate something like *Constantine*, or if they'd have to expand the structure to fit the new style of flagships one day.

Hopefully, his ship was decades away from being decommissioned, since it had only just begun to fulfill its purpose. As they walked down the space between the dozens of immense cruise ships, Tom wondered how many vessels hadn't made it to retirement. How many Concord fleet personnel had been killed while on duty? From what he could recall, only one vessel out of five had served for fifty years at the beginning of the Concord era, but that number had flipped to four out of five before the Statu War.

From here, the vessels were gargantuan, and Tom tried not to consider how massive the archives were to house so many of these relics.

"Are they still operational?" Tarlen asked.

"I guess they must be, if Keen was able to get four of them working."

Nee appeared pensive, and Tom asked him to speak his mind. "That, or Keen had a great engineering team. You saw how advanced some of their modifications were, and they made the changes in a very short period of time."

"Could you imagine if someone broke in and took all one hundred vessels?" Tarlen asked.

"That's why they now have patrol drones surrounding the entire station, and every single serious decision has to be approved by Chairperson Tess Longshade," Tom advised.

"The human woman that took over for Harris?" Tarlen would have met her briefly on Nolix, and Tom nodded. He had a meeting arranged with her while on Earon, and he was looking forward to the encounter. From his brief interactions with the woman, he sensed she was a strong leader with ideologies that aligned with his own.

They continued to walk, and Nee remained quiet, thoughtful even, his mind likely on something else.

"This is incredible." Tarlen's voice was small, and Tom watched the skinny Bacal teenager walk over to an old Callalay cruiser, setting his hand on the landing gear that had been added to accommodate the bulbous ship.

"That's *Metaz*. She was the second ever…"

nabbed her attention. "Hello, Executive Lieutenant Daak," he said.

"Whatever you do, don't tell me I can't go to bed." She stretched as she walked over to him.

"You can't go to bed."

Reeve bit back a sarcastic retort. "What is it?"

"Dinner onboard *Shu*. Be prepared to leave in an hour." Constantine disappeared, and Harry responded with a sympathetic nod.

"Fine. At least one of us can relax tonight," she told him, and Harry followed Reeve to the elevators. He continued on to his quarters, while she headed to the cafeteria for a pick-me-up. It was quiet on their ship, with most of the crew utilizing the station's many facilities.

Reeve found a ServoBot behind the cafeteria counter, and she ordered a hot cup of Raca, opting for the high-caffeine beverage over a normal coffee. The human drink was powerful but not as good in a pinch. She saw her reflection in a screen and fidgeted with her hair. She looked terrible.

Reeve hurried to her quarters, peeling off her uniform. It wasn't often she went without wearing it. Ever since she'd been posted on a real Concord cruise ship crew, she'd donned the clothing with pride at all opportunities. She tossed it in the hamper and pulled a fresh set from her closet.

After twenty minutes, she was in the outfit once again, and checking herself out in a mirror. She pouted her lips and forced a smile. "What in the Vastness are you doing?" she asked herself. "He's an idiot. Not worth your time." Cedric had once been nothing more than a distraction, and she was in too deep now to let him be one again.

Still, she added a few shades of makeup, something

she rarely cared to do, and made sure her hair was tied behind her shoulders. It had grown out just enough to do this, and it showed her usually hidden ears. Cedric had always liked her hair like that...

She pulled the tie loose, the hair falling into its normal place, and she smiled at her reflection.

Reeve met the others in the hangar right on time, and she was relieved to see Ven standing among the rest of the executive crew. He'd been so off since returning, and it was good to find him somewhere other than the bridge or his suite.

"What have you been up to?" she asked her brother.

"A little sleuthing at the archives. And you?" She noticed Brax had shaved his head for the occasion, opting for some oil on his pate.

"You'll see in two days," she whispered to him, and the captain turned to face the crew.

"I want this to go well tonight. These days, it's rare to find a cruise ship where we don't recognize someone from our past or have longstanding disputes between crews, but these are trying times. The Concord is stuck in a delicate position, and we're going to battle with these people very soon." He glanced at Reeve, and she gave him a knowing nod. He seemed to acknowledge the message she was passing about the wormhole being nearly ready.

"Yin Shu was my captain for years, and you're aware of what she did to sacrifice herself and *Cecilia*. Let's honor her tonight by being class acts and really exemplifying what it means to be the executive team of *Constantine*, all right?" Tom sealed his lips together in a final gesture, and they agreed in unison.

"Good. Let's head over there now. They're expecting us." Tom was the first to arrive at the transport in the corridor outside their cruise ship, and Reeve was about to enter ahead of Tom when he stopped her.

"I heard that the team is travelling to Earon for a test?" he asked.

"That's right."

"Have you heard from the Prime or the admiral?" Tom asked.

"No. I haven't been in touch with either of them… is this something I should be worried about?" she asked, seeing a distant look in his eyes.

"Nothing like that. I was only curious to see if they were in the office on Nolix. I'm sure she'll respond soon." Tom smiled, letting Reeve board the transport. He hated waiting so long for a response about Luci from the admiral, but he had no choice but to learn patience in the matter.

ELEVEN

$S hu$'s restaurant was much the same as the fancy eat-in dining hall on *Constantine*, with the exception that it primarily served cuisine from the Far Moons. The food was spicy, the drinks cold, and the company warm. Tom watched as the two crews intermingled, the *Shu* officers welcoming his people with open arms.

He noted that Reeve sat as far as possible from Shu's Tekol, and that Brax glared at the man a few times, but as the courses were eaten and the libations partaken of, any tension from earlier in the night melted off their shoulders.

The room's décor was full of bright, colorful designs, created to mimic the Far Moons' over-the-top attitudes. They were places for the Concord's elite to vacation, and Tom had been lucky enough to visit the Moons twice in his life. Constantine had always hated the gaudy architecture, but Tom adored it, if only for the mindset it placed him in.

"Enjoying yourself?" Rene Bouchard asked from behind him, and he gestured to the empty seat beside his. Ven was across the room, talking with *Shu*'s chief of security, a small but sturdy Callalay woman.

Rene took the offered chair and set a hand on his arm. "Baldwin, who would have thought you and I would be leading the charge to fight the bastards we thought were annihilated five decades ago?" She blew an errant hair from her face, and he gripped his Vina with his left hand, swirling it in the glass.

"What I struggle to believe is how they kept this quiet for so long. Imagine that on your conscience." Tom guessed it pained the previous Prime Phan to no end, but he didn't blame her as much as he blamed Admiral Keen, Lark's grandfather. He'd been the one to order the entire cover-up, and had bribed or disposed of the crew of *Andron*.

"I can't imagine it, Baldwin, but we didn't live through that. I suppose you're the closest thing to a War survivor now, aren't you? How did it feel when you first saw them?" Rene asked. Her red hair was neatly braided, and the end hung over her left shoulder.

"It didn't seem real. We were sent to Greblok on a diplomatic mission." He laughed. "I could barely recall my own executive crew's names; that's how fresh we were."

"It could have ended badly," she said.

"That's right, but we pulled through, got the job done, and…"

"Now we have to return to finish what you started," she said.

Tom could tell the rest of the crew was wearing out, and he noticed Cedric trying to inch closer to Reeve, who was talking quietly with Commander Kan Shu. "How is he?"

"Kan? He has his mother's instincts, but he's still raw. His Academy grades were at the top of his class, but there are some things you don't learn from books." Rene smiled, and Tom remembered what had made him dote after her all those years ago.

Maybe it was the freshness of seeing Seda again, or

the realization that he was over forty with no second thoughts of a wife and family, but Rene was making him wonder if there wasn't still a spark left to explore.

"You're right. Some things you must experience yourself," he told her.

Rene glanced around the room, and Tom saw what she was doing: making sure no one was nearby and listening. She leaned closer and spoke softly. He strained to hear her. "We're going to be heading into a serious battle, Baldwin. Maybe we should have a private strategy meeting."

He raised his eyebrows, gazing at his half-full glass of Vina. He couldn't. Not now. Not with Luci to protect in his suite. He pushed the drink away and stood, brushing crumbs off his pants and dropping the napkin on his plate. "I'd love to, but not tonight, Rene. Maybe... before we ship out."

Tom saw the disappointment in her eyes, but it vanished quickly as she rose to join him. "Thank you for coming, everyone. I'm pleased you were able to attend, and strengthen our bond. We're the first two of a new era of flagships, and together we're going to make a difference, and strive to improve the Concord along the way."

The executive crews from both ships were silent as she spoke, and they all raised glasses – some water, some empty – and Tom was glad to see everyone making an effort.

"I don't like them," Brax told her. He wasn't kidding either. His first impression of the captain was solid, and she had a way with words, but Brax also had heard about how reckless she was on missions, how she stuck her nose into business she didn't need to, and how because of this, she'd been relegated to safer Border patrols over the last few years as commander of the *Traveler*.

"May I ask why?" Ven lifted his fork with his mind, and Brax stared at the floating utensil before replying.

"First off, you have a captain that's never had a mission under her while wearing the red collar," Brax said.

Ven's fork lowered, and Brax followed it. "Captain Baldwin had never worn a red collar before Greblok."

"Good point."

"This was also my very first posting, much like the Callalay youth, and from what I gathered, he is very intelligent and analytical. A good combination," Ven said.

Brax wanted to be annoyed with Ven's commentary, but he was being truthful, and his assessment was logical and accurate. "What about Cedric? That guy is…"

"He has a decade of experience on executive crews and, from what I've read, is one of the Concord's finest pilots," Ven said, and Brax decided to stop trying to persuade the Ugna.

He opted to eat some of the breakfast on his plate and change the subject. "What are you doing while we're on Earon?"

Ven seemed to pale, if possible, and Brax watched him closely as he replied. "I'm taking a couple of days to myself."

"Is that so? Old flame? They seem to be popping up all around us," Brax told him.

"Nothing so exciting, I'm afraid." Ven continued eating, his gaze avoiding Brax's.

He didn't have to be a mind-reader to know something was off with his crewmate. "Do you want to discuss it?" Brax asked.

"No. I would rather not. What about you? What are you doing on the human world?"

Brax searched the mess hall and saw his sister eating with Harry near the exit. "We're going to check out the lead on Curator Peters. He traveled to Aris during the fumigation at the archives, and we have reason to believe there might be a group of the Assembly hiding on the planet."

"Be cautious," Ven warned, and Brax told him he would. "We depart soon. Join me on the bridge?"

Brax drank the last of his lukewarm beverage and rose, heading to their shift with a bounce in his step. He was anxious to see what they'd find at Aris, and he was also glad Treena was going to join him on the endeavor, even though she claimed to need a day first.

That was fine with him. Aris was a coastal city, and Brax could use a day in the sun with the water lapping on the beach. He was looking forward to that part of the trip. From what he'd discerned, they were going to be leaving for their mission in less than a week, as long as the device from Leria was functioning properly. According to Reeve, it would work as planned, and he never bet against his sister's assessments.

The bridge was a bustle of activity as *Constantine* prepared for departure from Earon. The last two days had been a whirlwind of tasks, meetings, interviews, and dining, and they'd left him exhausted. It was a good thing the trek from the station to the planet at localized speeds would only take an hour or so.

Shu was remaining at the station, and they were to return as soon as their business on the Founders' home planet was completed.

The previous shift crew stood, allowing Brax and Ven to relieve them, and Treena smiled at Brax as he settled at the left edge of the bridge at his console. Reeve was no-where to be seen, but she'd likely stay below deck with her Star Drive. It was hard on the best of days to separate the two of them, and today seemed to be no exception. Brax hoped she'd make time to head to the surface while they were at Earon, but he doubted she would once Zolin and Yephion arrived.

Captain Baldwin strode onto the bridge, looking like he'd had a long night, even though he'd returned from the dinner at the same time as them. The man had a lot on his mind and had probably had a restless sleep. Brax was glad to have the ability to sleep soundly under most circumstances.

"If everyone is here and accounted for, let's begin our disconnection with the docking bay," Baldwin said, taking his seat.

"Yes, sir," Lieutenant Darl said from beside Ven. "Releasing the clamps now."

The ship shook ever so slightly and began to drift from the outstretched arms of the dock. Through the viewer, Brax saw *Shu* lingering in place as Ven backed them away from the station at a very slow pace. Once they were clear of the security drones that circled around the region from all angles, the thrusters were activated, sending their cruise ship toward their destination.

Brax sent off probes, using advanced technology to detect any remnants of dangerous materials or hidden vessels. Earon reminded him of Leria in the simplicity of its orbit. On Nolix, a transport freighter might wait an hour for clearance and a lane to enter orbit, due to the high-volume traffic.

Here, most of the business was done with the station acting as the intermediary. The closer you flew to the planet, the fewer spacecraft were nearby.

Earon was a recent colony, at least compared to the other Founders. Humans had begun settling it a few hundred years ago, and though there were huge cities like Aris and Tauros, there were a lot of spread-out villages and smaller communities. It was one of the draws for retired Concord fleet members to settle there. In the early years, Tekol would always retire on Nolix or the Zilph'i on Leria, but as time passed, more and more would seek varying homes among the other Founders.

Brax had no idea where he wanted to plant roots once his time was done, but at the rate he was going, he didn't expect to live to the ripe age of retirement.

"Ease us in," Treena said, and Brax realized he'd been staring at the screen for the last twenty minutes, his gaze idly running over reports from the probes, displaying nothing out of the ordinary.

The image of the planet below was beautiful, and he gawked at it from their current position. There was thick cloud cover along the magnetic poles, clear skies between, and a massive body of water separated two nearly identical continents. The Twins. He and Reeve had always wanted to visit them, and he took a screenshot, shooting a copy to his sister in the boiler room, knowing she'd get a kick out of the inside joke.

Aris was along the east coast of the warmer Twin continent, and the capital, Tauros, was on the west coast of the other. They were at equal latitude, with over a thousand kilometers of ocean between them.

Ven moved them to orbit, far enough away so that they moved in pace with the rotation of the planet below.

The viewer buzzed, and Ven put through an incoming message from Tauros.

Tess Longshade appeared, a genuine-looking smile on her face. She wore a white robe over a Concord uniform, and spoke with an unplaceable accent. "Hello, *Constantine*. I hope your journey was peaceful."

Thomas stood in the center of the bridge, addressing the human leader. "Yes, Chairwoman Longshade."

"Please, Tess will do. Feel free to use your shuttles to venture onto Earon. We have approved all of your crew's ID tags for entrance, so they have nothing to fear while on the surface. I look forward to our meeting today, Thomas," Tess said.

"As do I. Thank you for the welcome," the captain said, and the screen flashed, once again showing the image of the planet below.

Captain Baldwin clapped his hands together. "This is it, people. We're going to be heading away soon enough, and some of you have important tasks to complete before we rendezvous with the Ugna fleet and *Shu*. Please, stay vigilant while on the surface." He glanced at Brax, implying he was concerned about his operation to track down the Assembly cell.

Brax rose along with everyone else and headed to his quarters to gather his pack.

———————

The shuttle landed, and Ven was glad when the doors opened, letting fresh air inside. The space had been cramped, with over fifty of their crew opting to use their time to explore Zealand. The city was constructed along the coast of a tiny continent within the southern hemisphere, known for great food and idyllic temperatures.

Ven was there for another reason. Elder Hamesly had sent that message privately for a reason, and even thought the Ugna had shown some of their cards to the Concord,

Ven suspected many secrets stayed hidden away.

When Baldwin had asked him what he was doing, Ven had only mentioned a private meeting with an old acquaintance. The intelligence in the captain's eyes expressed that he understood it was related to Ugna business, and he hadn't pressed any further.

Ven had never been to the human planet before, but he'd studied it as he'd studied each of the Founders' history in the Academy. The race was the last to join the Founders, and Ven wondered if the humans ever truly felt at home on this colony planet, having left theirs behind, living in various settlements before determining Earon as their final landing spot.

Ven watched the crew members teaming up, walking away from the shuttle to smaller hovering transports, and he felt a stab of loneliness. It seemed everyone here had at least one other person with them, and he was once again relegated to solitude.

He'd felt different since his rebirth, staying in his quarters, meditating on his life, so he hadn't done anything to help his isolation. But he did have friends now and considered Brax and Baldwin, along with the others, to be his new family, and that felt good to think of.

Ven slung his pack over his shoulder and searched the hovering vehicles for one heading to the Temple of Sol, but saw none labeled as such.

"Whatcha after, fella?" an older man asked. He chewed on something, his teeth covered in a brown liquid.

"I seek the Temple of Sol."

"One of those nutballs." The man looked Ven up and down, a sneer on his lip. "Shoulda figured. You're gonna want the number nineteen. It'll take you a couple blocks from there. Once off, you'll have no trouble finding it."

"Thank you," Ven said, hurrying toward the parking lot. Some of the vehicles were already leaving, and he spotted the one labeled with the proper numbers on the side. The thrusters hummed and glowed yellow, indicating it was leaving, and Ven chased after it before it took flight.

The door opened, and a woman's smiling face greeted him. "Welcome."

He climbed on board, seeing no others from *Constantine* among the ten or so people inside. The transport lurched, propelling Ven into a seat, and it rose from the ground. It was midday, the sky bright. He stared out the window as they traveled a hundred meters above the surface, riding along the white-sand coastline toward their destination.

It only took twenty minutes, and they settled, the doors springing open. He said his thanks and exited, peering around for the temple. The obnoxious man had said it would be easy to spot, and when the hovering vehicle shut the doors and took off, the brightly glowing orb on the roof spire came into view.

This was it. With renewed energy, Ven hurried toward the temple, eager to find Elder Hamesly. The streets were quiet here, the roads paved and well-kept. He strode along the clean sidewalks, past rows of two-story residences with balconies facing the water. He'd been so enthralled with finding the temple that he'd forgotten how close they were to the ocean. Ven had grown up in the middle of a jungle, isolated from bodies of water greater than a river, and he was drawn to the sounds and smell of it now.

He diverted his path and moved to the sound of crashing waves, delighted to see people playing along the beach. This was where all the locals were. Children ran in the water, giggling and shouting as currents tickled their legs. He spotted some hovering craft in the distance, hanging directly over the water a short way out.

"Do not be distracted from your purpose, Ven," he whispered to himself, and turned to walk the remaining block to the temple.

The entrance was grand, the doors ten feet tall, double wide atop the flight of steps that led into the main room.

"Can we help you?" a thin youth asked. He wore a white vest, a logo of a burning star on his chest.

"I seek the Elder," Ven told him, and the boy's lips sealed as he nodded quickly.

"You must mean the Father. Come with me."

Ven followed the boy through the rows of seating, which all faced the podium and stage where someone likely preached their religious beliefs to a congregation. At this point, the temple was all but empty, and Ven was glad that was the case.

They found offices in the rear of the building, the door frames carved from a light wood that Ven expected to be from a local tree. It smelled hearty in here, like soil and vegetation somehow, and when his young guide knocked on the door, it opened in a hurry.

The man that greeted Ven was familiar, but a far cry from the Elder he'd known as a child.

"Welcome, Ven Ittix. It is wonderful to see you again." Elder Hamesly reached toward him with hands too dark to be Ugna.

"What have you done?" Ven asked, appalled as he peered into eyes that were no longer red, but green.

TWELVE

Smuggling the girl to the surface had been a challenge, but they'd somehow managed to do it. Treena and the captain waited until most of the crew had departed, leaving behind only enough people to maintain the ship for a few days.

Once the coast was clear, they'd brought Luci to the last remaining shuttle, and Tom piloted it while Treena sent a communication to her mother's home. She didn't respond, and Treena was anxious about surprising her with the news.

"What do you think?" the captain asked from the front seat. "Do we drop by now?"

Treena glanced at Luci, who was staring with wonder out the side windows at Treena's old hometown below. They were in the middle of nowhere, farther from the coast and the warmth of the lower metropolises. When the world had been settled, they'd found the wood of this region to be the strongest and most durable to use among the salty coastal cities, driving a settlement to this area.

Treena had loved growing up here in Riverton, and happily gazed out the window at the tree coverage of the quaint logging village. In the distance, she looked at the deforestation regions, bereft of vegetation. Out the other window, she saw a region that had been logged some time ago, the trees far beyond saplings and gaining strong roots.

"I can see where the name comes from," Tom told her as they moved overtop the river that dissected their village in half. A long bridge crossed the bustling expanse of water, allowing foot traffic to traverse it with ease. She noticed a few people walking across it, strolling the cool morning away.

It was always chilly here in the north. When she was a young girl, she'd dreamed of living along the coast, feeling the sun on her face as she sat on a pier; but now, she found herself longing for this kind of quiet existence instead.

Treena wondered if the Concord would allow her to keep this artificial body if she left their ranks. That was at least a few years away, and she pressed the concerning thought from her mind.

"Keep going, and bank right after the town's last store," she said, remembering all the times she and her friends would hang out at the local restaurant, eating too much food and listening to live music on weekends.

The trip was quick, the town so much smaller than she'd thought it as a kid. Tom lowered the shuttle to the edge of her mother's property and sent the door wide open. Luci's face showed her trepidation, and Treena reached for her hand.

"This is where I grew up, Luci."

"It is?" Luci asked, seeming to warm up to the idea of disembarking the ship.

"That's right. See that house? That's where my mother lives. My room was on the right. That's my window." Treena held the girl's hand and directed her outside. The air had a chill, and she urged Luci toward the house.

"Should I come in?" Baldwin asked, and Treena laughed.

"Why wouldn't you? This might actually go better with you by my side."

"Why are we here?" Luci asked.

Neither of them answered the girl, and Treena wondered where her mother was. Karen's vehicle was gone, but the yard was immaculate; sturdy yellow flowers lined the walkway up to the ranch-style house. It was built with the very wood they were famous for, and Treena saw that her mother had painted the shutters recently. Compared to their environment on Concord, the village felt so antiquated, but the people here had opted for the historical charm of their heritage. She had no idea where the influence originated, because Treena had never seen the style anywhere else.

Luci ran forward, stopping at the entrance. She ran her hand along the side of the door, as if seeking the keypad.

"You have to knock." Treena leaned over the girl and used her knuckles to tap the slab. When no one answered, she checked the handle. The door slid open. Of course her mother hadn't locked the doors.

Treena had stayed here during her healing from the destruction of her cruise ship, so stepping inside wasn't as surprising as it once would have been. It was familiar and neat, almost the same as it had been throughout her entire childhood.

The floors were wooden slabs and a digital fireplace crackled along the living space wall. She waved them inside. "Come on. I'll make some tea."

Luci skipped into the house, humming an unfamiliar tune. "What's tea?" she asked.

"You'll have to taste it to find out," Treena said.

"Okay."

"Treena, I have that meeting with Longshade today. I

should be going," Tom told her.

"That's fine." She'd really wanted him here, but maybe time alone with her mother would be a good thing.

"Luci, I'll see you later," Tom said, but Luci was already off exploring the home.

Treena leaned in and whispered to him, "Did Benitor reply?"

Tom shook his head, his gaze darting to the door. "Not yet." He spoke too quickly, and Treena had spent enough time around the man to sense he was lying.

"Captain… Tom… what aren't you telling me?" she asked.

"Okay, I did hear from the admiral. She said there was no chance of changing her mind or the Prime's. Luci and Seda will remain on Bolux Nine," Tom said, his jaw clenching.

"What are we doing here, then? We have to return her!" Treena realized she was shouting, and lowered her voice.

The door opened, and her mother walked in, followed by their version of a ServoBot carrying bags of groceries. "What a surprise!" her mother exclaimed, and Treena glared at Tom.

"We'll figure it out," Tom whispered before turning his attention to Treena's mother.

"Mom, this is Captain Thomas Baldwin. Tom, this is… Karen," Treena said, moving to embrace her mom. She pulled Treena tight before breaking the hug, her hands settling on Treena's cheeks.

"You're here. You're really here. What brings you all the way to Riverton?" Karen walked to Tom and gave Treena's captain a hug, kissing him on the cheek. He stood there, grinning quietly.

"Mom, we have…"

"I like it here. Is this my new home?" Luci asked, running into the living room from the hallway.

———————

$\mathcal{A}$ris wasn't quite what Brax had expected. Humans were everywhere. It wasn't quite like his home, where the Tekol people were the majority, but there were countless other Concord races living among them. Here, he felt out of place in his uniform and was glad he'd brought a few changes of clothing.

The main city was on a peninsula, with beaches and ocean on either side. The effect was mesmerizing, and Brax walked with Tarlen and Doctor Nee as they sought their accommodation.

"This is perfect. We get a night in Aris before meeting my counterpart, and you do whatever it is a chief of security does while searching for thieves," Nee said with a smile.

"Believe me, I'd rather be talking with a scientist than doing this," Brax said.

Tarlen gawked at their surroundings, and he tugged at Brax's sleeve, his excitement palpable. "I wish I could join you and the commander tomorrow, but I have to be there for Belna."

"Don't sweat it, kid. We'll be fine without you," Brax told him, hoping it didn't come off as too flippant. "It's better for you to be with your sister."

They'd been invited to stay at the local Concord Academy for the duration of their visit, and Brax had been happy to. He loved the energy around the learning facilities, though he doubted he'd have time to invade one of the training operations as he had when they'd been in

Ulia.

"What do you figure, Brax?" Nee asked as they passed a guard at the gates. The facility was widespread, the buildings short and flat. It was placed directly at the edge of the peninsula, creating the illusion of being at the end of the world.

"I figure I wish we had more time here," he said, letting his pack slide to the ground as he walked between two beige buildings, coming to a wooden walkway that led to the water. The others were close behind, and Tarlen gasped at the view. Sunlight glimmered off the mostly still water, and Brax thought he saw a plume of ocean blow into the air from some underwater creature a short distance from the pier.

"Hello," a meek voice said from behind them.

Brax turned, preparing to reach for his PL-30. There stood a wisp of a girl, a couple of years older than Tarlen. Her face was darkened from the intense sun, her hair bleached blonde, and Brax couldn't tell where one freckle ended and the next started.

"Hi," Brax said. "Can we help you?"

Her eyes were dancing, and she opened and closed her mouth twice before saying another word. "Are you the ones from *Constantine*?" she asked.

"That's right." Brax folded his arms at his chest, wishing she'd get on with it. He wanted to jump out of his uniform and find the sun for a few hours before it set.

"I'm... My name's Madie. I..." She waited for a uniformed student to walk by before continuing. She was noticeably without Academy clothing, opting for pink shorts and a white tank top. Was she even a student?

"Look, we're tired, so if you have questions for us or..."

Resolve filled her expression. "I can help you."

"Is that so?" Brax raised an eyebrow and glanced at Nee, who was frowning.

"You're here about the missing ships, right?" she asked quietly.

"How can you help us?" he asked.

She shook her head. "Not here. They might be watching. I can't tell if they're still around."

"Who?" Tarlen asked, and the girl peered at him, as if she hadn't realized the Bacal boy was there.

"The Assembly," she whispered.

"Wait... what are you saying?" Brax stepped toward her, but she darted away from him.

"Tomorrow. Place called Beaches, by the hotels. Sunrise." She was off, long legs running quickly down the shoreline.

Doctor Nee shook his head, watching her go. "That was interesting. Now how about we find our rooms and something to eat?"

Brax stared at the empty sand, wondering if the girl was laying a trap, or if she really wanted to help.

———————

"And you're sure no one's been told of her whereabouts?" Karen asked.

Tom liked Treena's mother. She seemed no-nonsense and had a strong head on her shoulders, much like her daughter.

"We wouldn't ask you to risk yourself," Tom told her.

She sipped her coffee, Tom noting the slight tremble to her hand. He'd feel the same way if their roles were reversed.

"And how long would she be staying here?" Karen

asked.

"Mom, we haven't figured that out. We couldn't leave her there, could we? You would have done the same thing," Treena said, and her mom nodded.

"I don't blame you. I'm just getting on in years, and the last thing I expected was a child to come under my care," she said.

Tom looked to the living room, where Luci was holding two toys, one in each hand, making them have a conversation with each other.

"You took care of me last year," Treena said.

"That was different, and you know it. Oh, Treena, it's great to see you like this. After you lost your... I'm just glad to see you in good spirits and so passionate about something. If you could only go back two years to tell yourself you'd be okay."

"Well, we can't do that, but I *am* sorry for everything I put you through while I was here," Treena told her mom.

Tom wanted to sink into the chair and vanish, feeling like an intruder on a very private conversation.

"You have nothing to apologize for, sweetie. As for that cute little girl, of course I'll care for her. I still have a bunch of your things stored away that she can have."

Tom pictured a closet full of his commander's clothing and toys, preserved in top condition by her doting mother. She resembled the real Treena, but her hair was longer and darker. She wore a simple necklace, her clothing in muted earthy colors.

"You can't tell anyone who she is," Tom said.

"What do I say?"

"Tell them... she's the orphaned child of one of my crew members, and when you heard, you offered to help," Treena suggested.

That was the best alternative they'd come up with on their journey, and it sealed the deal. The panic evaporated from her mom's face, and her hand was steadier on the next sip of coffee.

"I'll be honest, I have been a little lonely out here," Karen told them. "Maybe this will be the fuel I need to keep going."

"Are you doing okay? That doesn't sound good." Treena reached beside her, taking her mom's hand.

"I'm fine. I don't need to work anymore, not with the income from the mills rolling in, and I can't keep volunteering my days away forever. This will be good for me, and for the poor girl. Her parents are that notorious?" She said the last bit quietly, with a hand beside her mouth.

"They are." Tom didn't elaborate. They'd agreed that their names and affiliation with the Assembly would remain secret.

"Then it's settled," Karen said, sending Tom to his feet.

"I have to be going, but it was a real pleasure to meet you, Karen Starling." Tom nodded to her, and she seemed disappointed he wasn't staying.

"I can't stay either, Mom. I have business in Aris in the morning," Treena advised, and her mother's eyes welled up.

"I wish you were here longer, but promise me you'll visit sooner rather than later." Karen peered over at Luci, who was still doing a good job of keeping herself occupied.

"I promise, Mom."

With a quick goodbye to Luci, Tom left the house, opting for the fresh air while Treena said her goodbyes to the girl and Karen.

He stared at the sky as the sun began its descent and

took a deep breath of crisp forest air. As much as he loved being in space aboard a cruise ship, he found Karen's setup refreshing. She was far enough from the city to actually find peace on a planet.

It was the perfect place for them to stow the girl until he could convince Admiral Benitor to heed his advice. Tom strolled toward the shuttle, and a few minutes later Treena jogged toward him.

"I'll drop you at Aris," he told her as he brought the engines to life.

It was a few hours later by the time Tom found the Concord offices at Tauros. He'd already messaged Tess. indicating that he was running late, and it was dark when he entered the skyscraper lobby. It was a far cry from the rustic home of Karen Starling. This was opulence and style paired as one.

He could picture Harris loving a place like that and wondered if that was what had drawn the previous Prime-in-Waiting to the position on Earon.

"I'm here to see Chairwoman Tess Longshade," Tom told a desk clerk sitting behind an energy shield.

The elevator beeped open, and an AI appeared behind him. She was wearing a white pantsuit, and her hair was pulled up tightly in a bun. "Please follow me." The AI flickered as she entered the elevator, and Tom smiled at her, not saying a word. It seemed that AI projections were gaining popularity elsewhere, not just on their spacecraft.

The elevator stopped some time later, and Tom turned to thank the AI, but she'd dissipated, leaving him alone on the fiftieth floor.

"Thomas," Tess said from down the corridor. The lights were dimmed, the offices empty at this time of the evening. CleanBots roamed the floor, picking up debris and washing the tiles, and Tom stepped over one as he walked to Tess' office.

"I'm glad you could make it. I hope it was no trouble," she said, and Tom nearly laughed. He'd had nothing but chaos since he'd started this role as captain, but he only shook his head, saying what was expected of him.

"No trouble at all."

She led him into the office, and he whistled as he saw the view. The city was lit up below, the expansive panoramic windows giving him not only a view of Tauros, but of the dark, star-littered sky. "Do you like it?" she asked.

"I don't visit cities often," he told her.

"I've heard that about you. Does that have anything to do with your parents, Tom?" she asked, motioning for him to take the seat opposite her desk.

He choked back a retort. "I don't follow."

"Your parents were killed while living in a big city. I thought maybe you were…"

Tom's blood began to boil, and he had to fight to keep from leaving. "If it's just the same, I'd rather keep this focused on the task at hand. Unless you have a private tragedy you'd like to dive into?"

This caught her off guard, and Tom reveled a little in the twisting of her expression. It was gone in a flash as she regained her exposure. "I didn't mean to offend. And here I was, so looking forward to this. I'm sorry for starting out so poorly."

Tom could see she was nervous for some reason, and he decided to give her a pass, for now. "Think nothing of it. I've had a tense few days."

"Met the new crew? I haven't been able to yet, but I hear they're good," Tess said.

"Rene Bouchard and her team will do a great job. What is it you wanted to discuss?" he asked. She'd given him no indication of her objectives, and he hated being left in the dark.

"I understand you were there while Harris was killed," she said.

"That's correct."

Tess' eyes narrowed, enhancing the wrinkles around them, and Tom realized he might have misjudged her age by a few years. "Let me cut to the chase, Tom."

"Please."

"The Concord may have all four Founders, but there are still cracks in the foundation. Humans have been on the bottom for so long, and we were nearly able to rise in the ranks. We were in line to become the Prime, and Harris would have made some real advances for us," she told him, her passion for the subject evident.

"Is that so?" Tom didn't love where the conversation was going.

"We managed to convince the admirals and Prime Xune to make another human captain of *Shu*. They were only too happy to oblige, since we were slighted so hard with the entire Harris scenario," she told him.

"Harris was killed."

"But not until after he was stripped of the Prime-in-Waiting title." Tess intertwined her fingers and set her hands on the desktop.

Tom stood, not wanting any part of her agenda. "I have a lot to prepare for. If you'll excuse me, I should be going."

"Thomas Baldwin, you owe it to your people to make a stand on humanity's behalf. If you use your recent celebrity…"

He cut her off, growing wearier of her voice with each passing second. "Celebrity? I've done my job, and my crew has done theirs as well. What you think is fandom is appreciation for us keeping the Concord safe. I don't care what you're trying to pull here, but we're Founders, and I'll never work against the others to benefit humans. You know nothing of the Concord fleet and what we stand for." He turned to leave, and heard Tess clapping behind him.

"Very good. What a show. The grandson of a traitor, and he thinks his morality is pure," she said, and he kept walking, not willing to engage.

The elevators couldn't take him away soon enough. Whatever Tess had been working at, she'd reminded him too much of Lark Keen as she'd talked with him, and it was something the Prime had to be alerted to.

THIRTEEN

"Now do you understand, Ven?" Elder Hamesly asked, only he was no longer Elder Hamesly; he was Father Hamesly.

"Perhaps, but I do not agree with you," Ven told him.

The man's news had been a revelation, and Ven found he knew next to nothing about his own people. The mere fact that so much of their existence was hidden made Ven appreciate the openness of the man across from him. That didn't mean he needed to align with Hamesly's beliefs.

"I didn't expect you to, but I did want you to consider what I've said." Father Hamesly's eyes bothered Ven the most.

"And you're saying that without En'or, with abstinence from the Talent, we can eventually return to our intended states?" Ven asked, unsure of how that could even work.

"That is correct." The man's hands were much darker than Ven's, his skin pigment that of an average Zilph'i. "The Talent is what makes us albino, but we can choose otherwise. We can choose to abdicate from our calling."

"Why would we do that?" Ven asked, still confused by the preaching of this self-proclaimed "Father."

"Ven, for one so bright, you're being quite dull. The Ugna are on the verge of gaining their own independence.

For the first time ever, they'll be out of the shadows. Already they're recruiting those from the Founders. Have you heard they have human, Tekol, and Callalay among them now?" Father Hamesly's eyes were wild.

Ven waited a moment to reply. "I'm aware."

"Really? I should have assumed you harbored more information than the average Ugna, given your rise to the ranks as executive lieutenant aboard a Concord cruise ship," the man said.

Ven finally found the courage to ask the question that had been burning inside him for the last few hours. "What happened, that you decided to forsake your people?"

"You still don't understand, after all these years, do you?" Ven shook his head, and the man continued to speak. "The Elders have been tearing children from their families for centuries, offering a pittance in exchange for their offspring. They're using us."

"To what end?" Ven asked, curious at the man's point of view.

"To create this." Hamesly pointed at the high ceiling, where a solar system was painted in intricate detail.

"I don't follow."

"The Ugna wanted numbers. They want power, and by taking children, forcing them to grow addicted to the drug, they control their people. Do you not see? They've managed to convince the Concord to allow them their own planet, which means they're now officially their own race."

Ven considered this but still didn't see what was so wrong with it. The children they brought in were special, heavy with the Talent, and if they were left to their own devices, they were a danger to themselves, their families, and others around them.

"I can see you don't agree with me but, Ven, you're in a position to change something. Be a voice to the Ugna, show them that you can break free," Father Hamesly said, his fingers resting on Ven's shoulder.

"What would you have me do?" Ven asked.

"Abdicate. I can already tell you're not taking En'or; that is the first step," the man told him.

Ven listened carefully, unsure of what his response would be. "How can you be certain?"

"Your eyes. You've already gone through the Vastness, haven't you?"

Ven blinked, recalling the patterns of light behind his eyelids. "I have."

"Then you know you can do this. Free yourself from the clutches and ambivalence of the Ugna cult, and…"

Ven rose, his limits reached. "And what? Join your new one? Just what is the Temple of Sol?"

"It's not mine, Ven. It's an ancient human religion, one that morphed to align with our Vastness belief system under my tutelage. You can join, break away from the Elder's poison, and stop this."

"Stop what?" Ven asked, giving the man one last chance.

Hamesly looked every year of his advanced age as he spoke. "The colony world, Ven. Don't allow them the power. It will only solidify their foothold and give them further reach on the Concord's children."

Ven's boots echoed around the open temple room as he moved for the exit. "I'll meditate on it." He would, but nothing the man could say would make Ven believe his people were evil.

"*A*nd do you trust her?" Treena asked, blinking away the rays from the rising sun.

"Are you kidding? Not in the least, but…" Brax stopped.

"But what?"

"There was a desperation in her voice, a spark in her eyes," Brax said, hoping he didn't sound too foolish for saying so.

He'd never seen Treena outside of her uniform, sporting a pair of blue pants and a bright green shirt. She carried a bag around her shoulder, as was the style on Earon, and he was confident there was a PL-30 tucked inside. Her hair was loose, hanging over her shoulders, and he could almost mistake her for a tourist.

His own gun was strapped to his hip – he was unwilling to go unarmed – but he was in a pair of shorts, comfortable shoes, and a button-up shirt, undone at the top to keep the already hot morning at bay. Beads of sweat were already forming on his head, and he wiped them away as they walked down the sidewalk near the beach.

"We're late," Treena said.

"I know. I didn't have the best night's sleep," he said.

"Dormitory life." She laughed, and wasn't wrong. Things were louder around the campus than Brax remembered, and the opposite of the peaceful, silent sleeps on *Constantine*.

"There it is." He pointed to the patio overhanging the ocean. The water broke against a rocky barrier, sending drops of water misting in the air just outside the restaurant.

The girl was leaning against the railing of the open-air establishment, right near the water's edge, her legs crossed as she stared toward the horizon. When she saw

Treena, she frowned.

"It's okay. She's with me," Brax said, but the words did little to ease her mood.

"I wasn't expecting you to come with anyone." Madie walked away, heading for the road.

"What? I thought we were eating," Brax called after her, his stomach grumbling at the sight of patrons consuming their food.

The entire area was full of resort-style hotels. Floating hover boats tethered to a drifting pier a hundred meters away, and already the tourists were flocking to the beach and breakfast joints.

Treena followed the girl, and Brax jogged to catch up.

"You know where they are?" Treena asked the girl.

Madie shook her head without looking back. "*Were*. I know where they *were*."

Treena glanced to Brax, who shrugged, following Madie across the street, where they waited for a public transport to arrive. Madie was watching everyone around them with distrust, and she stepped from side to side, rubbing her hands together as the vehicle neared.

"Are you okay?" Brax asked her quietly.

She met his gaze, and her eyes welled with tears. "No. My brother is with them."

"With the Assembly?" Treena asked the moment the doors to the transport opened, but she didn't receive her answer. The hovering bus was empty, and they sat at the front, Madie refusing to speak until they exited ten minutes later.

The sun was a little higher by then, and Brax's shirt clung to his back as they walked onto a quiet street. It was far less appealing here, the buildings older and in disrepair. A man leaned against a wall, grinning at them as they walked by, and Brax made sure to keep his hand near his weapon, glancing behind to see that the guy was gone.

"I don't like this," Treena whispered to him.

"It's our only lead."

Madie turned down an alley, and Brax stopped. "Hold on."

"It's this way. Trust me. I need your help," she said.

"I don't think so. I'll go first. Treena, keep an eye on her, would you?" Brax grabbed his gun, more confident with the metal in his grip.

Madie suddenly appeared much younger than her twenty or so years. "He's gone. They're all gone, and I need you to find them."

Brax started forward, and the others had no choice but to follow. The alley was narrow between two beige stone-walled structures, each with glowing energy barriers over their glass windows. The roadway was grimy here, the entire area smelling off, and Brax stepped over a bag of garbage.

"It's over there," Madie said from behind him, pointing to a metal-framed doorway alongside a boxy white two-story building. Brax glanced around and saw an old woman watching them from a window on the fourth floor across the alley. She didn't break her gaze when Brax caught her.

"Madie, if this is a trap…" Treena started.

"It's not. They left, but I thought you might be able to help…"

"When was this?" Brax asked.

"Two months ago. He didn't even say goodbye." Madie started for the doorway, and Treena set a hand on Brax's chest, stopping him from following.

"I'll go in. At least I'll be safe," she said quietly, but Madie looked at her inquisitively. There was no way the young woman could see Treena wasn't really human.

"No. It's my role. Stay with her." Brax made sure they were staying outside, and he stepped into the building.

The room was dark, and he pulled a LightBot from his pocket; the tiny drone hovered above them, illuminating the area. The place was a mess: wires hung from the walls and ceiling; consoles were left behind, smashed; and in the next room, twenty single-person bunks were lined up, reminding Brax of his time enslaved to the Statu. He pressed the memory from his mind and kept walking, searching for anything.

When he found nothing of use, he returned outside. "I hate to break it to you, Madie," Brax said.

"Break what?" the girl asked, her freckles bunching as she frowned.

"Two months matches our timeline. If your brother was with the Assembly, he's either dead or he's currently in prison."

She only stared at him, posture slumped, hope vanished.

---

*D*octor Nee followed Vicci DeLarose through her facility on the twentieth floor of R-emergence. The place was gorgeous, immaculately kept and brightly lit. If there was one thing Doctor Nee appreciated, it was sterile environments.

"This is all quite the feat, Vicci. Did you ever think you'd be heading teams like this?" he asked her.

Vicci was slightly older than him, her dark hair cut short, her eyes as intense and focused as ever. She held a tablet at her side and grinned at his comment. "And you aboard *Constantine*? A Kwant? Talk about breaking down borders."

Nee glanced at his gloved hands and smiled. "I never intended to be a voice of my people. I only wanted to work on a cruise ship and do my part."

"From the files you sent, it seems you've managed to do more than heal sick people, Nee." She tapped her tablet and showed a set of graphs to him. "What you've done with this" – she looked at Tarlen and kept talking – "Bacal girl is amazing. If what you're telling me is true, I think I have the solution."

"You do?" Tarlen blurted.

"Yes, Tarlen. I think I can help fix your sister's pathways. You see, we do things a little differently here. We're dealing with creating AIs from memories, much like the Constantine you see on your vessel. It's a very complicated process, and it took us several decades to perfect.

"Then we've also managed to create hosts, like the one your Commander Starling uses. This opens up a lot of opportunities for people around the Concord with disabilities or illness. Of course, at this time, Treena is one of two using the technology."

"One of two?" Nee asked, curious. "Who's the other?"

Vicci smiled again, and waved a finger in the air. "That's confidential, Nee. You wouldn't expect me to share that, would you?"

"I suppose not."

Tarlen stopped near a window, where three lab assistants were surrounding a robotic arm as its hand rotated. "But you can help Belna?"

"As I said, we're doing things differently, but from what I can tell, all you need is a neural link to be installed," Vicci said.

"Installed?" Tarlen asked.

"Perhaps that's a poor choice of words. We'll do a minor surgery on your sister that will connect her brain to her nervous system. The scans suggest that link had been fried by whatever these Statu do to their captives," Vicci told them.

Doctor Nee had been hoping for something along these lines, and he couldn't hold in his excitement. He grabbed Vicci, giving her a quick hug, and let her go a second later. "When can we do the surgery?"

Vicci stared at Tarlen. "Why, we can do it now, if you'd like."

---

*T*he *Savior* was bustling with activity as Ina was led through the corridors. She could sense a change in the Adepts over the last few days, but she was doing her best to work with them. Already, at least half of her Group had been taken, either at their morning duties or while they slept. She wondered if they were being brought to a higher purpose, and if she and the ones remaining were lacking something the Adepts wanted in their army.

The cloaked Adept stopped and waved her forward. He spoke quickly, his mandibles clicking away in earnest. "Ina, we see great things in you. You are stronger than most."

"I am?" she asked, using their language.

"Yes, we've watched you for some time."

"You have?" She slapped a hand over her mouth, feeling foolish for asking such simple questions.

The warship shook and vibrated as it lifted from the surface near their city entrance. "We have something to show you. You will not want to witness it, but you need to understand."

Her heart raced as he took her hand, his long fingers cold, his eyes black and lifeless. They stopped at a doorway. A large Adept guarded the passage. He stepped aside at the sight of the other Adept, and Ina followed him into the space.

There were at least twenty people gathered there, each of them fearful and panicking. "Ina, you have to help me!" Carl shouted, and she grimaced as one of the guards jabbed the end of their gun into his stomach. He fell over with a grunt, and it took all of Ina's inner strength not to rush to his aid.

"These people don't have your vision, your compliance to our cause. You are one of the chosen we're going to trust with an important task during our upcoming battle with the Concord," the Adept said. He motioned for the guard to grab Carl, and Ina went with them to the next room. There was a bizarre device in the center of the space, and they shoved Carl into the metal pod.

"Ina, help me. Don't let them do this!" he shouted before the lights flared in the pod. Carl tensed, letting out a slight muffled scream, before the tendons on his arms returned to normal.

"As you see, some serve their own purpose," the Adept said as Carl turned to face them. His eyes were no longer brown; only white remained, and Ina stepped away from her old friend.

The ship shook again, and the Adept gently took her hand, walking with her past the remaining captives. They were still crying and fearful, but after seeing Carl attacked, they'd quieted. Ina was ashamed at herself for not meeting any of their stares, but those people had brought this on themselves. If they were good and obeyed the Adepts like she did, they wouldn't be in there.

"Welcome to the next step." The Adept pressed a keypad on the rough wall, a secret door sliding open. He walked with her toward the edge of the *Savior*'s highest arm, where clouds floated directly overhead. They were so high, the air was hard to breathe. "Not that... look below."

She glanced toward the ground, a wave of vertigo hitting her. She clutched at the Adept, and he only chittered away, his mandibles moving excitedly. An army was lined up, endless masses of figures stood in rows, and she noticed the Adepts floating around on hovering platforms.

"What is this, Adept?" she asked.

"This is the beginning of our victory, and you're going to help us achieve it. You may call me by my name, Adept Feerez."

He let go of her hand, and she wiped it on her pants, unable to remove the coldness from her fingertips.

FOURTEEN

Reeve had never been more ready for something in her life. While everyone else was on Earon enjoying themselves, she was fifty thousand kilometers away, in the Ugna vessel Yephion and Zolin had been escorted in.

The ship was almost as sophisticated as *Constantine*, but everything was a little too dull for her tastes. The Ugna were a subdued people and strictly utilitarian in their design concepts.

Harry slid his helmet on, and Reeve helped make sure it was sealed tightly. It beeped, and she put hers on while Yephion did the same. "Are you sure you won't join us, Zolin?"

He smiled, the sight awkward as his scarred face bunched up. "One of us needs to remain here."

"Suit yourself." Reeve entered the modified cruiser. Originally, they'd planned to use a shuttle, but the sheer mass of the machine made it twice the shuttle's size, so they opted for the much larger cruiser, a Concord model from a decade earlier. It had the most space inside the cargo hold and would easily fit their needs.

"This is quite the device." Harry ran a gloved hand over the generator, and Yephion clicked his agreement.

Reeve still had reservations about working with the Statu on the project, but she was confident he was on their side and had been from the start. He'd been nothing but a pleasure to work with, and the entire team on Leria adored him, according to Zolin.

They said goodbye to Zolin and sealed their ship tight. This test was going to decide whether the war was about to occur or not. Everyone was counting on this working, and Reeve was only too happy to go down in the history records as being the sole Tekol on the development team.

"This is going to change everything," Harry said as she powered up the device.

Lieutenant Basker's voice carried through the intercom. She'd conscripted the fighter pilot to fly their cruiser for the important mission, and he was glad to assist in any way he could. "We're leaving *Intonation* now."

The generator hummed, and a soft blue light glowed around the circular disks that had begun spinning. The system was over ten feet tall, twice as long, and protruded from the rear of their cruiser.

Reeve pressed the communicator. "Basker, notify us when we're safely away from the Ugna. We need a hundred thousand kilometers to be safe." The true calculation was eighty-four thousand, but she'd decided to round up.

Yephion was busy at work, doing his part, and Reeve ran through the calculations on her console near the exit. The numbers were right; they had to be. Everything was telling her this was going to succeed, but they were also trusting that the engineering had been completed to perfect specifications. She trusted Zolin and his team, though, and she was sure they'd done it correctly.

Her nerves were almost on fire when Basker advised them they were far enough out. She checked the viewer on her console and saw nothing on their radar for quite some way. They were alone in Earon's system, and it was time to test the wormhole generator.

The inside of the device was lined with Greblok ore, the material that had brought them into the Concord's attention in the first place.

It was only a matter of time before the warships and their evil leaders found a way to return to Concord space, so Reeve and her people needed to win the sprint. Perhaps they'd manage to surprise the warships and Statu. That would be ideal.

"I wish we were testing this for the real Statu system," Harry said.

They'd discussed this in earnest, but once they used it on their final destination, they needed to be ready for the assault, and they weren't yet. Instead, they set their objective for somewhere outside the Denetron system, the future home of the Ugna colony, which was on Driun F49, a Class Zero Nine planet.

"Are we prepared?" Reeve asked.

"We're ready," Zolin said through her helmet's speaker.

Reeve stood on the side of the generator, peering through the window along its edge. Inside, blue light was flickering and stirring, swirling as the ore amplified the procedure. She confirmed the destination location and took a deep breath. She wished the captain was there to witness the first Concord-created wormhole, but they all had other tasks at hand. It was her job to complete this mission. With the slightest of trembles in her hand, she touched the screen, activating the final phase of the generator. Light blasted inside the cruiser's cargo hold, temporarily blinding her, and Zolin gasped through the speakers.

"It worked!" he shouted, and Reeve blinked away the dancing light from her eyes. The computer showed green lights along all of the mission parameters, and she rushed to the exit console, Harry directly behind her. The viewer showed what they'd been hoping to see: a swirling wormhole, one that could be turned on and off with the press of a button.

"Basker, send the probe," she ordered the pilot, and he quickly responded.

"Deployed."

Reeve had been the one to develop this particular probe. Before, they'd lost connection with anything that traveled through the space rift, but this one was self-contained, ordered to traverse until the energy readouts were different from the inside of the wormhole. It was to record and return. Simple instructions, but Reeve was tense as they watched the screens, waiting for the tiny drone to traverse the invisible tunnel. Even Yephion looked nervous, his mandibles clicking slowly inside his helmet.

"It's been too long," Harry said after ten minutes.

"Give it time," Reeve whispered, her hands shaking with anticipation.

Basker's voice cut through. "There it is. The probe's returned."

Zolin let out a cheer from his position on *Intonation*, and they followed suit, hugging one another. Reeve stared at the mouth of the wormhole, the beautiful cascading light giving the Concord a tool to win a war they'd thought was over nearly five decades ago.

She powered the device down, and the wormhole vanished as the destabilizers shot through the entrance. A few minutes later, there was no indication the rift had ever existed.

Now all they needed was a fleet.

---

*T*homas Baldwin landed in Aris as the sun began to set. After a restless sleep, he'd taken the day to relax and visit Tauros. The only thing it did for him was remind him that *Constantine* was his new home. His grandfather had never liked Earon, and Tom realized he was more like the old man than he'd care to admit.

Their other shuttle was nearby, and Tom stepped from his own to find Treena, Brax, Doctor Nee, and Tarlen standing there staring toward him. "Been waiting long?" he asked.

"No. We're just ready to leave," Brax said, his expression unreadable.

"How did things go?" Tom asked, not expecting a positive answer.

"Fine. The Assembly was here, but there's no sign of them now," Treena informed him. She wasn't wearing her uniform and neither was Brax. It was strange seeing them like that.

"Then I suppose that case is closed," Tom said.

Brax frowned and opened his shuttle's door. "We didn't apprehend all of them, but we don't have time to investigate any further. Their ringleaders are gone, and Keen and his family are sealed up tighter than an Eganian tourist's credit account."

Treena glanced at Tom, and he changed the subject. "That's reasonable. And you, Doctor Nee?"

"We have a guest coming…"

A hovering bus with "R-emergence" stenciled along the side came to a halt beside the shuttle, and out walked a stunning woman in a lab coat. "Load it up, boys," she told a few workers in coveralls, and Tom raised his eyebrows in question.

"This is Doctor Vicci DeLarose," Nee said, and Tom stepped over, smiling at the woman.

"Hello, Doctor. I'm Captain Thomas Baldwin of *Constantine*," he told her.

"Well met. I'm looking forward to seeing your vessel. Nee has told me many good things about you," she said.

"He always has been a bit of a storyteller," Tom said, wondering why he was blathering.

"Captain, we believe Vicci has a way to heal Belna," Nee said, and Tarlen's face lit up.

"And perhaps we can alter the slaves we find when we meet the Statu," Brax added.

"That's fantastic news. I don't know about you guys, but I'm ready to leave Earon," Tom advised, and they all echoed his sentiment. The rest of the crew visiting the planet had another day before they were returning to the ship, and he'd let them have it. They were about to head into yet another dangerous situation, and they deserved respite before the battle.

"Do you mind if I ride with you, Captain?" Treena asked, and Tom shook his head.

Once the large crates from the R-emergence van were loaded, Brax and the others filed onto their shuttle, and Tom closed the door on theirs. Treena was already in the front seat, and he noticed she was upset.

"What is it?" he asked.

"My mother. I hate asking her to do this. If the Prime doesn't agree with your petition, what'll happen? Will she be in any danger from the Concord?" she asked.

"No. I'll take full responsibility, Treena. Karen is a resourceful woman. She'll be fine," Tom assured her.

"I know. It's just… with my father passing, and her having to care for me while I was… *am* bedridden and miserable, she's been through a lot. And she's always worrying about my well-being, along with raising a little girl. She's supposed to be able to relax now. She's done enough."

Tom remained quiet and lifted from the ground a few minutes after Brax departed. They moved for *Constantine*, Tom glad that another pit stop on their way to the Statu was over.

"Captain, we have word from Earon Station." Constantine's voice carried through the cockpit.

"Go ahead, Con."

"The Ugna are here. The fleet has arrived. And Reeve has returned as well."

Tom's blood pumped harder, and he asked the question: "Was her mission successful?"

Con didn't speak for a moment, Treena and Tom meeting gazes as they broke out of the atmosphere and moved toward the distant, orbiting cruise ship. "She brings word that it was a full success."

"It seems we're ready," Tom said to Treena, and she nodded, staring out the viewer. It was time to finish the war his grandfather was supposed to have won fifty years earlier.

———

"Don't fear for her, Tarlen," Doctor Vicci DeLarose told him as they moved Belna onto the table. His sister was sedated, but they'd explained to her what they were attempting. Tarlen was given a few minutes to speak with her before they injected her with the dose, and it hadn't been enough time to say what he'd needed to.

"She has to make it," Tarlen told the doctor.

"She's in good hands. Nee, would you care to begin?"

Vicci asked, and Nee walked to Tarlen's side, speaking softly.

"We're going to ask you to leave the room for this, okay, son?" Nee asked him, and Tarlen peered over his shoulder as Vicci activated a tube-like machine.

"Can't I stay?" he asked, but the doctor was adamant.

"It's for her benefit that you're absent for the duration of the procedure, but you can observe from the other room, okay?" Nee had always been so kind to him and his sister, and Tarlen believed he was telling the truth.

"Sure thing. Just… take care of her, would you?"

"I'd never let you down," Nee said confidently, settling the lingering doubts in Tarlen's mind.

With a final glace to his sister as she entered the tube, Tarlen stepped near the door and left the operating room in the medical bay.

He was surprised to find Commander Starling there, sitting at the observation window. "Hi, Tarlen," she said, patting the seat beside her.

"I didn't expect you," he told her.

"And miss such an important moment of your life? Never. Come on; it's starting."

Tarlen sat, watching with interest as Vicci's machine slid Belna inside it. The contraption was long, a shiny white tube with glowing blue lights inside. There was a screen near him, and Tarlen tapped it to life, seeing a life feed from the interior of the surgical tube. There were half a dozen robotic arms adjusting controls, and one rolled Belna to the side. With a quick and precise movement, it shaved the back of her neck, cutting away some of her long dark hair.

"She's going to hate that. She loves her hair," Tarlen joked, and realized it had been so long since he'd allowed himself hope for her recovery. Was this really going to work?

Another robotic arm slid up the wall, and a thin blade reflected light from it. He looked away as it cut a straight line in her neck. He concentrated on Doctor Nee instead, who was standing beside his counterpart as she controlled the mechanical limbs doing the surgery.

Tarlen saw his sister's vitals, and they remained stable, according to what Nee had told him was normal under this kind of duress. "Come on, Bel. You can do it," he whispered.

A clear object appeared in robotic digits, and the arm placed it inside, sealing it with some kind of organic goo. It was mere minutes later and the surgery was completed. Judging by Vicci's and Nee's satisfied expressions, it had gone well, but they wouldn't confirm results until Belna came out of her anesthetized state.

Tarlen stared at her as the tube spat her out slowly, and glanced at Treena. "Thanks for coming."

"It's the least I could do," Treena told him. "And you're welcome. Plus, I needed to get out of the captain's hair. He has a million things coming at him, and I've managed to have a lot directed at me instead, to ease his stress levels."

"Then what are you doing here?" he asked.

She laughed, the sound a pleasant noise. "Hiding."

"How's everything coming along with the preparations?"

Treena rose from the seat and brushed her pants off. "They're good. By all accounts, the wormhole is ready to operate. We have the *Shu* prepared for the mission, and the Ugna are sending twelve of their fleet along to ensure we can't lose."

"Will that be enough?" he asked.

"We hope so. From what we could tell, there were

only a few of the warships remaining."

Tarlen nodded, recalling it vividly. He'd been on ground level as they'd rescued the Bacal; only they'd been too late for Belna.

"You can stay behind, Tarlen. The captain has already expressed his concern with bringing non-crew along on this mission. Your friend Kriss and the others won't be coming. They'll be staying on Earon Station." Treena headed for the door, and Tarlen wasn't sure what he wanted to do. He needed to wait and see what the results with his sister were.

———————

*I*t was the first time Ven had witnessed so many Ugna in one place. The twelve of their cruisers were docked near *Constantine,* and after a couple of days of anxious planning and message relaying, everyone was finally gathered in a giant amphitheater on Earon Station.

The place was made to seat over five thousand, and the stage was large enough to land a freighter on it, so their group was unremarkable as they piled into the first three rows near the dais.

Ven sat with the executive crew of *Constantine* beside their counterparts from *Shu,* and the Ugna captains and commanders were all together, waiting silently for the last of the parties to arrive. Captain Baldwin and Captain Bouchard sat on the stage, and Ven let his senses seep out.

The room's mood was impatient, the people all afraid of what was to come. He directed the tendrils at *Shu*'s captain and sensed her unease at the huge responsibility. She wondered if she was good enough, and he saw her glance at Baldwin, feeling inadequate at his resume. Ven considered the detail he was consuming, and realized he was nearly reading their minds, even if he wasn't. It was more of an emotional detector that translated at a higher level. Interesting.

He was about to check Baldwin, when he stopped himself. It felt too invasive, like he was doing something unethical, and he ceased, cutting off the tendrils. He shifted in his seat, catching Brax and his sister whispering to each other. He couldn't hear them but knew they were as ready for this to happen as everyone else.

Captain Baldwin rose, his shoulders broad as he strode to the lectern. "Thank you for your patience, everyone. We're about to start, but we're still waiting on a few guests."

The doors to the rear of the stage opened, revealing Prime Xune and Admiral Jalin Benitor. The gathered crowd rose, Ven along with them. He'd heard they were attempting to make the trip in time, and it appeared as though they had.

"Prepare to be inspired," Brax whispered to Treena, who waved him away.

The Prime stopped at Bouchard and Baldwin before heading to the center of the stage to speak to the Ugna captains and the Concord cruise ship crews. "Thank you for waiting. I do apologize for the delay, but as you know, we've been struggling with stretching ourselves too thin these last few months. Amid all the chaos, we're still having to stay extra vigilant along the Borders, as outsiders seek to take advantage of our situation.

"We thank the Elders for allowing us access to the Ugna fleet, and to the captains and commanders here and heading on this imperative mission, I thank you." He nodded to the Ugna, and Ven felt a rush of pride at the acknowledgement, even if it wasn't him being targeted by the comment. Contrary to what Father Hamesly had suggested, they were a great people and deserved their place among the Concord.

"I'm new to this role, but I've learned an awful lot about the Concord in a short time." Xune paused, setting his hands on the podium. Ven leaned forward, drawn to the man's charisma as he spoke. They'd done well in choosing the Prime. In Ven's opinion, this one was far more suited to the task than the human named Harris had been.

A screen lowered behind the stage, and simulated images of their fleet appeared. "The wormhole generator has been completed and tested by our team of experts." Ven noticed Brax patting his sister on the shoulder in front of him. "Tomorrow, we leave. We'll embark on a mission more important than any of us truly realize. There's a chance the Statu would never return here, but sadly, that's not the reality. They *will* fight us; they will come to Concord space once again and attempt to duplicate what happened back then. Many of you were around in the years shortly after, some even during…" He glanced at Admiral Benitor, who was seated beside Baldwin.

"The Concord was shaken in the aftermath, and this already feels similar. We were complacent for too long, too happy to forget our past, too lazy to carve a future. But that era is over. When we return from defeating the Statu, we will be ushering the Concord into a new era, one with stronger connections, with morals that stand the test of time and with great leadership."

Someone clapped, and Ven noticed it was the one named Cedric, from *Shu*'s crew. He stood, and the rest of his team joined him.

"What a suck-up," Brax said, standing too. Ven did as well, and soon they were all risen, clapping at the encouraging words from their new Prime.

He raised a hand, silencing the crowd, and smiled at them. "What I ask of you is absurd. The burden you carry on your shoulders is not for the weak of heart, but I believe you can all handle this task with poise and determination. I recognize many will be unable to return, but those who do will claim satisfaction at the future you've helped secure for our next generations."

More clapping, and Ven felt a surge of elation from the people inside the room. He glanced at the Ugna, and a few were bent over, the emotions possibly too intense in the room.

"Stay vigilant and remember: *There are two sides to every conflict, but know in your heart, the rightful will prevail.*" Prime Xune stepped away, moving toward the center of the stage, where he motioned for Captain Baldwin to take over.

Ven watched the captain settle at the podium, and he spoke with passionate determination as they went over their plan, step by step. He showed them visuals and 3D projections of battle plans, and when they opened it to the floor, the one-sided conversation turned to hours of discussion and strategy tweaking. Ven said his suggestions where he saw fit, and noticed that the one named Cedric had a mind for confrontation with their enemy.

When Ven thought the discussions were coming close to an end, Brax stood up, getting everyone's attention. "This has been very informative, and using their past movements and strategy will probably work, but we have to bear something in mind."

"What's that?" Captain Bouchard asked. She sat on the edge of the stage beside Baldwin, the Prime, and the admiral in the front row as the conversation had shifted to the war details.

"The Statu are unpredictable. They seem to be almost robotic in their ways and are rarely seen themselves. Why did they go to such lengths to hide the fact that they were sending our people against us?" Brax asked.

"So we wouldn't stop fighting them?" Commander Shu asked.

Brax nodded slightly. "Could be. But would we have stopped even then?"

Cedric spoke up. "No, but maybe there was another reason."

Ven rose, thinking he might have the answer. "Because they didn't want us to be aware of how few soldiers they truly had."

"That's correct," Brax said.

"Then why the war at all?" Commander Starling asked.

Captain Baldwin took this one. "People have been asking that question from the very start, and no one has come up with a conclusive answer."

Ven thought he might have an idea, but he didn't want to say it yet, not in front of everyone. He'd wait until he could speak privately with his crew members.

"Okay, back to the point. We have to assume they're weak, they don't have many slaves, and we took the ore they stole from Greblok. They're as good as decimated," Brax said with confidence that Ven no longer felt.

FIFTEEN

Tarlen woke to a gentle shaking of his shoulders and blinked away the sleep from his eyes. "Nee?" he asked, seeing the white-haired doctor over his bed.

"It's time," Nee said, a smile spread across his handsome face.

Tarlen bolted from the patient bed, tossing the heavy blanket to the floor as he darted from the room. Nee laughed, following close behind, and they moved from the rear of the medical bay to the surgical chamber.

The doors slid open, and Vicci was there, standing in front of someone, blocking his view.

"Belna!" Tarlen called, hoping the surgery had been a success.

Vicci stepped to the side, and there was his sister in a patient gown, sitting on the table, her eyes still pure white. He slowed, chin lowering to his chest. "It didn't work," he said softly.

"What do you mean, Tarlen?" It took him a moment to realize the voice came from her mouth, not the speakers beside the bed.

"Belna... is that you!?" He ran to her, and she slid off the bed, landing on uneasy legs. He caught her in an embrace and lifted her from the ground.

"Be careful, Tarlen," Nee warned, and Tarlen set her on the floor.

Belna stared at him with blank eyes and smiled. "It worked. I can think, and move, and speak again. You have no idea how scary that was, but you came for me. You saved me from that dreadful planet and never gave up." She hugged him, squeezing until he could hardly breathe.

"This is unbelievable. Thank you, Doctor Nee, Doctor DeLarose." Tarlen turned to see the two faces smiling widely at the two Bacal siblings.

"We're going to send you two to Earon with Vicci, where she's going to insert pigmentation for Belna's eyes and run more applicable tests. We want to ensure this is a permanent fix," Nee said, and Tarlen nodded along.

"That's good." Tarlen was fully aware that *Constantine* was heading off to war today, and maybe it was for the best that he and his sister were remaining behind. Her awareness was fresh; he didn't want to lose her again. Not after they'd lost so much in the initial attack on Greblok.

Belna shook her head. "I appreciate what you're saying, but I can't go."

"Why not?" Tarlen asked.

"Because there are too many people over there that need our help," she said.

"What are you talking about?" Nee asked. "Over where?"

"On the Statu world."

"We already … dealt with them," Tarlen said, recalling the destruction as they'd killed so many of the brainwashed slaves.

"Not them. There are more. I was in a facility briefly. I saw the people, but they weren't Bacal. There were ones like… him." She pointed at the Kwant doctor. "And there were humans, like Vicci here. Some with bald heads and ruts on their foreheads. And tall thin ones. So many."

Nee crossed the room and grabbed Belna's cheeks softly with his gloved hands. "Are you saying there are Kwants as slaves over there? And others?"

She nodded. "They don't seem like slaves. I heard one of them call themselves Groups. They hardly spoke Standard. They clicked."

"They clicked?" Tarlen asked.

"Yes, like the Statu." Belna's hand was shaking, and Tarlen feared the worst.

"Maybe we should stop; she's nervous. She's had too big of a day," he said, but Nee kept asking questions.

"They spoke like the Statu. Were they young, old?"

"All sorts of different ages," Belna said.

Doctor Nee turned almost as white as his hair. "How many? How many did you see?"

"There were thousands, but that was only one area. I think there might have been more," she told him.

Tarlen tried to understand what he was hearing.

"Someone find Captain Baldwin, now!" Nee shouted out the door at Kelli.

———

"*T*his changes everything, doesn't it?" Reeve asked.

With the technology R-emergence had created, they might be able to recover and repair the Concord slaves, and because of that, this had turned from an all-out battle to a rescue mission. Tom rubbed his head and looked around the room.

The executive crew was all present, and he'd wanted to discuss it with them first, before bringing their findings to the rest of the fleet. "Belna was sure there were pockets of these Groups all over the planet. She overheard a conversation in Standard when they'd first arrived. It sounded like not all the slaves they held were too keen on being rescued. Many of them still displayed their iris color, and yet chose to fight alongside the Statu."

"It's a textbook syndrome, if you ask me," Nee said. The doctor sat at the opposite end of the meeting room table from Tom, with the twins on the right side, and Ven and Treena on Tom's left.

"Can you explain?" Tom asked.

"Throughout history, there have been many cases of a group of people being invaded and enslaved, the captors treating them well enough for the prisoners to entertain the notion that they're being cared for, even loved. The enslaved have the delusional sense that they're in the wrong and deserve their fate, ensuring they'll do anything for the invaders, even kill or die, perhaps." Doctor Nee folded his hands on his lap and shrugged.

"I didn't know you were a therapist too," Brax said with a smirk.

"I may be wrong," Nee said.

Ven tapped a long finger on the table, drawing Tom's attention. "What is it, Ven?"

The Ugna appeared surprised to be called on, or maybe he'd been deep in thought. "I've been thinking a lot about the Statu since our meeting last night. I think with this new information, I have a theory."

Tom was glad everyone was concentrated on this problem. They were going to need all the skilled minds they had to solve the issue. "Can we hear it?" he asked when Ven didn't continue.

"The Statu arrived six decades ago, and we fought them for ten years, correct?" Ven asked.

"That's right," Brax replied.

"We always seemed to be fighting on even ground,

never with the odds completely against us. They would send a few warships into a system, draw us in, then leave or end up being destroyed, quite often obliterating our ships simultaneously.

"They also attacked a lot of planets early on, leaving craters and destroyed cities, which we now understand meant they used their Movers to steal thousands, or tens of thousands, of slaves. They then used these slaves to control more warships and kept repeating the same motivations the entire time. Eventually, they used a wormhole and departed, after Yollox."

"And then they came back a few months ago. This is common knowledge, Ven," Tom said, trying not to sound short with the Ugna. Tom was growing weary of the discussions and wished the mission was over already, before it had begun.

"To obtain the ore."

"So they could return with the ability to make wormholes?" Treena asked.

"I think they have a formidable population," Ven said.

Tom leaned forward. "We were over there. They had a dozen warships, and we destroyed a few, even stole one. We understand the ships' capabilities and the trick of the slaves. We're prepared for them."

Ven didn't appear to buy it. "It doesn't add up. They came the first time to steal our people. They waited two generations before attacking Greblok."

"Are you implying they were aware of the mineral under the Bacal ocean, when the Bacal didn't even know it was there?" Treena asked, and Ven nodded.

"I believe so."

"Yephion told us their neighbors were devious. Imagine how many of these Groups they could control between those two planets. And if they had thousands then, what if they made them breed?" Brax asked, and Tom cringed at the thought of all the slaves being made to procreate.

Reeve frowned in distaste. "That *is* plausible, and some of them would be third-generation captives. Those would be the ones speaking Statu and believing in the cause."

Tom's headache was growing worse with each passing theory, and he drank deeply from his glass of water. "If all of this conjecture is true, what's the worst outcome you can think of?"

Brax glanced at Ven, then back to Tom. "If this was their plan the entire time, they might have a veritable army and fleet over there. We didn't check the neighboring planet for warship construction. And what about the twelve that came from the depths of that system when we arrived? Where were they coming from? We were in such a time crunch; we had no way to investigate."

"Maybe we should open the wormhole and send a scout," Reeve suggested.

As much as Tom liked the idea, it wouldn't work. "Then they realize we're coming, and we have no element of surprise. As it stands, they likely expect us, but they have no clue when we'd come. And since the generator was created so quickly, we're probably far ahead of their estimations. We can't do a reconnaissance mission, unfortunately."

They were scheduled to leave in four hours, and if this speculation was even close to reality, he needed to speak with the admiral as soon as possible. He stood, tapping his knuckles on the table as he walked past his crew. "Prepare what you can. Brax, make sure our weapons systems are attuned to any of the vulnerabilities we learned from our stolen warship."

"Captain, we checked those a dozen times," Brax told him.

"Check them again, and bring Reeve with you. We can't have any errors." Tom left them chatting amongst themselves and went to find the admiral.

He found her on *Shu* a half hour later, talking with Rene Bouchard. He waited outside her office on the bridge, shifting from foot to foot while seconds stretched to minutes and minutes to a half hour. Eventually, he located Commander Shu, and the young Callalay must have heard the importance in his voice, because Admiral Benitor opened the door moments later, her gaze meeting Tom's.

Rene exited her office, visibly rattled. He'd recognize that look anywhere. He wondered if she'd tried to transfer her command of *Shu*. That wouldn't do them any good.

"Baldwin, in here. We don't have much time now, do we?" Benitor waved him in, and Tom shut Rene's office door behind him.

"Admiral, we may have some news…"

She lifted a finger, stepping closer to him. She was a good half-head shorter than he was and at least three decades older, but she still caused him to react at the movement. "Did you think we wouldn't find out?"

Tom swallowed hard. It was clear he'd been caught, but it might not be about Luci. "You're going to have to be clearer."

She cast her gaze to the door and brought out a device he'd never seen before. It was half the size of her palm, and she pressed a button on the edge before placing it in the center of the desk. "We can talk freely without fear of being heard."

"You think Rene is bugging her own office?" Tom asked.

"I think that this ship has the AI of a very intelligent woman, and one of the best captains this damned Concord has ever seen, and Bouchard has a checkered history with authority."

"Then why did you name her captain?" Tom asked. "Was it the whole human thing, because Tess Longshade seems to think…"

"Tess Longshade needs to watch what she says before she ends up beside Harris," Admiral Benitor said quickly. He'd never seen her this agitated.

"Look…"

"The girl. We're aware she isn't on Bolux Nine. What did you do with her?" The subject change caught Tom off-guard, and he uttered some nonsense. "Tom, I vouched for you after Greblok. I really did. There were some that wanted to string you up and blame your grandfather for the aftermath of the Yollox Incursion, but I stood by you and your name. Don't make me regret it, please."

She sat down, and he saw her years adding up in her posture, in the way her skin sagged around her eyes, and he nodded, sitting opposite her. "I'm sorry. I didn't have many options."

"You could have done what we asked and left the girl with Seda."

"If you knew me at all, you'd have expected it," he said.

She smiled: not a happy gesture, but one of resignation. "Perhaps it might be better this way. On Bolux, she was sure to die, but we might need bait one day."

"Bait? For what?" Tom asked.

"Keen."

"He's not going anywhere, Admiral. What are you…"

"It's come to my attention, from one of your crew members, that Keen is privy to key contacts outside the Concord's reach." The sparkle had returned to her eyes.

"You mean the angry aliens he bartered with, trading stolen Concord property for technology?" Tom had heard enough. "Why can't you let the mother have the girl and keep them contained somewhere instead?"

"I heard you had a relationship with Seda. Is that true?" she asked, and Tom slammed his palm on the desk. Benitor didn't so much as flinch at the action.

"What in the Vastness does a crush from twenty years ago have to do with anything?"

"Everything, Tom. Everything. The girl stays where you stashed her." The admiral didn't advise if she was aware of the location, and Tom wasn't about to offer it, so they proceeded to stare at one another.

"Come back alive, Baldwin. Contrary to what you think, I support you and always will. You have a good heart, even better than the old codger had when he was at it," she said. "You leave in three hours. Make it count, Tom. Finish this war."

He sighed, the fight gone from the room, and he told her about their new theory. She listened with care and disagreed with the hypothesis.

"What if we're right?"

"We don't have the people. We're rebuilding. You can't be right, and if you are, you have to win regardless. You have the two finest vessels the Concord has ever seen. You have the element of surprise and a fantastic crew. You can do this, Tom. If there's any hope left, it's you."

Tom rose, deciding the meeting had to be over. "I'll do my best."

"*Effort equals results. Give your all; you shall receive as much in return.*" Benitor came to stand by him, and she set a hand on his arm. "Tom, there's one more thing. I'm giving you a promotion for this mission. You are now Fleet Captain, the direct leader of Captain Bouchard and all twelve Ugna vessels. We can't have any more subordination in this unified battle."

Tom stood proud and nodded his understanding. "I think that's for the best."

"These events have been culminating for some time. Let's see us begin fresh when you return. I have a fun mission for you next," she told him.

"Not going to tell me what it is?" he asked.

"In due time."

---

*T*reena watched the wormhole expand to life; the swirling colors were even more beautiful than the one the Statu had created. The rift was focused, the spectrum array breathtaking to behold. It was also the single most daunting thing Treena had even seen.

Even though her real body was up in her suite, the hands of her artificial body shook. Real habits were difficult to break.

Shu was in position beside them, the twin vessels flanked by the dozen smaller vessels of the Ugna fleet, and everyone was waiting on Fleet Captain Baldwin's word. Treena sneaked a peak at the man as he paced the bridge, hands behind his back, his posture perfect, his eyes set in the slightest of frowns. She'd known him for a long time, and there was no one she'd trust to lead them as much as Tom.

Reeve's voice carried from the boiler room, where she was in contact with Harry on the cruiser connected to the generator. "Captain, the wormhole has stabilized. Waiting on word from the probe."

Treena and the rest of the crew lingered impatiently for word that they were targeting the proper system, and she ran her gaze across the executive team. Brax was in his spot on the left edge of the bridge, his hands anxiously flexing. Ven remained in the main helm position. She was really beginning to like the odd man, even more so since he'd opened up slightly around everyone. His ideas and theories about the Statu had been well-calculated, but that didn't stop her from hoping he was wrong.

Lieutenant Darl had taken Zare's position after she'd proven herself a traitor to the Concord. A small part of Treena felt saddened by her suicide, but she tried not to give it a second thought as she once again watched the wormhole.

Constantine's AI observed it all with a sort of bemused grin on his face, his arms crossed as he stood at the right side of the bridge.

"Captain, we're good to go. The wormhole is stable and is leading us to the Statu home world." Reeve's voice held a nervous tinge.

"Very well. Ven, send communication to the others. This is Fleet Captain Thomas Baldwin," Tom said. The admiral and Prime would be listening, along with any Concord officers on Earon Station, and Treena listened intently as her captain spoke. "We're about to embark on something I wish we didn't have to do."

It was starting out rocky. He turned to look at Treena and offered a confident expression before facing the screen again. "The Statu threaten our way of life. They've ruined worlds, stolen our people, killed our families. I consider our mission as one not of vengeance for the lives we've lost to the Vastness, but one of thanks for their sacrifice. It's unknown what happens when we die" – he paused and glanced at Ven – "but I'm prepared to risk my own life to save the people of the Concord. Today, we end the War our predecessors couldn't or wouldn't, and tomorrow, we start over with new leadership, new ambitions, new partners like the Ugna. We each have a legacy, and today, we start ours."

Brax nodded, sitting firmly in his seat, and Treena sensed the mood on the bridge improving. She gazed at the captain with admiration, as the others all did.

"Ven, lead the charge. Until we meet in the Vastness," Tom said, ending the communication.

"Until we meet in the Vastness," the entire crew on the bridge echoed, and the captain returned to his seat beside her as Ven brought them toward the wormhole.

"How'd I do?" he asked from the side of his mouth. "Couldn't have done better." Treena closed her eyes as *Constantine* entered the wormhole.

SIXTEEN

*I*na immediately knew something was wrong. The ship, *Savior*, had lowered toward the neighboring planet of the world she'd inhabited her entire life. When Adept Feerez showed her the screen with images from outside the vessel, her heart skipped a beat. The ships were huge, arms protruding at all angles. But what really caught her off guard was the sheer number of them.

She tried to count but lost track after around thirty. "Where are we?"

Adept Feerez stood proudly, his cloak draping over his shoulders. "We are at our birthplace," he said.

"Where did I live?" she asked.

"At the traitors' world."

"The Concord?" She was confused.

"No. Centuries ago, our cousins lived below ground there. We didn't share a vision, so we disposed of them when they caused trouble." He said this with detached emotion, his expression unwavering.

If they'd kill their own cousins so easily, what did that say for her people? Her mother's words rang through her mind. *This isn't our way. You're human, Ina. Your grandfather was from Earon, a lieutenant in the War, the same War that ended with him captured. We are slaves. Don't forget it. Never forget.*

It was one of the last things she'd heard from the woman, and true to her word, she never did forget it. "What do you want me to do?"

"Things have escalated. They will be here soon."

"Here?" Ina looked around, as if expecting trouble to

storm through the corridors.

"No, my girl. Not here, but out there." He pointed to the sky.

She failed to understand, his words familiar to her, but the meaning of them beyond her capacity. Growing up below the surface and having little interaction with the Adepts was a predictable disadvantage. "What do you have to fear? Surely they cannot compete with this." She pointed to the screen, where dozens of the immense Adept ships hovered across the open sand. The land was different here than home, and she wondered what it would have been like to be raised here among the Adepts rather than in their numbered underground city sections.

"Sorry, you haven't answered my question, Adept Feerez. What do you need me to do?" she asked.

He gave her the strangest version of a smile, his mandibles clicking together a few times wordlessly. "You, my sweet Ina, will be the face of your people. You're going to stand before this camera and tell the Concord exactly what I say."

She glanced to the right, where one of the Adepts grunted, this one wearing choppy armor. It pointed to a screen, where clusters of red lights moved closer to two planets on what she understood to be a map of some kind. She was suddenly nervous. "I am?"

"That's right." He set a hand on her shoulder, and she cringed at the touch, trying not to let him notice. "Here's what you do."

———

"Ven, what's on the radar?" Tom asked the moment they emerged from the wormhole. *Constantine* shuddered as they slowed, entering the Statu system. It felt like he'd just been here, and Tom almost expected to find Captain Yin Shu in *Cecilia*, defending their escape.

It was quiet now; nothing but their own fleet occupied the space.

"Captain, there is no indication of the…" Ven started, and stopped as something did appear on their screen. It was a solitary warship. "There's one, sir. And it's moving toward us."

Tom rose, walking toward the viewer. "Get me *Shu*."

"Yes, sir." Ven tapped his console, and half of the viewer filled with the other flagship's bridge. Rene was there, her face pale.

"You made it without incident?" he asked her.

"We're fine. You could have warned me about that. I thought the effect was immediate," she said, her voice shaking.

"Sorry," he told her. The fact that the trip took somewhere around ten minutes must have slipped his mind while they'd talked strategy. There were too many moving pieces to remember them all.

"Captain, the Ugna vessels have checked in, as requested, and are in working order," Brax advised him.

"Good."

"What do you make of this, Baldwin?" Rene asked. "Why is there a solitary ship?"

"I don't know, but we've deployed the probes." Tom waited as they flew toward the planets, their tiny jump drives sending them there far faster than any other device could have made the distance. With the recent discovery of the Nek mines, the Concord would be able to implement the technology into the cruise ships eventually, but not until they'd been tested, which would take years on a safety hazard like that.

"Sir, the probes are revealing the first planet to be much the same as it had been. Some life forms are active." Brax pushed the details onto the viewer, and to *Shu* and the Ugna fleet.

"What about the other planet?" Tom asked. They hadn't had time to investigate it their previous visit, and he hated going in blind like this.

"Sir, there's too much atmospheric interference for the probes to do their job," Brax advised.

Rene was still on-screen, and Tom heard her mumbling something, catching the words "big surprise."

"Do you have something to say, Captain Bouchard?" he asked.

"Why is there one ship heading for our position?" she asked. "It moved swiftly, as if they'd been expecting company."

Tom considered this. She might be correct.

"Sir, there's something else showing up on the sensors," Ven said.

"What is it?"

Ven changed the image on the viewer and used the zooming feature to show chunks of metal floating halfway between them and the planet. "Readings tell me they're Statu, sir."

Tom blinked, walking closer to the screen. There had to be a dozen warships' worth of debris there. "Who did this?" he asked, wondering if someone else had already done their dirty work.

"There are no residual Star Drive particulates around them, so it had to have occurred at least two weeks ago," Ven said.

Tom tried to take in the whole picture but was struggling to piece it together.

"Seems like we're almost done here," Rene said, her

color returned to her cheeks. "Let's blast these bastards and go home heroes."

Tom stood thoughtfully. "I think we need to consider the world below. We can't be sure they're all destroyed."

"Baldwin, the evidence is there. You thought there were upwards of ten or so remaining, and we have proof of at least that many being destroyed, halfway to their home world. We've already won," Rene said.

"Stay where you are, everyone. I'll reconvene in a few minutes," he said, and Rene looked about ready to interject when her image dropped from the viewer.

"Commander, what do you think?" he asked Treena, who appeared deep in thought at her seat.

"Too early to tell. The warship is bearing down on us, and we have to assume that's an act of hostility, so I do agree we need to destroy it, but we can't leave this system until we properly investigate their planet. Plus, if Doctor DeLarose and R-emergence are capable of repairing the damage done to the slaves, we have a chance to rescue the Bacal we left behind, and anyone else we find on the surface," Commander Starling said, making perfect sense.

"Very good, Commander. Ven, on screen." Tom waited until he saw *Shu*'s bridge reappear, and the heads of all twelve Ugna captains in two rows on either side of the viewer. "We'll intercept the warship, fend off any attacks, and return to the planet where we left the Bacal. Folks, this has turned from war to a rescue mission, and we're going to take our time, ensuring we save every life possible."

Rene seemed irritated at the suggestion but kept it internalized, only nodding her understanding.

"Ven, set course for interception," Tom ordered, taking his seat once again.

"Course is set, sir."

"Time to intercept?"

"One hour, sir," Ven advised, and Tom stared at the images of the debris, trying to determine who or what could have caused the damage.

---

*T*arlen walked closer to Belna, her movements unsure in the aftermath of the surgery. She stumbled and he caught her, urging her through the corridor.

"Will I ever get the hang of this again?" Belna asked.

"Yes."

"Why are you so optimistic?" Her blank eyes stared at him, and even though he'd been assured countless times that she was able to see just fine, he kept thinking she was blind.

"Because you've managed to survive this long, so learning to walk again is nothing." Tarlen hoped he was right and led her into the courtyard. They'd survived through the wormhole, and Tarlen had made Belna stay in her quarters for the duration of the trip.

She stopped at a viewscreen along the edge of the courtyard entrance, watching as the image showed the incoming warship. "I don't like this," she whispered, holding on to his arm for balance.

They were at least a half an hour from contact, but Tarlen had a sinking feeling in his gut as they neared the ship. "Constantine," he said, trying to get the AI's attention.

The projection appeared behind him, and Tarlen jumped at the sudden movement. "What is it, Tarlen? Weren't you supposed to exit the ship with Doctor DeLarose?"

He shrugged. "Belna wouldn't let us, even though I told her it was the best idea for her health."

Belna turned to Constantine and placed her hands on her hips. "The Statu are distracting us. I know it," she said.

Constantine pointed toward the warship on the screen. "We found debris from many more vessels. There was a battle, and they lost."

"Have you attempted communication with the warship?" Tarlen asked.

"We have, but we're showing… wait, there has been contact." Constantine flickered, as the AI could be up to twenty places at once. There was bound to be a version on the bridge. "I must go."

Constantine was gone, and Belna shook her head slowly. "Something's wrong."

———————

*I*na stood exactly where Adept Feerez had told her to, and when the timer counted down to zero, she touched the button. Words scrolled over the computer in Standard, and she read them, having practiced for several hours.

The image would be transmitted to their bridge, he'd said, and as much as she'd been fearful of the Adept, she almost wished he was there to support her as she began speaking.

"My name is Ina. I am human and come from Casonu One. We managed to escape, stealing this vessel after a mutiny transpired. My Group took to the skies in their ships, and we were chased down, nearly all of us being destroyed on both sides. We're injured, in need of food and water, and there are numerous others on Casonu Two, from what we've been told. Please, I beg of you… help us." Real tears streamed over her cheeks, and she hit the button again with a shaky finger, ending the communication.

Now all she could do was wait.

———

*T*reena watched the girl's face, trying to decipher it. The message played for the third time. "Please, I beg of you… help us." Ven paused it at the end.

Brax was the first to speak this time. "Ina. Do you hear that voice? What kind of accent is that? She's clearly human, but… remember what Belna said about some of the slaves having their minds unaltered, yet siding with the Statu? If this Ina was born there, she might be working for them."

Treena had thought the same thing, but the tears and fear in Ina's eyes felt real enough. Tom hadn't said anything in a few minutes, and she noticed him sitting patiently, clenching his jaw. He'd been under a lot of pressure and was being careful to make the proper decision.

"Play it again," he said quietly, and Ven started the short message from the beginning. When it was over, Tom rose, pacing the bridge. "She said they had a mutiny, and that they took to the skies, implying they were pursued from Casonu One. That's where Yephion and his people used to live, the same planet Treena chased through the underground cities, before using the hovertransports to rescue the Bacal slaves."

"If this is real, we have nothing to fear," Ven said.

"Can you get a read on her, Ven?" Tom asked, and

the Ugna man shook his head.

"Not from this distance, sir, but perhaps if we were in a room with her," Ven suggested.

"It may come to that, but I worry that if there's a trap, then it'll be too late," Tom told them.

"Sir, Captain Bouchard is trying to reach you," Ven said.

"On screen."

Rene's face was hardened, unreadable. "Captain Baldwin, it's decision time. Do we blast it?"

Treena shuddered. Rene always had been a bit of a wildcard, but it was clear she wanted to shoot first and ask for forgiveness later.

Tom crossed his arms, looking confident as he spoke. "We're going to stay out of range. We'll send her a message, informing her we're sending *Cleo* and a specialized team to investigate and offer supplies. Lieutenant Commander Brax, see to it," he said.

Brax nodded, and notified Doctor Nee he was wanted on the bridge.

"Fine, do it your way, Fleet Captain Baldwin." Captain Rene smirked and whispered to her crew. "We'll send our own team to rendezvous on their warship. Better to have extra muscle, don't you think?"

Treena half-expected Tom to decline her invitation at assistance, but he didn't. "Good thought. The ships will need to be scoured for signs of Statu, so bring a discreet contingency of guards under the guise of medics."

"If you trust her, why the cloak and dagger?" Rene asked.

"No one said I trust her. The whole scenario feels like a trap," Baldwin said.

"Then I stand by my first suggestion…"

Tom raised a hand, stopping her from finishing. "We

have our plan. Now set to it."

Treena crossed the bridge as the *Shu*'s crew dropped from the viewer. "Brax, we know the ships better than anyone else. I'll join you." She didn't add that she was the only one that could be resurrected in a new body with her mind intact.

"I'd welcome your company," Brax told her.

Tom sent a message to Engineering. "Reeve, how's our wormhole doing?"

Reeve Daak's voice was clear and concise over the speakers. "Stable and strong, Captain. Nothing to report from here."

"Good. Everyone to your tasks."

---

*B*rax was fastened behind *Cleo*'s pilot's seat, once more leaving on a dangerous expedition. It was part of his role, but he'd come perilously close to dying as a Statu hostage, and he didn't want to relive the experience.

Cleo was packed with his guards. Kurt, his newest deputy, was taking the lead on the sweep of the warship's upper half. He was a square-jawed human with a dirty blond buzzcut and a trimmed beard, making him appear older than his thirty years.

Treena Starling was all business, sitting beside him, her hand settled on her PL-30 at her hip. She was ready for this, even more so than Brax. The hangar opened, and Brax remembered flying the stolen Tuber into one of these ships only a few months ago. He closed his eyes after breaching the energy barrier and lowered *Cleo*, the expedition ship from *Shu* directly behind them.

Two of the Ugna vessels lingered close to the warship, shields on full and weapons at ready in case something fishy was going on here. Brax hoped it didn't come to that, because with the firepower the Ugna brought, compared to the low-tech Statu warship, he expected there wouldn't be time for an evacuation.

"Don't worry, Commander," he assured Treena. "It's like we've been here before, but this time, it's different."

"We should have checked the planet first," Treena said softly.

Brax stood, blocking the commander from exiting. "If you had another suggestion, you should have told the captain before we'd boarded the enemy ship."

"No, it's not that. Just my intuition. Maybe we should have brought Ven. He could have read the girl," she said.

"That's true, but even the captain doesn't want to risk everything on Ven's emotional premonitions." Brax turned to Kurt and grimaced at the task they were about to endure. The ten men and women were armed, lined at the exit, and ready to enter the warship's hangar. "Deputy, we're heading to Deck Ninety, where Ina told us we'd find her. You split the teams into groups of three and comb the ship. Tell them to all keep in touch with you, and you relay to me. Got it?" None of this was new information, but it was Kurt's first foray as deputy, and Brax wasn't taking any chances.

"Done. We'll begin right away," Kurt said. His people carried water and various medical supplies with them, and formed a line near the elevators.

"Lookie what we have here." Cedric strode over, holding an XRC-14 over his shoulder, the barrel pointing at the ceiling behind him.

Brax tried to push away his dislike for the man and forced a grin. "Cedric, I'm surprised they let you out without a leash…" Commander Kan Shu exited their expedition ship, and Brax let out a laugh. "Never mind. There's the leash."

"You think you're so funny, Daak? I'm surprised they didn't name your sister chief of security. She packs more punch." Cedric smirked.

"That's the first thing you've ever said that I agree with. Okay, people. We have our orders. Move out." Brax waved them forward, and the four executive officers found the elevator first, the rest waiting behind so they could gather into position.

"Stay vigilant," Treena told the guards as the elevator doors closed, and they lifted toward Deck Ninety.

Brax's jaw tensed, his hand clutching his large weapon tightly, and the trip felt like it took far too long. By the time the elevator stopped, he was beginning to feel cramped in the confined space, with the other three crew members surrounding him. He pressed off first and saw their contact.

Ina was even smaller than her image on the viewer, her brown hair shoulder-length and thin. Ina's face was narrow, and she lit up at their appearance. She rushed forward, and Brax lifted his gun to aim at her, but Treena stepped between them, accepting the girl's hug as she almost jumped into the commander's arms.

"You came. You really came. My mother always said the Concord was honorable, and that they'd come for us eventually. I…" Ina looked around as she let go of Treena, and must have noticed the huge guns in the Concord crew's possession. She stepped back warily, her eyes darting around the room.

"What is it?" Treena asked.

"I… have you seen anyone else?" Ina asked.

"What do you mean?"

"On this ship, have you seen anyone else?" Ina asked

again.

"Not yet. We only just…"

Brax tapped his communicator, holding the piece in his ear. "Deputy, what have you found?"

"People. No one seems injured, and not that many are speaking Standard. Their speech is…"

Brax eyed the slip of a girl. "Statu?"

"That's right. We're going to keep moving. So far, the other teams are reporting pretty much the same thing," Kurt told him.

"Okay, keep going. I'll be in touch." Brax ended the conversation.

Treena walked to the girl, who didn't move this time, and reached for her hand. "Ina, what happened?"

Ina broke her gaze and glanced at Brax, meeting his stare for a moment before looking at Cedric. The big Tekol stayed motionless, his gun resting on his shoulder.

"We escaped. Fought them, but they were too powerful. We stole seven of the ships, but they brought three. The odds were in their favor, but we managed to remain on the outskirts of the battle. We lost hundreds, thousands of us, but we think that was all of them." Ina was crying now, her face contorting as the tears fell.

"Where were you going?" Brax asked her, and she answered through the sobs.

"We didn't know. We planned it for years and finally gathered the courage. I hoped to find the Concord, but we didn't have any coordinates," she admitted.

"And you said we need to head to Casonu Two?" Brax asked.

"We believe there are more slaves there, yes," Ina said, her composure slowly returning.

"And the Statu?" Cedric asked, his free hand resting on his hip.

"They're gone, from what I've heard. We attacked them on Casonu One, and the ships were the last of the Adepts," Ina told them, and Brax breathed a sigh of relief.

"Come on, then. Let's move your people to safety, and we'll take it from there," Treena said, ushering the girl toward the elevator.

Brax peered around the computer room, seeing the screens along the walls, and he remembered flying the other craft away from the Statu world. He didn't want to pilot another one.

"Kurt, can you come up to Ninety? I have a job for you."

SEVENTEEN

*I*na's tears had been real, but her story was false. For a brief moment, she'd considered telling them the truth, but deep down, something had told her she'd die a horrible death at Adept Feerez's long fingers. The second the big strong Concord crew members arrived, she'd felt something lift in her chest. She was free. She could spill the plan to them. Surely Adept Feerez had been mistaken to trust her with such an important task. Why had she been asked?

He claimed to have prayed on it, and his gods had advised him to seek her out. When he'd found her as a small child on Casonu One, he'd recognized her, and he'd left her there to live underground with her Group.

She'd asked him about her mother being killed, and he'd assured her none of them were murdered, only repurposed. She thought about the blank white eyes after Carl was put through the machine, and it made her question if her mother was now like that, a mindless drone for the Adepts.

Adept Feerez had explained the Concord's hatred, the evil they carried, the fact that they were indeed wraiths, and that the Adepts had managed to save her people from becoming the same. He'd told her that just because they were born to evil didn't mean it couldn't be cleansed out of them. He'd said that once they defeated the Concord, they'd be able to return to their enemy's space and end the injustices for good.

Then Ina would be given a throne for her involvement, and Adept Feerez would single-handedly train her in their ways. She could become an Adept herself, saving her soul for eternity.

Ina thought about the evil Vastness the Concord spouted, a place where their people and enemies would burn through the ages. She dreaded the Vastness and had dreamt of it last night. A place where she couldn't breathe, but only gasp as she tried to swallow air, and when she screamed, the blood vessels burst in her eyes, but no sound emerged from her throat. She'd told the Adept about it, and he'd reiterated the importance of her task. "You must not fail, my child. The fate of everyone falls in your young hands." He'd left her with that, sending her away in *Savior*, to do precisely as the ship's name demanded.

"Captain, what are your orders? There are about twenty-five escaped prisoners here," the blonde woman said, snapping Ina into reality.

She could only hear this side of the conversation, but it was imperative that she lure them to Casonu Two. If she failed, Adept Feerez had assured her the Concord would drag her into the Vastness, and the thought alone was enough to make her skin crawl.

"That's right. Ina claims…" The woman turned from her, but Ina stayed close, not wanting to be out of earshot. "Claims that there are a lot of refugees residing on the second planet. Yes, not Yephion's, but the other twin world. The one we haven't been to." She glanced at Ina, who cast her gaze to the ground to appear meeker.

"Okay, we'll leave the warship where it is, under our control, and take one of the ships to check it out. We'll be returning with Ina and the others. Yes, sir. We understand we need to keep them under supervision." The woman motioned for Ina to follow, and the girl did just that. She needed to convince them to bring all their ships. It was clear the Adept wanted that.

"You know my name, but I don't know yours," Ina said to the woman. The big Tekol that seemed in charge was barking orders to his people, and Ina noticed how quickly they deferred to him. This woman seemed to be more emotional, more apt to listen to her pleas.

They strode across the hangar, toward two space-crafts. She'd seen the cylinder-shaped ones the Adepts used, but nothing compared to these. They reminded Ina of smooth rocks, long and lean, with curves and not sharp edges.

"I'm Commander Treena Starling of the Concord cruise ship *Constantine*. That's Lieutenant Commander Brax Daak, and those two men are Executive Lieutenant Cedric and Commander Kan Shu, of the cruise ship *Shu*," Treena told her.

"What's a cruise ship?" Ina asked. "Is that one?" She pointed to the waiting vessels, and the commander laughed lightly but not cruelly.

"No. Those are our expedition vessels. Ina, tell me about the Statu," Treena said, leading Ina onto the vehicle. Some of her people were already inside, and the Adept swore they were to be trusted. She didn't recognize any of them, but they were all of right mind, each having colored irises. Ina noted how young they were, most even younger than her.

"The Statu?" she asked.

"The ones that held you captive. Do you know anything about us?" Treena asked.

"We only knew them as the Adepts, and they told us

about you." Ina let this truth slip through, aware she'd need to sell her cause.

"Adepts…" The woman whispered it. She brought Ina away from the rear of the ship, past the other Adept-coached people, and to the front. Everything inside was far more advanced than she was used to, and Ina found her eyes being drawn to the blinking lights and her ears pleased at the soft chimes.

"Can I speak with your captain?" Ina asked.

Treena's eyes narrowed, and she sat Ina down, taking the seat on the bench beside her. "Why's that?"

The one she'd called Brax Daak strode onto the vessel, setting his huge weapon into a case along the wall. She eyed it casually and gawked back at Treena. "I have information that can assist you to recover the rest of my people. Of your people. Lest they find their way to the Vastness." Ina said the last with distaste, but used the keywords Adept Feerez had engrained into her.

Treena smiled. "I expect he'll want to speak with you."

"Strap in, everyone. Time to go home," Brax told them.

———————

"What's your assessment, Doctor?" Kelli asked.

Doctor Nee stared at the readouts, the young boy unmoving in the scanner. "By all accounts, what we have here is a healthy Callalay boy of around thirteen years. There are some signs of malnutrition, likely related to diet restriction. Otherwise, his brain activity is sound; his comprehension of the images we shared with him were as strong as one could expect from a boy trapped on a strange world, born in captivity."

"And the language?" Kelli asked. The boy only spoke a smattering of Standard, and opted for the clicks and grunts of the Statu. It was the strangest thing. Nee hadn't thought the Callalay physiology compatible with their intricate speech, but the Tekol and humans they'd checked spoke the language as well.

"It's remarkable what one can learn when not given a choice in the matter," Nee said as he powered down the scanner. The boy automatically slid from inside the machine on a flat white bed, his eyes wide and fearful. Nee gave him a smile, and the boy relaxed slightly. "You're okay, son. You can join the others." One of the guards posted outside the medical bay entered, escorting the thin Callalay to the cargo hold, where they'd placed a series of bunks to house the newcomers.

If there were thousands to be rescued, the Concord had prepared them for that. *Shu* would house most of the refugees, with the entire Deck Six being temporarily designed to take on such a load of passengers.

If that failed, they always had the warship they'd just received, though Nee didn't expect the captain to be so hot on shoving the slaves into those terrible pens like animals. That was how their own, Brax, had been brought to the planet the first time, and no one deserved that kind of treatment, with the exception of the Statu, perhaps. *A little taste of their own medicine.*

Kelli walked away, nursing a patient who'd been experiencing a fever. He was one of the guards that had set foot on the warship, and only two hours later, he was burning up. Nee followed her, with the medical bay empty save the single man on the patients' bed.

"How are you feeling?" Nee asked while Kelli stared at the tablet beside his bed.

The tablet clattered to the floor, the noise loud enough to startle the patient, but he remained unmoving. "Doctor, he's not breathing!"

Nee rushed to his side, the machines no longer beeping along with his vitals. "What in the Vastness happened?" The patient hadn't been sick enough to warrant the full array of tests, and Nee kicked himself for the lack of effort.

"I don't know…"

The door sprang open, and two officers basically dragged a Zilph'i woman between them. "She's burning up. Says she can't breathe."

"On the bed!" Nee pointed to an empty cot, and they settled her onto it, her eyes burning red, her lips pale and cracked.

"What's your name?" Nee asked, using a small pocket light to check her pupils.

She coughed, the sound thick and sticky-sounding. Something was wrong. "Get her a medispray, I need her vitals, and…"

The door opened again, and more people staggered in. Doctor Nee had a feeling things were about to escalate.

———

*T*om had listened to the girl's story a few times now and decided they would indeed send both cruise ships into the atmosphere to rescue the others. Their radars still showed no Statu warships in-system; the only thing bugging him was the lack of probe readouts from Casonu Two.

He peered at the viewer, seeing the planet as they neared it. Everything was calm, peaceful, and he wondered how long the mission would take. The desire to leave here was thrumming in his veins, and he glanced to Constantine, who stood behind Commander Starling, observing the entire meeting.

"Thank you, Ina. We're grateful for your time and assistance," Tom told the girl, and she looked around, as if unsure where to go.

Treena rose and guided her out the door, shutting the executive crew in behind. Rene Bouchard was there with her, Commander Kan Shu beside her, and she appeared ready to explode.

"That girl is up to something, Baldwin. I recognize a lying woman when I see one," she said.

"And how do you know that?" Tom asked her.

"As if you'd have any idea. You have no clue how many times I've lied to men over the course of my career… my life. Sometimes it's the only way to make someone to listen to you. Her story doesn't add up. And do you really think that the warships operated by those skinny kids could have defeated the real Statu?" she asked.

Tom noticed Ven shifting in his seat. "Ven, what do you think?"

Ven's glass slid closer, and he took a drink before speaking. "If this is true, my theory about them having far more people than we had predicted is false."

"Rene, if they're still around, where are they?" Treena asked.

"The interference. They could be hiding inside the atmosphere," she said.

Brax drummed his fingers on the table. "Captain, we could send a fighter in, get the lay of the land first. There's no harm."

"But with the interference, we might not be able to

contact them," Tom said.

"That's right, but if there's nothing to fear below, the fighter comes straight out and reports it to us. If there is, they escape and bring word," Brax suggested, and Tom nodded along.

"Fine. Send Basker. He's the best we have," Tom said.

Rene shook her head. "I think Cedric is better."

"Fine, send your guy. I don't care. Just get us some surveillance beneath all this atmospheric disturbance," Tom barked. The planet was covered in clouds, and the few spots they could zoom in on from orbit showed nothing of use.

Rene smiled at this, always one to take a win. Tom didn't feel the same way as she did. He only wanted everyone to make it home safe, regardless of who took what steps to make it happen. "With any luck, we'll find nothing, and we can begin our rescue efforts. Everyone understand their roles?"

Constantine buzzed, flickering away, then back. "Captain, the doctor needs to speak with you."

"On screen." Tom stood, striding to the front of the meeting room, where Nee's face appeared. His white hair stood on end; his usually composed face was twisted in stress.

"Captain, something's happening." Nee's voice was frantic, and there were at least a dozen patients inside the medical bay behind him.

"What is it?"

"There's some kind of virus hitting our people. I think it's a contaminant from the newcomers, but I can't be sure at this time. We've had three fatalities so far, but for now, we're trying to contain those potentially affected: the guards that were in contact with the kids and anyone that was around them. We need assistance and another cargo hold cleared out for a quarantine room," Nee said in a rush.

"Brax, get your men on this. Suit up; we don't want this spreading. Make sure Ina is with the others, and seal them in. Nee, you know what to do." Nee nodded, the screen going dark, and Tom rubbed his hands, as if cleaning them of any potential sickness.

"She could have infected us," Captain Bouchard said, her eyes wide.

"We can only speculate at this point. Send word to your ship, Rene. Has Cedric returned there yet?" Tom asked.

"No. He's still in the hangar," she advised.

"Good. For the time being, you and Kan will remain with us." Tom moved for the bridge, knowing they weren't going to be able to leave until Nee figured this one out. As if he needed more to worry about.

"Tell Cedric to make his way to Basker. Treena, get Lieutenant Basker to prepare a fighter for the executive lieutenant," Tom ordered, and with that, everyone broke from the meeting room, returning to the bridge and their positions.

Tom walked over to Ven and leaned over. "Do you stand by your theory?"

Ven peered up. "I read the girl. She's difficult to sense, but there's deception beneath her surface."

That could mean a multitude of things, but Tom was going to err on the side of caution. "Let me know when Cedric is ready to take off." He sat in his chair, hoping Nee was able to get a handle on their situation.

---

*C*edric squished into the fighter. One thing he'd always hated about them was how cramped the cockpits were. They weren't made for a male Tekol's wide frame, and he'd been lucky enough to have his old ship modified to accommodate him. This one wasn't to his specs, and his shoulders rubbed against the seat's edges; his hips fit tightly.

His mission was simple, and he was glad Captain Bouchard had volunteered him for the role. It was the first time he'd been part of an executive bridge crew, and he wasn't going to mess it up. He saw the way guys like Brax Daak looked at him. He'd liked to pick on Daak back in the day, but the truth was, he'd been jealous of the man.

Brax had always been at the top of his classes, even if he was the last one done at each exam. At any given time, Cedric could find him studying away in the Academy libraries, while Cedric was more interested in finding a woman to share his bed.

And at the end of the day, they'd both ended up on state-of-the-art Concord cruise ships, so Cedric was fine with the amount of effort he'd put in to get here.

Basker patted the side of the fighter and pointed to the exit, indicating the coast was clear. The big Tekol closed his eyes, as he always did before leaving in a fighter. "Until we meet in the Vastness." The engines kicked on, and adrenaline coursed through his veins as he anticipated the trip.

He slid the ship out, sending it through the barrier and into space. They were still a few thousand kilometers from the planet, and he stared at his target through the viewer, seeing nothing but dense fog or cloud cover.

It was a simple mission. In and out. If there was nothing to see, he'd quickly make the trek back to *Constantine*. Cedric raced toward the world, his blood pumping harder than he'd expected it to. The news of the virus spreading on the ship was disconcerting. The twenty-five slaves had showed no sign of illness, so there were other implications behind it.

It lingered in his mind as he entered orbit, letting his ship ride along with the gravitational trajectory, and lowered slowly while orbiting around the planet. Cedric thought about Reeve Daak as he waited to enter the atmosphere, and he rubbed his jaw, recalling where she'd punched him. He'd deserved it. He'd been younger then, more interested in a quick relationship than anything long-standing, and Reeve wasn't supposed to find him with the other girl. Cedric tried to remember the fling's name, and he was drawing a blank. This made him laugh. "Bridge, can you read me?" he asked.

"This is *Constantine*; read you loud and clear," Brax replied.

"I'm about to make my descent past the clouds. I'll try to stay in touch as I break through." Cedric hadn't felt this free in a long time. He'd always been stuck on guard assignment during his previous posting and recently couldn't escape bridge duty. Part of him felt like he was meant to fly, and that had always been his biggest draw to joining the Concord.

The trip was going smoothly, and he checked his elevation. Ten thousand meters and lowering. The clouds were thickening, and he suspected it would be this way until he broke free around two thousand meters, below the stratus cover. "Can you read me?" he asked, and heard no reply. His contact had been disrupted.

Cedric pushed all thoughts from his mind, not worrying about postings or the Daaks; just the task at hand. He visualized the flame. *The flame is life.*

His fighter shook and rumbled as he kept the thrusters at three-quarter power, easing up slightly in his descent. The ship beeped, and he saw there were finally items appearing on his radar. His nerves jolted as he erupted from the cover, unable to stop staring at the radar screen, where dozens of lights were flashing. He glanced up from it, and there they were. Tubers. At least thirty of them, hovering near a giant warship.

"*Constantine.* The Statu are here. I repeat, they're here. I see…" His gaze went distant as he saw another warship on the horizon. He zoomed out on the radar, and his breath caught in his throat. How many were there? And this was only one section of the planet, the one he'd randomly selected to poke his nose into. He needed to spread the word!

Cedric began to turn around, but the Tubers had caught sight of him. Ten of them broke formation and began the chase. Cedric considered fighting them off, but even his own ego didn't convince him it was possible. No, he had to escape. That was top priority.

The thrusters burned hotly as he swung the fighter away from the warship ten kilometers away, but just when he thought he might be able to outrun his tails, he noticed another ten lights blinking toward him from the other direction. They were on a direct course to intercept.

He slammed a gloved hand onto the dash in anger and made a decision. If he couldn't escape, he could at least take down as many of them as possible. He set his sights on the closest warship and raced toward it, remembering that the most vulnerable stop on it was at the very bottom, where the drive met the thrusters.

Tubers surrounded him, and Cedric shouted a primal war cry, the sound loud in the compact cockpit. His ship was hit, sending him reeling sideways, but he recovered, his grip tight on the controls. He urged himself on as another struck, the wing cut in half. He was close.

He was lowering to the ground, but Cedric pulled up, bringing his nose to face the center of the warship. Gravity would do the rest. He fired everything he had, the first few shots running errant, but the torpedoes hit with a satisfying detonation, and Cedric closed his eyes, letting go of the controls as he neared the gargantuan vessel. He'd woken up that day expecting a far different outcome, but he welcomed the Vastness now. A calm encircled him as another Tuber blast struck the rear of his ship, but it was too late. His target was in line.

Freedom is not to be taken for granted. Sometimes one must fight to have peace. Cedric mouthed the words to the relevant Code saying as he crashed into the warship.

EIGHTEEN

"What's happening down there?" Tom asked, standing behind Brax.

"Sir, there's no response. We lost him." Brax kept trying, but nothing was making it through.

"He should have returned by now," Rene said from the other end of the bridge.

"Maybe we should send Basker," Tom suggested, but Rene shook her head.

"Send one of the Ugna in," she said.

Tom weighed her words and was almost willing to do so, but didn't want to take the chance. Their relationship with their new partner was already wearing thin, especially after Tom had allowed *Triumph* to be destroyed by the Assembly.

He glanced around the bridge, noticing all eyes falling on him. He was the fleet captain, tasked with ending the Statu war; only he hadn't been expecting any of this to greet them on the other side of the wormhole.

Anything could have happened to Cedric, but Tom sensed the trap was lying beneath the cloudy atmosphere. "Engineering, this is the captain," he said, wondering if Reeve could assist.

"Captain, it's Reeve."

"Reeve, is there a way to disperse the cloud cover from here?" Tom was getting desperate for a solution that didn't put him in immediate danger.

Reeve didn't reply for a moment, but when she did, her voice was full of optimism. "I think it's worth a shot, Captain. How long do I have?"

"You're not going to like my answer," he told her.

"I'll begin immediately, Captain."

Tom sat in his chair, staring toward Casonu Two. This was the home of the evil Statu, the same race that had devastated the Concord fifty years ago. This race was the reason Yephion and his friends had fled five hundred years earlier. If Ven was even half correct about his theory that there were far more Statu than they'd ever let the Concord believe, they were down there, hiding below.

Ina had done a great job of convincing them to head there, and she'd also conveniently brought a deadly virus on board to infiltrate his crew. Tom was growing angrier with each passing heartbeat.

He had half a mind to blast the world from here. If their entire fleet battered it with an assault, Casonu Two could be wiped from the history books once and for all. Unfortunately, the tiny part of his mind that thought there were slaves below that needed rescuing kept ringing in the recesses of his brain.

He'd wait and see what Reeve could concoct before making any rash decisions.

———————

"These drones could be too heavy for the task. Once they're inside the atmosphere, they might not be able to rely on their miniscule thrusters with the added mass of the propellers," Harry informed Reeve, but of course she'd already taken all of this into account.

"I've tweaked the position of the thrusters by thirty degrees to accommodate the reverse force of the propellers. It'll work. At least enough to carve a path through these damned clouds," Reeve said, proud of all she'd been able to accomplish in two hours' time.

More of their crew had fallen ill, and Reeve was glad she'd managed to avoid everyone by isolating herself in the boiler room. It was another perk of being in the bowels of the ship.

"I still think we need something stronger opposing it. Once these propellers are going at full bore, we're going to have an issue," Harry advised.

Reeve ran the numbers, but they were only rough, since this hadn't been tested before. He was right. "Harry, you're coming for my job, aren't you? Fine. We'll piggyback one of the TEL-1509 drones on the modified ones, programming the thrusters to variable power."

Harry grinned and keyed in the new parameters. They received green lights in the basic testing simulator. "I knew you'd figure it out. Come on; we need to start the mods."

Reeve followed Harry to the workspace down the corridor on Deck One, and to the right. The room was enormous, workbenches lining the walls along with a full array of manufacturing drones, as well as robotic printers of all sizes. She found various raw materials, choosing an alloy from Nolix that was durable and lightweight. She loaded the sheets using a remote-controlled robotic arm and set the supplies into the second-largest printer they had.

Harry plugged the keycard in, downloading their schematics, and they gathered the appropriate drones while it created the propellers. By the time they were done, Reeve was sweating, the room smelled like solder and grease, and they had their drones, all four of them in a row.

"That's it." Reeve stood, wiping her hands on her pants, leaving black streaks over the thighs. "They're not pretty, but they'll do the job." She assessed the devices and almost laughed at the absurdity of their function. "Dispersing clouds."

"Dispersing clouds for the safety of the Concord, may I remind you," Harry said, patting her on the back. "Let's get them outside."

With the assistance of four more crew members, the drones were powered up and sent through a probe release hatch under *Constantine*. The moment they were out, Reeve activated them, sending them toward Casonu Two.

Now all they could do was give it a try and see what was hidden below the planet's dense atmosphere.

———————

Ven waited for the results to come in. "Captain, the clouds are indeed artificially created." He wasn't convinced at first, but the probes had gathered the data at the peak of the ice crystals and water droplets. He ran it against all known data points on various planets' cloud composition and found too much metal inside. It would be possible on a metal-dense world, one with little greenspace and tree cover, but the brief images captured from their initial spin into the system showed Casonu Two to be as lush as its twin.

"That's what I thought," Captain Baldwin said. "Reeve, what's our update?"

Reeve's voice carried from far below, thanks to her choice to stay away from the possibly infected areas of the ship. "Captain, we're breaching the atmosphere and have visual." The viewer cut in half, with feeds from the four drones centering on the left side of the screen.

They moved smoothly, ever toward the wispy white cover, and already Ven saw the propellers begin to swirl. The drones shook more and more as the speed increased, and eventually, they were in position.

"Come on; all we need is a window," the captain said, and Ven found himself clenching his hands.

He'd only just met Executive Lieutenant Cedric, but the man shared a rank with himself, and he'd hoped to become allies at some point. Ven vowed to make someone pay for the man's death, because he was positive the fighter had been destroyed.

The clouds began to dissipate as the fans blew. Reeve directed them closer to the ground as they broke through the sky, and Ven sat at the edge of his seat as they advised the bridge that the drones were at three thousand meters.

"Give us a vantage point..." Captain Baldwin was standing too close to the viewer, his hands at his sides.

Ven saw it: the ground, a forest of treetops like garden vegetation, all blending into one. "There it is, sir."

"Keep gusting, Reeve. We're almost there." The captain leaned forward, and Ven thought the man was holding his breath. The entire bridge seemed to be, and Ven took a deep inhale, as if to counter them.

A surge of emotion, so angry, so strong, sent his mind reeling. Ven pushed away from his helm console, striking the ground and landing on his side.

"Ven!" Brax shouted, rushing to his aid, but the pain was too much. Ven could sense thousands of minds, each solely focused on the destruction of all Concord affiliates. He groaned, pointing toward the viewer as the clouds spread apart, revealing the tiny forms of Tubers. Behind them was a warship.

"Warship…" he croaked, and all eyes left Ven and settled on the viewer.

Captain Thomas Baldwin moved swiftly to his seat, reaching out to the other ships, as Brax helped Ven to his position. "This is Fleet Commander Thomas Baldwin. Abort. I repeat, abort. Rendezvous thirty thousand kilometers out, at our muster position."

Captain Rene marched over to him, hands on hips. "I think we should reconsider. They killed Cedric. We can take them, Captain, we can…"

Ven noticed Captain Baldwin point to the screen, and the right edge of the viewer where a section of the planet was magnified. Warships were rising from the clouds, at least twenty of them. Once they had passed by the safety of their interference, the radar began to chime as each warship entered nearby space.

The onslaught of emotion was gone, replaced by a steady determination from the Statu, and Ven did his best to block it out and concentrate. He urged *Constantine* away, moving as fast as the Star Drive would allow.

"Captain Bouchard, I agree we'll fight them, but we have to know what we're up against first," Captain Baldwin said.

Ven was glad they hadn't been lowering through the atmosphere when they discovered the Statu had a veritable fleet hidden below. Ina had to answer to her betrayal, but the captain didn't have time for that now.

"Brax, how many are we looking at?" Baldwin asked.

"Captain, I'm counting forty, and there seem to be more," Brax said.

"Forty…"

Ven wished he wasn't right about his theory. They'd been hiding their numbers from the Concord, and all of their moves felt like an extremely patient trap. And the Concord had played directly into it.

———————

*D*octor Nee was glad they'd been able to quarantine the new passengers, as well as the guards who'd come in contact with them, but after that, he knew others on the ship had made some level of secondary interaction. The good news was that no one had died in the last hour.

The bad news was, they'd lost five since the beginning of the outbreak.

He was tired, his limbs aching, his mind turning to mush. He poured another cup of Raca and took a long drink, wondering if he should inject something to keep himself focused and on task. Kelli was such a trooper, and Belna and Tarlen had arrived, volunteering to assist in any way they could. He'd only let them in after they'd put themselves in quarantine uniforms, and so far, they'd been a big help.

Nee watched the magnified sample and recognized how rudimentary the virus really was. The Statu had hoped for an epidemic, and it was strong, transferring quickly, but Nee already had a very similar cure on board, and after several tests, was prepared to experiment on one of the symptomatic patients.

"I need a volunteer, someone symptomatic and willing to be my test subject," Nee told everyone in the medical bay. The room was cramped, with over twenty people inside, not including the bodies they'd already disposed of.

"I'll do it," a middle-aged woman from Leria said. So far, only the Zilph'i and humans were showing any kind of effects from the virus, and this particular antidote met the same criteria.

Doctor Nee motioned for her to enter the private room at the far left corner of the medical bay, and Kelli followed him inside. "Thank you for volunteering..."

"Zola. I work in on the security team, mostly shift scheduling," she said, and Nee nodded, preparing the medispray with the proper vial.

"How are you feeling now?" he asked. Her skin was pasty, her lips dry and cracked, and her eyes were rheumy, just like the rest of those suffering in isolation.

"Not well. I want to sleep, but I'm too scared to," she said honestly.

"Okay. There's a chance this won't work, but we need to try it on someone, Zola. We don't have time to wait," Nee said, and she nodded her understanding.

"I'm ready." Her voice was meek, but she held her head up high as Doctor Nee pressed the device into her neck.

She slumped instantly, the medication entering her bloodstream. It was powerful, and she was a slight woman: tall and thin. Kelli held her upright, and Nee lifted her eyelids, seeing a slight improvement in the redness. A minute later, she gasped, maybe breathing more evenly than she had been.

"I... I feel the same," she said, running a clammy hand over her face.

Nee smiled, a tired but well-meaning expression. "It needs time to course through your body and work with your immune system."

"I'm afraid to sleep."

"You'll be fine, I assure you. When you wake, I'll be here." Nee turned from her, facing Kelli. "Let's get everyone injected and count this one a victory."

Kelli helped Zola up, and Nee glanced at the screen on his wall, seeing that *Constantine* was racing away from the planet they'd only just arrived at. He reached out to the bridge, curious to see what was going on.

---

*B*rax should have known better. They'd talked about this for hours, and had all agreed to be cautious. Now they were being chased by a massive fleet of Statu, and time was running out on their options.

Each of the Ugna were on screen in the meeting room, and Captain Bouchard and Commander Kan Shu were still on board, the other captain having elected to take a medispray antidote back to her ship when the meeting was over, in case any symptoms arose.

"Do we leave them behind again?" Reeve asked.

"Not an option," Tom said firmly. "We were sent to fight them, but things have changed. We've never seen a confluence of warships like this before. While I think we're capable of taking three- or four-to-one odds, I don't think we should risk it on their terms. Within that planet, they held the upper hand, likely with suborbital defenses in place and numerous other potential traps. We avoided that, but we need to be careful now.

"They cannot enter the wormhole. It's powered by the generator in Concord space, and we could have it disabled with us on either side of it," Tom said, and Brax bristled.

"You want to send an expedition ship through and tell them to turn it off? With us over here?" he asked, trying to see how deep they were in this battle.

"Not necessarily." Tom tapped the desk console, and

a 3D image of the nearby region of the system appeared, showing over sixty warships on the radar, all trailing after the Concord Fleet. "But I do have an idea."

Brax noticed that Captain Rene Bouchard had lost her bluster, seeming disenchanted, her posture worse, her voice small as she spoke. "I didn't sign up for this to come and die on my first mission, Baldwin."

"None of us did, Rene, but the truth of the matter is, we've been put in this position because the Concord trusts us to win this battle and to end the war!" Tom shouted, catching Brax off-guard.

"Or more likely, found us to be disposable. Maybe they wanted you to lose… did you ever think of that?" Rene asked, and Brax fought the urge to tell her off. By the look in the captain's eyes, he was close to doing so himself. "I say we hightail it out of here and tell the Concord they sent us with far too few cruise ships. This Prime doesn't know how anything works. Harris would have…"

"Are you capable of leading your ship, Commander Kan Shu?" Tom asked, not addressing *Shu*'s captain.

"Yes, sir," Shu said, and Rene barked a laugh.

"You have to be kidding me, Baldwin. You don't have the authority to…" Rene started, and Tom nodded to Brax.

"Put her in a suite and make sure to guard the door," Tom said, and Brax grabbed her by the arm.

"Just hold on." Rene lifted both hands in front of her. "I'm sorry for my rash words. I didn't mean it, Baldwin. I can do this, you can count on me," she said softly.

"Rene, you're lucky I'm not throwing you in a cell," Captain Baldwin said. "Fine. We don't have time to dwell on this. Pull yourself together. We have a war to fight, and you need to be clear-headed."

"Yes, sir." Bouchard lowered her gaze, and she returned to her seat at the table.

"We have sixty of the Statu coming to intercept us, and we need to make this decision." Captain Baldwin turned to the Ugna. "Ven, we have a head start, but not by much. How far out of range are they now?"

Ven didn't need to use his fingers on the keypad, but opted to use his Talent instead. It was still odd to Brax, but the man had saved his life, and he could be as different as he wanted to be. "They are two thousand kilometers from range."

Brax sat on the edge of his seat, hands resting on the table. "Captain, we can confirm the warship range is slightly less than ours. What if we create a line, moving away from them at the exact right speed, allowing us to fire on them, but avoiding direct contact from their efforts?"

"That only works if they were lined up too, but the Statu will likely bunch together, sending a warship full of our slaves to the forefront of the battle, and when it's destroyed, they'll be in the proper radius to attack," Treena offered.

"Captain, with all due respect, we can't give quarter to any of the warships now, slave-filled or not." Commander Shu didn't look pleased as he said this, but he had a point. "We're outnumbered, and we have no choice but to attack them relentlessly if we want to end their fleet."

Brax nodded, showing his support for *Shu*'s young commander. "Captain Baldwin, you said you had an idea earlier, before Bouchard showed her true colors. What was the plan?"

Thomas Baldwin still stood near the 3D image, his expression grim, but a faint smile crept onto his face. "It won't work."

"At least let us hear you out. Maybe we can all think of a way to make it happen," Treena said.

Tom glanced at his commander, and Brax saw a flicker of hope in his eyes. "Fine. We don't have enough firepower to fend off sixty enemies today. We never had anything remotely close to this during the initial War, is that correct, Constantine?"

The AI nodded. "That is correct. The largest battle was at Vilinar, where we lost five cruise ships while stopping eight warships from entering their neighboring system. We saved billions of lives that day."

"Five against eight. We do have better technology now, and the Statu appear to have remained stagnant out here, but we need help," Tom said. "We have a wormhole generator outside Earon, and in retrospect, the admiral may have been short-sighted to suggest operating it so close to the human settlement."

A notion occurred to Brax, and he didn't want to believe it. Perhaps the Concord was aware of how many Statu remained, and they wanted them to enter the wormhole, to return to Earon and destroy the human race. He shook the worrisome thought from his head because he had enough to be concerned about.

"Captain, we have that under control. We can shut it down if necessary," Reeve advised him.

"How? We're too far to relay a message in this system from the wormhole to the planet…"

"We planned for that. We brought the Nek Drive shuttle with us," Reeve said, and Brax smiled, wishing he'd thought of that sooner.

The captain's eyes grew wider, and he leaned over the table, palms pressed to it. "You did? We can jump to the wormhole and send word to them?"

"That's right. We can be at the entrance in a split second. It'll be a total of twenty minutes from our hangar to Earon Station," Brax told the captain.

"Then prepare it," Tom said, smiling again.

"What's the plan?" Rene asked.

"We're recruiting the backup we need."

NINETEEN

*T*he sight of the radar was daunting, and Treena cringed as she watched the blinking red dots culminating on *Constantine*'s position. They were two hours from reaching the wormhole, and they'd even contemplated moving away from the entrance to lure the Statu somewhere else. Tom was confident the warships wouldn't follow; that they'd travel to the wormhole regardless. Their enemy's goal was entering Concord space, meaning they were far less worried about the small opposing fleet that had entered their system.

Treena strode through the corridors, alarms gently chiming throughout the entire ship, keeping everyone on alert and on edge.

"Treena, I want to come with you," Tarlen's distinguishable voice called from down the hall, and she slowed to allow him to catch up.

"It's always dangerous traveling through the wormhole, and this time, we're doing it in an old modified shuttle. I don't think this is the best idea, Tar." She stopped at the hangar, the guards stepping away to grant her access as soon as they recognized her.

"Don't let him through," she commanded, and Tarlen remained behind, stuck in the hall as she strode toward the Nek Drive shuttle. "Sorry about this, kid. I'll be back really soon. Tell you what, go to my room and watch over me. Tom was going to send Kelli, but she's got her hands full with the sick patients. I'll relay when I've successfully traversed the wormhole."

"I'll be there!" the Bacal teen called as the hangar doors slid shut, and Treena made her way to the deteriorated shuttle. There hadn't been time to fix it up or test it again since Brax and Ven had used it at the Tingor Belt, but there was no choice. If Tom's plan had any chance of working, she needed to make this trip.

Treena entered through the lifted door, not needing to wear the full EVA armored suit the others would have donned, since her body was robotic, and it allowed her more space to move around. The Nek Drive took up half of the ship, adding substantial length to the shuttle.

Treena took the pilot's seat, strapping in, and the shuttle powered up with the press of a circular red button. She glanced over the controls, having only been briefly told how the Nek Drive operated. She almost wished Brax was here with her, but he'd been through enough deadly missions over the last few months. The dash had a thin layer of grime over it, which didn't bode well for its functionality.

"Be glad you're not blowing yourself up this time," she whispered to herself, and the ship rumbled, shaking as she lifted from the hangar floor. "At least, not on purpose."

Once outside, she avoided looking at the shuttle's radar, not wanting to be reminded how many enemy warships were on their trail. Tom's plan was as solid as she could ask for, and she adjusted her trajectory, pushing away from *Constantine*'s massive hull. She flew between two beautiful Ugna vessels and realized she'd never stepped foot on one.

That would have to be remedied when the battle was

over, but she had bigger worries now. This technology was so new, so untested, that it had the potential to explode or send her far from her target zone. The controls were simple enough, and Treena set her destination, which was a thousand kilometers from the wormhole opening.

She waited as the drive powered up, needing to generate enough momentum to send her there in a quick hop rather than a trek. This shuttle would take twenty-nine hours to make the same trip at regular propulsion, and that wasn't going to work. Their entire fleet would be destroyed by then.

The dash told her the drive was prepared, and she blinked a few times, trying to regain her composure. She heard something inside her head, her real mind, and knew Tarlen was at her bedside in her suite on *Constantine*. It was somewhat of a relief to know the boy was there, like she was no longer alone on this daring mission, even if she was by herself on the shuttle.

"Here goes nothing," she whispered, pressing the jump key.

One second, Treena was near their fleet; the next, all of the radar icons were far away on the map, and the swirling wormhole stood waiting for her arrival. She let out a quiet cheer, her mood still subdued, because the next part was just as worrisome. Treena needed to take the shuttle through the fold in space.

Every noise inside it seemed amplified, and she almost felt like the hull was going to fall apart as things groaned and clanged the closer she brought the shuttle to the opening.

With a deep breath this body didn't need, Treena urged the shaking shuttle into the wormhole.

"*T*ell me again," the captain said.

Ina had tried to stay strong, but everything had fallen apart. The longer she was separated from the others, left to her own thoughts, the clearer the real Ina became. She wasn't a bad person. All she'd ever wanted was to be free outside. To let the sun freckle her skin, to have the wind tousle her hair as she worked.

Not once had anything in her life been her own decision. She realized this now. Her cheeks were tight from the dried tears, and fresh ones threatened to come at any moment.

"Look. I'm not going to wait all day. Tell me why you did it!" The man slammed his hand against the table, sending her chin up from her chest to meet his angry gaze.

She'd seen anger before, but this burned like the entrance to the Vastness in his eyes. She suddenly wasn't sure what to tell him. "They told me I had to."

"Or what? They'd wipe your brain like the others? They'd kill you?" the man asked.

She only nodded, still meeting his stare. "That's right."

"You could have warned us, but you demanded we bring everyone to the planet. Mark me a fool for listening to a girl who grew up a slave to the bastards," he said.

"I am not a slave!" she shouted, resolve firming through her being.

"Is that so?" His expression shifted from angry to full of pity. "Did you have choices? Were you able to leave when you wanted? Eat what you chose? Spend time with anyone you wanted?"

She shook her head, because she hadn't been able to do any of those things. "No. I couldn't."

"See, you were a slave, Ina. They used you, just as they've used our people for decades, sending them to battle against us. I need you to tell me how many of our people are on these warships," he told her.

"I don't know." The answer was truthful. She'd seen some boarding the warships on the Adepts' second planet, but mostly, they had been Statu. "I don't think many." She tried to envision what she'd witnessed as the Adept had showed her the view from the top of *Savior*.

"Think, Ina."

"I grew up being told the Concord was evil," she finally managed to say. "The Adepts…"

"The Statu are manipulative. They're too scared to fight themselves, so they steal our children, our soldiers, our spouses, and turn them against us. We have a way to repair their minds. That's why I need to hear what we're dealing with. We not only want to destroy your Adepts to keep our people safe, but we want to free the slaves, even the ones you've seen with no color to their eyes," the captain said, his tone gentle.

Could it be true? Her mind argued with itself, and she pressed her eyelids closed tightly, feeling a tear squeeze past one. "My mother told me stories when I was a little girl."

The captain sat down finally, no longer tall and threatening across the tiny room. He didn't speak, but she could sense his urging her on.

"She told me my grandfather was a soldier in the War. That he was from Earon, and a lieutenant. She was born underground like me, but she knew this to be true," Ina said.

"Earon. We're only a few hours from Earon. You can

help me win this war, and I'll bring you there. Maybe you still have family on the planet. We can return everyone on this side to their families. Wouldn't you like to help them go home? To no longer be slaves to these...Adepts?"

She nodded, feeling so foolish for ever believing the Adepts' lies. It was so clear. "What of the Vastness? If I accept your truth, will I burn for eternity in it?"

He laughed, and she saw a smile break the lines of his face. He was handsome when he did this, and Ina felt herself drawn to the man.

"The Vastness is a belief system, a welcoming and wonderful place we're nourished by while we live, and reside in during the afterlife. Some of the Concord's partners believe different things, but many of us focus on the Vastness to guide us through our days. We live by the Code, an ancient set of texts that help shape our society, to put us on the proper side of ethics, to help one another in times of need. It's so much more than that, and I'm not the best person to explain it, but if there's one thing I know, it's that the Vastness is not to be feared," the captain said, and Ina's heart soared at the passion the man spoke with.

She made a decision, picturing herself walking free on the human home world, perhaps learning where her grandparents had once lived, seeing their village, their schools, feeling the same wind on her face as her ancestors had, rather than the stale underground air, she'd grown up with.

"I'm sorry, Captain Baldwin. I didn't know what I was doing. The virus was brought on by the others," she admitted.

"We know about that." The captain coughed, but he still didn't seem to understand.

She shook her head. "You don't."

"Our doctor has fixed it. It was an old strain, one we identified and have potentially resolved," the man said, coughing again. His eyes were turning red, and he finally appeared to comprehend what she was saying. "What is it? This virus…"

"I overheard Adept Feerez talking to the others about it before we left. It was a secondary defense that wasn't supposed to hit until you arrived on-planet," she told him.

"How do we stop it?" the captain asked, his skin already starting to shine with perspiration.

"You don't," she said sadly.

The wormhole was only an hour and a half away, and the Statu remained relentless in their approach. Captain Bouchard and Commander Shu had returned to their ship, and Brax was left on the bridge, trying to decipher their best course of action.

"Where's the captain?" Brax asked Constantine, and the AI flickered.

"He's interrogating the girl," Constantine said.

"I wish he'd left me to that task. I could have made her talk," Brax said.

The bridge was fully attended, and Ven met his gaze from his center helm position. "Lieutenant Commander Daak, they've deployed their Tubers."

He'd been waiting for that to happen. They were looking for a fight, and Brax wasn't going to disappoint. He hated the Statu fiercely. Growing up in the Concord, every kid wanted nothing more than to fend off the enemy, like Constantine Baldwin had at Yollox, and even though Brax understood the complicated details of that encounter, it changed nothing for him. He still wanted to fight and send them into the Vastness.

In the absence of numbers, we must have a multitude of ambition. The saying echoed through his mind as the Tubers' tiny icons appeared. There were hundreds of them.

Brax did the math. They'd brought an extra six fighters, along with the ten on *Shu.* The Ugna had different tools, and he'd only viewed the schematics and a computer-generated simulation of the drones. The pilots controlled them from inside the safety of their vessel, and they held about as much firepower and effectiveness as the Concord fighters.

The Statu wanted a dog fight, throwing their people, or perhaps the Concord's people, against them without a care in the world. Brax grinned as he thought about the Tuber he'd stolen and landed inside the warship. Bringing it back home had given the eggheads a lot to consider, and after a month or two, they'd developed a handy defense against the cylinder-shaped enemy craft.

Their fighters were now equipped with the technology, as were the Ugna drones, and Brax made the order in spite of the captain's and commander's absences on the bridge. With them away, he was in charge.

He set the communication to all of their fleet. "Concord, deploy Tuber resistance." They had the same equipment loaded into the flagships' weapons array, but they required close proximity to be effective. That was why they worked with better efficiency from the compact fighters and Ugna-operated drones.

Brax watched as over eighty of the Concord vessels flew from their position, heading toward the thick blots of the warships on the radar.

*D*octor Nee was beside himself. The medispray had been working. The results had been only temporary, and now everyone originally infected had returned as sick as ever. "I don't understand. We had it right, Kelli."

Her hair was pulled into a frizzy ponytail, her eyes lined and puffy even though she'd managed not to catch the illness. She wore the protective gear, as did the other helpers like Belna, but he found the medical bay with more occupants than it was created to handle.

The door opened and the captain strode in, his hand around a thin girl's arm. Nee had never seen the teen before, and she glanced around the room with fear in her eyes.

"Captain…" Nee saw the fever raging in Tom, and his shoulders slumped. They needed to get a handle on this.

"I caught it. The girl, Ina, will tell you everything she knows, but I don't think it will be enough." Tom coughed and staggered, setting a hand on the table ledge to steady himself.

Once Ina explained the Statu's plan, Nee rubbed his gloves together. So they'd hidden something inside it, a secondary level of infection. Doctor Nee had had to work twice as hard as all the other medical students at the Academy, being a Kwant. No one had wanted to partner with him, always fearful that he would touch them with his skin, killing them with his poison.

He'd grown to accept it as a challenge, and eventually, he made friends. By the time he was at his first posting, he had a reputation as a funny and charming doctor, as well as somewhat of a genius when it came to rare Concord partner diseases. Most of their medical field only worried about the Founders' illnesses, because that was who they would primarily be attending to on the Concord cruise ships.

Nee took the time to study all major viruses, infections, cancers, and organ diseases as he could in his spare time, and he ran across the room now, activating his cross-reference database. He'd carefully curated the information over the last decade or so, and he chided himself for not thinking of this sooner. The original results had come back with such clarity, he hadn't questioned the data.

He peered over his shoulder at Tom, who looked like he was about to expire at any moment. With a battle about to commence out in space, Nee heard the ticking of the seconds in his mind as he entered the details into the system once again, anxious to find a solution.

———————

*T*he trip had taken just as long as before, and Treena realized it didn't matter what size your ship was or the speed your engines were set at; traversing the wormhole took ten minutes, give or take a few seconds.

She let out a cheer and patted herself on the legs, making sure she was still in one piece. The shuttle groaned and creaked, but the system showed it was sealed and operational.

Treena closed her eyes, concentrating on transferring the message from her real body back to Tarlen in her room on *Constantine*.

"Tarlen, are you there?" she asked in her mind. It would relay through the speakers on her bed.

"I'm here." She felt a slight touch on her hand and assumed the boy was holding hers as her comatose body lay there.

"I made it through. I'm heading for Earon now," she told him, ready to break contact when he said something quickly.

"The captain is sick. The virus was devious, and everyone who's come in contact with the slaves is in rough shape. Hurry."

Treena wanted to say more, but needed her concentration in the shuttle and left her own mind. What did he mean? The captain was sick? That wasn't good, and it also meant she was the most experienced executive in the fleet, and she wasn't even in the same system as they were.

The shuttle moved toward Earon Station, and the trip took a while, moving past the wormhole generator. Treena reached out to them with her communicator, filling Yephion and Zolin, the Zilph'i engineer, in on what had occurred.

"Should we shut it down?" Zolin asked plainly.

"No. Our people are over there, and we have a plan," she said, not expanding on it.

"Very well," Zolin said over the speaker. "We will be prepared for destabilization on your word."

"Thank you," she said, ending the communication.

She reached out to Earon now, knowing the admiral and Prime remained there, and finally, after being passed to three stations, she was in touch with Admiral Jalin Benitor.

"What happened?" the admiral asked, and Treena told her everything.

"You cannot allow them to win. At any cost," the admiral said.

"I agree, but I need your help," Treena said.

"Anything."

"The archives and museum. We need access, as well as people." Treena wished she could have brought capable crew members with her, but the shuttle had no room. They were going to require a lot of trust in new people and old vessels.

"Bodies we have," Benitor said. "What do you want from the archives... wait, the decommissioned ships?"

"That's right. The only way we stop the Statu and live to return to Earon is by bringing the entire fleet of legacy ships over to fight," Treena said.

The admiral's voice sounded tired. "I knew we were stretched too thin. What were we thinking, sending two cruise ships and twelve Ugna vessels to fight this battle?"

Treena cut her some slack. "We misjudged their strength and intelligence. They fooled us again. But we have something they don't."

"What's that?" Admiral Benitor asked.

"We have our ancestors to fight with us." She smiled as she raced toward the station, seeing the massive archives where over forty retired Concord vessels sat gathering dust.

"Meet me there. I'll bring my finest," Benitor said, ending the call.

TWENTY

Brax zoomed on the battle, watching as the Tubers tried to lure the drones into a trap. The Ugna were smart enough to avoid the ambush, and one by one, Brax saw the icons of the cylinder ships vanish from the radar as their electrical systems were ended.

The pulses firing from the drones shorted the Tubers out, and Brax was glad they'd been able to finally target the exact right nodes. For years, their people had attempted to disable the enemy crafts with pulse, but had failed until their recently-acquired ship taught them there was indeed a single connection in the electrical system that could be waylaid.

It worked, and as soon as the Tubers realized what the Concord fleet was capable of, they eased off, most of the remaining cylinders returning to their assigned warships.

"This is Basker to the bridge," the lieutenant said through the speakers.

"Go ahead," Brax told him.

"We have visual. The Tubers are running scared. We're going to keep half our fighters and drones outside for quick reaction, should the bastards grow brave again."

"Good work out there." Brax smiled as they won their first encounter of what was sure to be many. They were still moving toward the wormhole, and he wished that Treena would hurry along. "Constantine, check with Tarlen in Treena's room. He told me he was there with her."

Constantine vanished, returning a few seconds later. "He says Treena has made it to Earon Station, and they're mounting the fleet now. It appears as though they're encountering some issues, but Tarlen is unsure what they are, specifically. She's pressed for time."

"Thank you," Brax told the AI, and reached out to the medical bay. "Doctor Nee, what's happening down there?"

"By the Vastness, I might have it. These Statu are far sneakier than I ever gave them credit. They layered this, likely testing it on their slaves over the years to perfect. I dread to think how many were killed in the process..."

"Nee, enough chit-chat. How's the captain?" Brax was impatient for results.

"He's resting, and we have him sedated, but..." Brax heard medical alerts ringing out through the speakers. "Brax, I'll get back to you."

The contact ended, and Brax returned his stare to the viewer, seeing the zoomed image of the gathered warships heading toward them. "Ven, you were right."

The Ugna man nodded, not breaking his stare with his console as he spoke. "I wish I hadn't been."

"You and me both," Brax said.

———

*T*he lights were bright inside the archives, and the entire place had erupted in a cacophony of noise as the relic ships were brought to life.

Treena walked down the main center line, with Admiral Benitor and Prime Xune beside her. "I'll be captaining *Remie*," the admiral said.

"*You?* Are you positive?" Treena asked.

"I'll have you know I was a great captain in my day," the old Callalay woman said, her ridged brow furrowing even deeper.

"I don't doubt that," Treena admitted.

"I'll take *Persi*," the Prime said, causing Treena and the admiral to stop in their tracks.

"I think not, Prime," Benitor said.

"If I'm to lead the Concord, let me do so by example. I will not hide while others do our dirty work. I'll take *Persi*; just place a competent commander on the bridge with me, so I don't endanger anyone." Prime Xune may have been the second choice of the Zilph'i delegates, but after the untimely death of Shengin, Xune had turned out to be a great candidate, and Treena saw the passion burning in his eyes.

"Very well," Admiral Benitor said. "I'll send retired captain Jake Barclay with you. He'll love that."

"It only seems fair these retired ships are led by retired officers, doesn't it?" Treena asked, getting a laugh from the Prime.

Treena watched as the very first ancient ship departed through the giant energy barrier in the side of the warehouse. It was necessary to move the vessels out one after the other; the planning on this alone had taken three warehouse foremen and a computer to calculate exit strategies.

"There are too many of them inside here, don't you think?" Treena asked, and Benitor nodded.

"Perhaps we were remiss to retire them all. We could have donated some to our partners, easily stripping them of weapons and our network data."

"The Concord has had a long history of preserving the past," the Prime said. "It's time for a change there as well."

"You may be right," Benitor said, agreeing with Xune.

The first ship was named *Titun* and was almost a square in shape, the thrusters jutting out from the sides of the box like hands. Treena didn't know much about the three-hundred-year-old cruise ship, but it was only large enough to hold a crew of twenty or so. Today, it was operated by a crew of three.

Treena walked along the sterile, dark gray warehouse floor toward the next craft in line to depart and saw an elderly Tekol woman in uniform, wearing a red collar. Her attire was the old model from decades ago, and Treena had to smile. "I bet she didn't wake up today expecting to be conscripted into the Fleet once again."

Admiral Benitor set a hand on Treena's wrist. "None of us did, dear."

Each of the vessels were brought into space, and Treena kept a close eye as various people were being ushered onto the cruise ships, cruisers, and freighters, some wearing old uniforms, some new, and others in maintenance outfits. Anyone that understood the functionality of a Concord vessel was asked to pitch in, and according to the lead recruiter, only the sick or injured were turning the offer down.

Everyone wanted their chance at revenge against the Statu. It was too good of an opportunity to avoid, and Treena felt the energy of the place increase with each passing minute. She checked the time and cursed under her breath. "We need to move now."

"The first wave is prepared to enter the wormhole," Benitor said.

"Then let's get to our posts and join them," Treena

said, leaving the Prime and admiral to board their own of the last three remaining cruise ships, the very same ones that Treena had helped escort back to Earon only days ago. *Andron* was the largest of the three, and there were some advanced modifications done to her. She recalled the layout of *Andron* well, and three officers were already inside.

"Commander Starling! We're here to help you," a girl said. She couldn't have been out of the Academy. Her cheeks were rosy, her hair curly and tied on the top of her head. "I'm Neve. This is Otto, and Blanche." She pointed to the other two students, each one appearing fresher under the collar than the previous.

"When do you graduate?" Treena asked them.

"This year," Otto answered. He was wide at the shoulders, thin at the waist: the kind of shape only a teenager could manage.

"Good." Treena led them onto the bridge, and she was surprised to see them take positions as if they'd worked together for years. "I take it you've done some simulations."

"We're at the top of our class, sir." This from Blanche, a snub-nosed girl with shiny black hair swept to the side.

"Then show me what you've learned. Take us out, Blanche." The girl sat in the primary helm position with Otto beside her. Neve took the weapons position along the edge of the bridge, and Treena accepted the captain's seat, feeling surprisingly calm aboard this old codger of a ship. She pictured Constantine Baldwin in his prime, barking orders as they fended off the Statu at Yollox, and grinned.

Andron followed *Remie* and *Persi* from the museum, and Treena didn't have to urge Blanche to bring them to full impulse; she did it on instinct, bringing them to the front of the line before the wormhole a short time later. The other ships waited for *Andron* as instructed, and Treena stood before the viewer, activating the communication stream visible to each ally around them.

"The trip is safe; ten minutes of turbulence and you'll be on the other side. We're cutting it close, and I expect our allies and enemies to be nearby when we exit. As discussed, the oldest of the fleet will remain behind, ten of you to defend our lines should we fail on the other side.

"Zolin will be powering down the wormhole should the Statu break through our ranks in their system, and you're tasked with destroying any warship on sight. Stay vigilant and fight with honor." Treena paused, wishing she didn't have to hear the following saying so often. "Until we meet in the Vastness." She ended the communication and pointed toward the viewer.

Blanche directed them to the wormhole, and Treena clutched the arms of the old captain's chair as they entered.

---

*T*homas Baldwin blinked, the room feeling too bright around him. Everything ached, and he smacked his lips, the flesh sticking together. "Doctor," he said too quietly. Nee was bustling around the room, a perfect combination of frantic and calm surrounding him. "Doctor."

Someone noticed Tom was up and motioned for Nee, who rushed over. "Thank the Vastness, you made it, Tom." His gloved hand snaked on Tom's wrist, and the captain tried to sit up.

"Am I…"

The doctor shook his head. "No. We managed to find a solution, sir. You're fine. The virus was strong, attacking you with vehemence, so it's taking longer for your body to recover," Nee said, and Tom only partially understood him.

"What time is it? Are we at the wormhole? What's happening out there?" Tom asked, but Nee waved his comments away.

"You need to rest and heal up," the doctor said, but already Tom was feeling slightly better. He sat up, his chest burning, and he found a glass of water beside him. He drank deeply, and Nee grabbed it, setting it down. "Not too much at once."

"I have to get to the bridge," Tom said.

"You are in no shape to go…"

Tom grabbed Nee by the collar. "Am I a danger to anyone? The virus… is it gone?"

"You're no longer contagious, if that's what you're asking," Nee advised, and Tom swung his legs over the edge of the bed. There were fewer people inside the medical bay now, and that was a good sign, unless they'd been transferred to the morgue.

"The others. Are they…?"

"We suffered two more fatalities before creating the cure," Nee told him, and when it was clear Tom wasn't going to relent, the doctor stepped to the side, helping Tom to his feet.

"Has the commander returned?" Tom asked, but the doctor didn't know and told him as much.

"Kelli, bring the captain to the bridge, please." Nee passed a medispray to Tom, and he clutched it to his chest. "If you get dizzy or can't think clearly, use this, but only in an emergency. I haven't verified what it will do when mixed with the antidote."

Tom nodded, staggering away from the bed, and Nee's nurse Kelli caught his arm, steadying him. "Come on, Captain. Let's get you there in one piece."

---

*B*rax sat in the captain's seat, and it was chaos all around him. The sounds of the ship's alarms had faded to background noise, and he was finally attuned to the scenarios they were encountering.

"*Trust* and *Shelter*, stay strong, don't let those three warships sneak past you!" he shouted to the two Ugna vessels holding the pass to *Constantine*'s port side.

He fired at the warship closest to them, the computer programmed to alternate between the nearest three targets with each pulse. So far, it was working well enough to hold them at bay while *Shu* and *Constantine* stayed a few hundred kilometers from the wormhole's entrance.

"Where are you, Treena?" he asked aloud, not expecting or receiving an answer.

Ven was quiet, focused as he maneuvered their ship, staying in the precise position necessary to defend the maw of the wormhole. He was almost in a trance, humming an unfamiliar tune while his lips moved, repeating a mantra of some kind. Brax let him be, not wanting to interrupt the meditative state keeping him on point.

The Tubers were out in full force, too many to stop at once, and a few of them made it by the fighters and drones. Brax watched as the closest was destroyed by the automatic targeting built into *Constantine*.

A few errant shots from the warships struck their shields, but they were holding at eighty percent. This was good, but considering they'd only destroyed five of the sixty, it wasn't great. It meant they might hold off half of the enemy fleet or perhaps even three-quarters, but fifteen or twenty of the warships would remain long after the Concord cruise ships.

Brax tried to gauge how the Ugna vessels were doing, and he was impressed with the dexterity and foresight from the small ships' captains. Another warship vanished along the starboard side, about two thousand kilometers from the center of action. Three more took its place, and Brax cringed as the Ugna vessels icon flashed and disappeared.

"We have a breach!" Brax shouted. "*Calamity* and *Perseverance*, cover them. *Shu*, hold your position. We're going to stop them."

Ven didn't have to be told twice, and *Constantine* backed up, the side thrusters rotating to push them away from the fray. Brax continued firing on the enemy, and one more warship gave up the ghost, pieces of the massive craft spreading wide as two fresh warships took its position. He felt the weight of what was occurring threaten to consume him. They were going to lose. *Constantine* was powerful, but there were just too many of them to stop. *Shu* destroyed one, but was pushed into retreating another hundred kilometers as a result, and Brax was only too aware of how close they were getting to the wormhole.

Another Ugna was destroyed, and the Tubers had managed to overtake the drones, leaving only a few remaining out there, trying to divert any Tubers they could.

"Basker, retreat. I repeat, retreat. I need you to…" Brax was cut off as one of their fighters raced in front of the viewer, three Tubers following. He tried to target the enemy cylinders, but they were too fast and close from this proximity, and the fighter was blasted, the ship exploding before his eyes. He caught one of the Tubers, sending it reeling, but the other two escaped, heading behind the enemy lines.

The bridge doors opened, and Brax peered over to see Baldwin there, sweat stains covering his chest and armpits. His hair was plastered to his head, and his eyes had a wild appearance, darting from Brax to the viewer. "I'm sorry, sir. There are too many of them." Brax rose, giving the captain his seat.

"*When faced with impossible odds, choose to play a different game.*" The captain winked at Brax, and the chief of security thought Baldwin might actually be off his rocker. He stood there, Kelli at his side, and pressed the open communicator to all in the area, not just the Concord.

Contrary to his disheveled appearance, his voice was strong. "This is Fleet Captain Thomas Baldwin. Stand down, Concord. Let them pass."

Brax's jaw dropped, and the captain shut the call off and took a seat.

---

*T*arlen watched the battle through the screen beside Treena's bed and could see they were losing. "Come on, Treena. Where are you?" he asked.

Constantine appeared again, grabbing his attention. "The captain has devised a plan, Tarlen. The moment the legacy fleet enters Statu space, they're going to encounter the warships. We've created a path to distract the Statu. They're so single-minded about getting to Concord space, they've already sent over half of their fleet in a direct line for the entrance.

"How much longer before they arrive?" Constantine

asked.

Tarlen checked his timer on the tablet, and he lifted a finger. "One minute."

"Then you need to advise Treena to relay these instructions the moment she arrives. Understood?" Constantine asked, and Tarlen nodded, ready to hear what Captain Baldwin had in store for the Statu.

———

Andron was a solid cruise ship, one of the best in the old fleet. It had once been a flagship for a new era, much like *Constantine* was now, and it showed. While some of the interior had faded and worn out, the bones of the vessel were as strong as ever, and it withheld the wormhole transition with ease.

The three kids kept it together quite well during the short trip, and Treena saw the timer she'd set, advising her they were about to exit. "Everyone on alert." She activated the alarm system, soft red lights flickering behind the bridge.

One moment, *Andron* was shaking within the colorful rift; the next, it pressed away from the exit, space greeting her. Treena gasped as they encountered seven looming warships.

She felt something pinch her hand, and she lifted it, seeing nothing before realizing it was Tarlen at her real body. Treena closed her eyes, focusing on entering her brain, trapped in her quarters aboard *Constantine*.

"Tarlen." Her voice pressed through the speakers.

"Treena, you have to listen to me. Baldwin set a trap. You have to split your forces and come at them from all angles. Our fleet is holding off, waiting for your arrival," he told her, and she left, returning to her artificial body.

The rest of the fleet were right behind her, and she sent a message out to the thirty old and undermanned vessels, hoping it reached them in time. "Alpha team, bank in my direction, Bravo opposite. We came here to play, so now's your chance. This is the real deal. Make our ancestors proud. Make this *our* legacy!" She shouted the last, and Otto pumped a fist into the air as Blanche guided them toward the coming warships.

Persi had been the one to destroy Treena's previous post, leaving her for dead while killing her entire crew, including the love of her life, Felix. He was now safe in the Vastness, and the irony that she fought alongside the vessel wasn't lost on her as they both sent an assault barrage at the first warship. The Assembly had added some powerful non-sanctioned weaponry from outside the Concord, and it showed.

Within two minutes, the warship was detonating, and they moved on to the next ship. Once Treena was confident her inexperienced three-person crew were capable, she reached out to *Constantine*. "Captain Baldwin, are you there?" she asked, and his image appeared in the corner of their viewer.

"Good work, Commander. I knew I could count on you," he said. She did a second take, shocked by his appearance.

"Captain, are you sure you should be on the bridge?" she asked.

"Nee handled it. Believe me, I feel better than I look," he said.

Treena assessed their situation and saw *Titun* destroyed. She said a silent prayer for the fallen crew and did a tally on the remaining warships. "Captain, there are thirty left."

Baldwin nodded. "Keep to it. Don't let any of them enter the wormhole."

"I know. I gave orders for them to destabilize it should anyone but us return," she said solemnly.

He didn't reply, but only stared at her.

"Captain, we're going to win the day," she assured him, chin tilted up.

"You're damned right we are." His image vanished, and Otto glanced at her.

"Was that…?"

"That was the best captain you could ever hope for," she told him.

———————

Reeve ran the diagnostics again, trying to find somewhere to borrow energy from. The backup system was a good option, but she didn't want to mess with it until she absolutely had to. The shields were under a lot of duress, and she twitched as they lowered to twenty-nine percent.

"Harry, where are we with our problem?" she asked.

He was sweating, running around the boiler room like a madman, issuing orders. "We're nowhere. Reeve, I'm up to my neck in minor repairs, and the maintenance crews are spread too thin. Even if we could find enough power somewhere, we don't have the manpower to manually reroute it."

Reeve thought about life-support, but that was the absolute last resort. They'd be able to survive for some time without it powered on, but that would be a final effort, after the backup source was depleted. "Think," she told herself, but was drawing a blank.

"Bridge, how are things out there?" she asked, hoping

it had improved in the last half hour.

To her surprise, Captain Baldwin replied instead of her brother. "It could be better."

"How bad is it?" she asked, bracing for the reply.

"We've lost eight legacy vessels, five Ugna, and *Shu* is under twenty percent shields. Rene's about to reroute their secondary system," Baldwin told her, and Reeve nodded, accepting the fact that she was going to have to do the same. "But we're down to twelve warships, and despite the losses, I'm optimistic. Are we going to make it?"

She glanced at Harry, and he gave her a wicked grin before rushing to the edge of the boiler room, where a screen began flashing. "We're going to make it."

Reeve continued her work, preparing the transfer of energy to their dwindling shields.

TWENTY-ONE

Ven directed the ship with a level of comfort he'd never before enjoyed. He felt at one with *Constantine*, as if his flesh and her circuits somehow merged to form one entity. The mantra he spoke didn't even make sense to his ears, but they were the proper words he needed at that moment.

The last few hours had been trying, and his bones ached; his shoulders were so tense, he could almost hear them creaking as his hands moved, and he used more Talent than he should have been able to as they fought the Statu with everything they had.

Twice Ven had moved to intercept *Shu* and give the less experienced crew and vessel safety from a barrage and desperate attack from the Statu. Captain Baldwin had attempted early on to communicate with the Statu, but as always, they refused to grant him access. Ven felt Baldwin's motives for wanting to offer the enemy a chance to surrender, but he only wanted to end them.

He'd sensed their hatred, their motivation for passing to Concord space, and now, with the Statu fleet all but decimated, they still had that single-minded desire to rush into the wormhole. At this point, it would serve no purpose. Ven and the others were aware of this, but it didn't seem to matter to the Statu.

Treena Starling had impressed everyone with her

leadership aboard *Andron*, and it had led the charge in the last couple of hours, fighting and assisting anyone near her, letting the two main flagships stay the course and defend the wormhole. So far, it had worked, and no one had been able to pass them.

"Captain, *Shu* is reaching out," Lieutenant Darl said from beside Ven.

"On screen," Baldwin said.

Commander Kan Shu appeared, worry across the ridges of his forehead. "Captain, our shields are at four percent." Ven saw Captain Bouchard behind him, rushing to the weapons position, leaning over an officer.

"Break away, retreat to safety. We can manage," Baldwin told him, passing sound advice.

"Sir, we can stop the last few," Shu said, and Ven noticed the AI of Yin Shu near the young commander.

"No. Do as I say and retreat to the sidelines. We'll be able to finish them off without you," Baldwin said, and Ven felt the satisfaction pouring from the remaining Statu on the last five warships. He tried to discern what could have made them so thrilled, but he couldn't grasp it. He wanted to warn the captain, but the man's attention was on other things.

Pieces of their fleet mixed with the destroyed warships, making debris everywhere in a ten-thousand-kilometer radius around the wormhole entrance, but they'd managed to stop them so far with minimal loss of life, in comparison to what the Statu would have done had they accessed Concord space with the same fleet.

Shu moved away, and the Statu stayed put for a few minutes before sending four of their warships after the shield-deprived flagship.

"Captain, they're trying to destroy *Shu*," Brax said, and Ven waited for directions.

———————

*T*om felt like he'd been hit in the head with a Bentom ball and stayed seated as he considered the problem. He couldn't let the crew of *Shu* die here, not after the woman he'd idolized had sacrificed herself.

"After them. Starling, Prime, Admiral; everyone, give them all we have. This ends now!" Tom stood, his knees buckling under the weight.

He still couldn't believe the Prime was on board *Persi*, or that the admiral was aboard *Remie*. He imagined the few crew on those ships were scared witless of anything happening to their leaders, but if it came to that, they'd all be in the Vastness together, so it wouldn't matter any longer.

Tom pushed the thoughts of death from his mind and tried to focus. *Andron* took the lead, and Tom noticed one of the warships had been left behind. It moved quickly, cutting directly for the wormhole.

"Damn it," Tom muttered. This was their plan. Send the Concord ships all reeling after the other four while they sent one through. But to what end?

Ven must have read his mind, because he finally spoke up. "Sir, I've been sensing excitement from them, and this is why."

"But what will it accomplish?" Tom asked.

"They must be aware there's a high probability that we'd shut the wormhole down if one of their ships emerged first," Ven said, and he was right.

"That is the case. We can't fend off a fleet of sixty Statu, only to be trapped over here. We're years from Concord space," Tom said. But it was too late. The warship was nearing the entrance, and *Shu* might be destroyed if they were to intercept the lone enemy straggler.

It became clear what he had to do. "Join the fray. Kill them, Brax. Kill them all." Tom ran toward the elevator that would take him to *Cleo*.

"Where are you going?" Brax shouted at him, mercilessly firing toward the enemy.

"To make sure we can get home." Tom disregarded his bridge's concerned calls and headed toward the expedition ship above the bridge.

A few months ago, he'd been fending off attacks along the Borders, stopping pirates from stealing freight haulers, without many concerns for what was happening outside *Cecilia*'s hull. Now he'd been through the wringer, and here he was, trying to end a war with an old adversary.

He'd managed to save the Bacal, uncover conspiracies, help shape the future of the Concord, disrupt the Academy, and prevent an ancient creature from becoming Prime. They'd done a lot in a short amount of time, and here was his chance to ensure the rest of them delayed their deaths and still had a way to arrive at Earon in one piece.

Constantine appeared beside him as he stepped foot into *Cleo,* named for his mother. His head was swimming, and he sat in the pilot's seat, powering up the expedition ship. "Con, what do you say we go on another journey?"

The AI sat beside him, smiling. "I'd say it's a welcome change from battle."

Tom lifted off, *Constantine* moving away from the wormhole as it bombarded the last few warships. One of them blew just as Tom spun the craft around, maneuvering it for the Statu as they entered the rift. They vanished, and Tom could only hope he had enough time. His head pounded and his vision doubled, a deep ache in his chest making it hard to breathe.

"Sir, are you going to make it? I can fly the ship." Constantine pressed a hand forward to comfort Tom, but it vanished as the projection passed through his arm.

He blinked, looking out the viewer, but the stars grew blurry. Even the swirling sight of the wormhole sent him into a bout of vertigo, and he fell over. Nee had assured him he was healthy enough, but his body had been beaten up by the illness.

"The medispray," Tom whispered to himself, recalling the last-ditch device Nee had given him. He found it in his pants pocket and pressed it to his neck. It hissed, and instantly, his head cleared, his heart beating fast like he'd taken an injection of adrenaline. He sat up, hands gripping the throttle, and he guided the ship into the wormhole.

The next ten minutes stretched on forever, and even though the shot had improved him, the effect began to wear off after a few minutes. Still, he didn't feel like dying any longer, and that was a good sign.

"Con, if this is it, I want to tell you something," Tom told the AI.

"Sir, I'm all ears."

"I love you," Tom said, grinning at how absurd it was to say those words to an AI projection.

"And I love you, Tommy. I always have and always will," Constantine said, returning the dumb grin.

"We really make quite the pair. Two Baldwins in over our heads, with nothing but high expectations. We're probably doomed to fail," Tom said.

Constantine lost his smile. "You haven't failed. Not ever, Tommy. I did, and it's one of my biggest regrets. The other is how I treated you and everyone else as I grew older."

"How about we concur that none of that matters anymore? If we make it through this, we put it all behind us." Tom glanced at the AI's eyes, and the young version of his grandfather nodded in agreement.

"Sir, we're about to exit," Con said, ending the moment of tenderness between a captain and his ship's AI.

Tom braced himself, expecting the wormhole to destabilize before they exited, trapping them inside forever. He was almost shocked when they emerged, and seconds later, the wormhole vanished behind him.

Pieces of the warship lingered, and he piloted around one of the vessel's huge arms. "It's me, Captain Baldwin!" he shouted through the communicator as the clunky old vessels surrounded him.

"By the Vastness, we didn't expect you, Captain Baldwin," Zolin's voice said, carrying from the modified cruiser where the wormhole generator was stored.

"Zolin, we need to reactivate it. They might need our help," Baldwin told them.

"Yes, sir. Give us a minute." The line went silent, and Tom raised his eyebrows at Con, who was staring at the old machinery.

"Feel good to be useful, you old dogs?" the AI asked quietly, not directing the query at anyone in particular.

Ten minutes passed, and Tom saw lights flash from the cruiser, but nothing remotely looking like a wormhole appeared. "Zolin, what's happening?" he asked.

"It's… the ore is depleted. We can't activate it again."

"For how long?" Tom assumed something needed to recharge.

"With this ore? Never."

"Then exchange it for some fresh supplies," Tom ordered.

"We can't." Zolin's voice was small. "Because we don't have any more processed Greblok ore on hand."

———————

$\mathcal{T}$reena stood in the center of the bridge as the last warship exploded. The three youths were on their feet, cheering and hugging. Treena watched them smiling and pumping fists in the air, and she wondered if she'd ever seemed so young.

"Captain, we did it!" Neve said, rushing to her side to hug Treena.

"It's Commander... never mind. Great work, you three. I see we have three of the Concord's finest in our midst," she said, and their faces all lit up at the praise.

The celebration was short-lived as Blanche noticed the wormhole no longer existed.

"No..." Treena walked toward the viewer, where the young girl had changed the image, zooming on the rift's previous location.

"Everyone, we seem to be missing something," Treena said. As thrilled as she was to have defeated the Statu, they were now stuck far from home.

She didn't think about all the losses they'd suffered this day, because there would be time for that later. Much later.

Bouchard spoke first. "We just made it. Our shields are at two percent. Thank you for helping us. On behalf of the entire crew, we appreciate it."

"Think nothing of it," Brax's voice said.

"Where's Baldwin?" Treena asked.

Brax's voice was strained. "He went after the warship."

Treena hung her head, her chin resting on her chest. "Then he may be lost to us."

The wormhole was to be destabilized if a warship emerged, and since one had, Tom was likely chasing behind it. Meaning that not only was Tom possibly dead, but the rest of them were trapped in the Statu system.

———————

Reeve kept her mind occupied by working. Two days passed quickly as they set to repairing the remaining fleet. Out of the thirty legacy fleet ships and the dozen Ugna, only fourteen retired vessels and four Ugna were left in the aftermath of the final battle. Even though the odds told her they should have suffered an even worse fate, that did little to ease her heartache.

"I'm sorry, Tom," she whispered as she stared into the Star Drive. She'd refused to leave the boiler room since it happened, and even Harry had managed to sneak away a few times to eat and sleep. Reeve was content to stay below, napping in her office when necessary.

For the time being, she was alone, the rest of the crew given some time off to rest. Footsteps carried across the room's floor, and Reeve recognized the sound of her brother's march right away.

"Brax, if you're coming to lecture me, I told you, I'm fine," she said, spinning in her chair to face him.

He looked tired, and he displayed a few days of stubble. He leaned over, pulling her into a hug. She had no choice but to stand into the embrace, and he squeezed her tight.

"We almost didn't make it," he said.

"You don't know that," she told him.

"I saw it. I felt the loss coming. I was in the fray, and I stood on the cliff of the Vastness, Reeve. It was close." Brax let her go, and his arms fell to his sides, like he didn't know what to do with them. "It's been too long. You need to meet with us."

"I have work…"

"Stop it, Reeve. I know you. You're mourning Tom and the others, but you can't stay isolated forever. You're one of the best minds we have here, and you need to meet with the executive teams so we can discuss what our next steps are," he said.

"You're right." Her shoulders slumped, and she grabbed her tablet, following him from her boiler room. "You did a good job up there, Brax."

Her brother stopped at the elevators and craned his neck to look at her. "You think?"

"I know." She patted his back as they stepped on, and Reeve finally felt ready to face the rest of the ship. It had taken her twin's presence to snap her into reality.

The elevator paused, opening one deck early, and on walked Nee, with Tarlen on his tail. The kid lit up at seeing them.

"Doctor, are we safe to be out and about?" Brax asked Nee, and the Kwant gave him a patented handsome smile.

"My friend, you were never in danger from it as a Tekol now, were you?" Nee said, and Brax shrugged.

"You know what I mean."

"The virus is dealt with, and if it resurfaces, I have plenty of medisprays loaded with the synthesized cure." The doctor turned from them as the elevator opened, and their group moved for the ship's largest meeting room. Reeve noticed Rene Bouchard pacing in the corridor, and she braced herself for what was going to become a very interesting conference.

———————————

Treena Starling was in charge on *Constantine*, but there were still three others in the board room that outranked her, making her role precarious at best. She was entitled to her opinion, but that didn't mean anyone would heed her advice.

The admiral seemed somewhat amused that Tom had nearly kicked Captain Bouchard off her own command. The rest of the executive crew from *Shu* was present, minus Cedric, who'd died on Casonu Two in the fighter. She knew Reeve and the other Tekol had been through some sort of a checkered relationship, but it was clear the chief engineer was upset at the loss.

Admiral Benitor sat at the head of the table with Prime Xune beside her, both of them appearing calm and composed. The remaining four Ugna captains were present, each of them on board *Constantine* for the first time. Two were male, two female, and each of them were tall and albino, but none were bald like Ven. They hadn't spoken a word yet, and Treena wondered how they were taking the losses of so many from their fleet.

Treena sat next to the Prime, Brax and Ven beside her, followed by Reeve, Tarlen, and the doctor. She'd been the one to invite Tarlen, and he sat there quietly, his big brown eyes wide.

"We're in a bit of a bind, aren't we?" Prime Xune asked. He wasn't quite as charismatic as Shengin, but he was a capable leader as far as Treena was concerned. He'd also stuck his neck out as he'd climbed into the fray of the final battle, and that made him even higher in her esteem.

"That's for sure," Brax said.

"The main thing is, we won. And I don't think we're understanding the value of our recent sacrifices." Admiral Benitor sat upright in her seat, her gaze moving from one to the next.

"The wormhole is gone, and we have to assume that Tom didn't make it," Treena said stiffly.

Reeve shook her head. "We didn't test opening and closing the wormhole as we should have. All we knew was that we had the power to activate or destabilize it. There's a chance that Tom made it, and that the Concord destroyed the last warship. They might find a way to return to us."

Treena hoped the chief engineer was right, but at that moment, it felt like a dream to think that possible.

"We have to prepare for the worst," Rene said. She was looking far better than before, her hair braided from the top of her head into a long ponytail. "We have supplies, but for how long? We have ships left, but we also lost a lot. We're going to have to head to the twin worlds."

"They're Class Zero Nine planets," Brax said. "We've been to Casonu One, and I'm confident we could find sustenance and water."

"But to build a new home? Do we risk it with the Statu possibly still out there?" Kan Shu asked.

"Are you suggesting we didn't finish this war?" Benitor asked.

"We can't be sure," Kan said.

Ven finally broke his silence. "I think we're done with them. I suspect we'll not find any more of their warships. This was their last effort. They put everything behind it."

Brax leaned forward, his fingers intertwined as he

rested his hands on the table. "I agree with Ven. If we find any, we kill them and move on."

"What about their slaves?" Tarlen asked, speaking for his people. Treena had almost overlooked them.

"And the girl, Ina? Do we trust her word any longer? Can we?" This from the Prime.

"I don't see how we can. She lied to us repeatedly. She brought a virus to us, trying to kill our crews," Brax said, his anger obviously still fresh.

Treena wanted to calm the room. "Let me speak with her. She was born into a life she didn't choose. No one deserves to be punished for things out of their control."

"Let's not forget she came clean with us, and her analysis helped me figure the whole virus issue out," Doctor Nee told them.

Rene Bouchard tapped her fingers on the table and sighed. "Why does this victory feel like such a loss?"

Treena knew. It wasn't because they'd been left years away from reaching Concord space; it was the fact that Thomas Baldwin may have been lost forever. The others had to be feeling the same way.

"We must remain vigilant. We sent many to the Vastness today, from both sides, but we are yet to make the trek. We have to cling to the flame and find our way. And I suggest it begins with scouring the twin worlds, seeking lives to save, and perhaps a place to call home for the time being," Prime Xune said.

Treena warmed at his words, passing him a small smile. "I agree with the Prime."

Captain Bouchard frowned, but relented. "I agree as well."

The Ugna looked from one to another, and the shorter of the female captains spoke for them. "We support your plan."

"Then it's settled. We'll remain here for one more day, then move on," Admiral Benitor said.

TWENTY-TWO

*I*na felt her world caving in. She'd never meant to harm anyone, but now, she felt the truth behind the Adept's words. He'd deceived her, and she'd been too simple to realize it. Her mother had fought them but had died for it. Perhaps Ina should have died as well, rather than go against her own people.

The door slid open, drawing her attention as a pretty blonde woman entered; her uniform was crisp and her face stoic. "I'm Commander Starling."

"I remember," she said, having met the woman before.

"Good. Can I sit?" the commander asked, motioning to the chair across from the bed where Ina sat.

"Please." Ina was nervous, and she felt like this meeting was going to decide her fate. "Where is the captain?" She'd liked the man. He'd talked to her like a person, and it was easy to sense his passion.

The commander didn't answer; she changed the subject instead. "Ina, we're going to Casonu Two."

Ina nodded, surprised at the news.

"What will we find there?" Treena asked.

Ina had to be truthful. "I grew up on the other world, underground. We lived in Groups, each in a different section of the city below the surface. Once in a while, we'd be given work duty above, and those were my favorite memories. I only saw the Adepts' planet for a short time, but it was terrible. There were what you call warships everywhere, thousands of slaves."

"Ina, we've defeated the warships. None of them survived," the commander said, and an immense weight lifted from Ina's shoulders. She folded over, head resting on her knees, and she cried.

"Are you sure?" the girl asked.

"We're sure. What will we find on Casonu Two?" the woman asked her again. This time, her voice was less friendly.

"I don't know. I think all of the warships will have been used. I also suspect the people I saw were on the ships you destroyed," she said, seeing the effect it had on the commander's expression. "I'm sorry. I don't mean to blame you for their deaths."

"But some might linger there, correct? It's worth checking?" Commander Starling crossed the room and came to sit right beside Ina.

"Yes. There might be more left behind," Ina told her.

"We understand why you did what you did, Ina. And we're going to give you the benefit of the doubt. The others from your ship haven't shown the same remorse. I'm sorry, but we can't let them stay."

Ina understood what this meant. They would be killed.

"We'll scour your old home, and if we deem it empty, we'll drop them off there to live out their days," Treena said, her voice soft and dripping with compassion.

"Why?" Ina didn't comprehend the words. "Why would you let them... us... live?"

"Because the war is over, and we're not animals. We're the Concord." The commander frowned, and Ina could think of nothing to say. "Would you like to join them, Ina? On Casonu One?"

She considered this and shook her head. "Not if it means living underground. I need something more."

"Then we'll discuss that at another time. I'm sorry, but you'll need to remain confined to your room," Commander Starling said.

"I don't mind." It was the truth. It was far better than she deserved.

---

*C*asonu One had clear skies over the region where Brax had been imprisoned a couple months ago. The probes had shown no warship activity; neither did the radar, and there wasn't so much as a Tuber flying within the atmosphere.

Brax guided the lander to one of the slave encampments he'd visited with Penter and exited the ship, carrying his PL-30 at his side. He didn't wear armor, just his uniform, and as he stepped from the expedition vessel, the hot air clung to him instantly. It was quiet here. Gone were the sounds of machinery or revving thrusters. A multitude of insects chirped from the safety of the treeline as he walked to the stone structure he'd slept inside when Reeve and Starling had arrived to save them.

The beds remained, some overturned, and there sat the rotting corpses of the Statu guards. There was nothing here for him, and he returned to the lander to make his way to the next site. Basker was doing the same in his fighter, and Rene Bouchard had taken it upon herself to scour in *Shu*'s expedition craft.

The process took hours, and by the end of the day, as the sunlight was waning, the three met near the ocean, landing on a flat spot overlooking the wavy water.

Brax was there first, and he watched as Rene climbed from her ship, her hair messy, her eyes sunken from exhaustion. Basker acted like he'd been having fun all day, and for a pilot stuck in a hangar most of the time, Brax suspected he'd enjoyed the freedom of his compact fighter.

"Well? We good?" Basker asked, his hand acting as a visor from the bright sun that was threatening to cross the horizon at any moment.

Brax pulled a tablet, checking on the drones. "Looks like our drones covered every square inch of this underground city, and they found some bodies, but no one alive. I guess Ina was correct. They took them all to the other planet and shoved them in the warships.

"Lieutenant Commander Brax Daak to the bridge," he said, using his communicator on his wrist.

"Go ahead, Lieutenant Commander," Darl said.

"We're awaiting the return of the drones, and then we'll be heading away from the planet. We're all clear down here." Brax ended the communication and found himself glad they'd encountered nothing out of the ordinary. He assumed there would be some pockets of resistance on the world's twin, but it was controllable.

"This is where Yephion and the others originally came from, is it?" Rene asked. She walked toward the cliffside and stood near the edge, Brax and Basker coming to join her.

"This is it. You can look at the drone footage of their city afterward, if you like," Brax said.

"The planet is beautiful. Why would you hide below the surface?" she asked, her voice whimsical.

Brax grunted. "Probably because of what's out there." He pointed up. "There are days I wish I could hole up some place too."

"I doubt that, Lieutenant Commander." Captain Bouchard met his gaze. "You did a hell of a job this week, Daak. With the others running around, I hear you were confident and in charge." She rubbed her throat, staring at the ocean as the sun finally crested the distant skyline.

"You did well too."

"I wonder if Baldwin made it through." Rene turned from the water, facing Brax and Basker. "You know, I always thought your captain was a bit of a blowhard. He's way older than I am." She paused, as if Brax was about to call her on that fact. The truth was, she was younger, but not by as many years as she claimed. "When he secured that position on *Cecilia*, I was crestfallen. I'd been going for the same role, and not only did he get it, he climbed to the executive team, then to commander, within a few years."

"Is that what happened between you?" Brax asked, knowing he was overstepping the line.

"No. Too many drinks is what happened between us. A part of me did admire him, though, and I only wish I could have spent more time around him. I may be the captain of a cruise ship, but I don't feel like I've earned it yet. Not like Tom did. I hope he made it, Daak."

"So do I," Brax said, turning to see the first of the hunter drones arrive. It had thrusters and lowered to the ground, its six long metallic legs clicking as it walked toward the cargo trailer attached to his lander.

"If I know the captain, there's a very good chance he made it through that wormhole alive," Lieutenant Basker said with confidence.

Brax cleared his throat, watching as the last of the drones entered their temporary home. "Time to go find out what's left for us on Casonu Two."

———————

"*A* month! You're telling me it's going to take a damned month?" Tom paced the room on Earon Station, not willing to accept the news. "We have no idea what might have happened to them over there. They were in the midst of battle when I left. I need to reach them, Zolin. Yephion, there has to be another way."

The two engineers sat still, unwavering in their lack of emotions. "We have done all we can. The shipment needs to be processed. We have the ore, but there are steps that must be completed to utilize it for the purpose of the wormhole generator," Zolin said, not for the first time that day.

Tom rubbed his head. "Why didn't you have more prepared?"

"We were rushed along for this. The Concord needed to make a show of power. With all the issues, the Prime and Admiral Benitor were adamant we end this Statu threat once and for all, and the Founders unanimously backed their plan. We had no idea what to expect, or that we'd need to reopen the rift so soon after destabilization."

Tom let it all sink in, trying to imagine what was happening aboard his ship, which was so far away. "Where is the processing happening?"

Zolin didn't hesitate to answer. "Outside Nolix, on the Moons."

"A month. I don't like this, not one bit." Never in a million years had Tom expected to not be able to reactivate and return via the generator, but at least he'd made it through and had been able to let the Concord know what happened.

"We don't like it either." The door was open. Admiral Molan was standing there, the old Tekol Tom had met while being told he was to escort Prime-in-Waiting Harris to Leria, what felt like years ago.

"Admiral, I was just…"

The Tekol's hair was short, gone gray, and he limped over to the table, still standing. "You did good, Baldwin. You think the others are alive?"

"I do."

"The Prime? Benitor?" he asked.

"They were putting up a fight when I left."

The admiral nodded. "Speed up the processing. I'll have one of the Nek shuttles ready to bring it here when it's ready."

Tom was surprised they had the technology ramped up so quickly. "You can do that?"

"The Prime made it a priority, and we're working on two prototypes," Molan said.

Zolin smiled. "Another project for the Zilph'i team."

"Why didn't I guess that? It would be nice if we weren't traversing the known universe with rushed wormhole generators and jump ships, but we don't have a choice. I only want to keep my people safe," Tom said.

"Our people," the admiral corrected him.

"Whatever you want to call them, they're the most important part," Tom said, frowning.

"The war being over… that's what matters." The Tekol turned, limping from the room. "If the Prime is dead, someone's going to pay, Baldwin."

The door slid shut, and Tom glanced at Yephion, who clicked a few times, his words translating. "You are a brave and honorable man, Captain Baldwin. The generator will be fixed posthaste."

"Thank you, Yephion." Tom rose, leaving the two engineers together to discuss their plans for expediency, and he walked the corridors of the station. What started out as a distracted stroll to clear his mind ended up taking him to Gideon's Grill, the most famous place to have a bite to eat on Earon Station.

It was busy inside, everyone talking excitedly about the rumors of the Statu war. The moment he stepped inside, he regretted wearing his uniform.

He heard his name whispered a handful of times before he sat at the bar, and he turned to face the gathered people. "I'll get this over with." He remained standing, placing his hands on his hips. Everyone hushed quickly, all eyes settling on him. "Yes, we were fighting the Statu, and yes, there were far more of them than expected."

"Why didn't the Concord send more ships?" a large man asked from the table closest to him. His forehead was sweating, his beer glass empty.

"We didn't think…"

"That's right, you didn't… Is the Prime truly dead?" a slick-haired woman asked from the back of the grill.

Tom shook his head. "No. I don't think so…"

"Why did you run away?"

"Are the Statu coming here?"

"What's happened to the Concord?"

The series of questions flew at him from all angles, and he sighed, turning to the bar to order a drink. When the bartender poured the shot, he downed it, leaving the glass.

"If you're all done fearmongering, I'll tell you what I'm certain of. The Concord is doing the best they can. The Statu deceived us again, but I'm confident we have defeated them once and for all. There will be no more Statu threat." He paused, seeing people begin to buy in to his speech.

"We're working on returning there to rescue the others, and honestly, the last thing I wanted to do was leave, but the warship was heading through, and the engineers were under strict guidelines to shut it down if the Statu emerged. If I'd stayed behind, we'd all be stuck there, and it would take years to return."

"You're a hero!"

"The Statu are dead!"

"This one's for you, Grandmother!"

"To Baldwin!"

The place erupted in cheers and chants of his name, and soon Tom was surrounded, bodies pressing against him, trying to shake his hand, pat his back, buy him a drink. He conversed with the people of Earon Station, learning a bit about them, discussing the Statu and the future of the Concord. It felt great to be among the hardworking people that lived on the Station, and hours later, Tom left, slightly drunk, extremely tired, and hopeful for tomorrow.

---

*V*en Ittix reached out with his Talent, seeking the same negative energy of the Statu, but found only minor traces of anything below. They were still too far from the surface, orbiting Casonu Two, but the artificial cloud cover was mostly gone, and the probes were sent out, returning information as they collected it.

"What do we have, Ven?" Commander Starling asked. Ven thought she'd stepped into the role as their leader with grace, and he was happy serving under such a good superior.

"There is some activity below. Tubers. They appear isolated to this region." Ven zoomed on the viewer, showing a small continent. He made the image closer, and it appeared like an above-ground city. They'd never seen the Statu cities before, only the underground one their cousins used on Casonu One.

"We may encounter more of their people," Brax suggested from the left edge of the bridge.

Ven shook his head. "I think we'll find only emptiness, Lieutenant Commander. They threw it all against us." He moved the angle of the image, noticing a warship near the city's outer boundary. It was only half completed, and it sat in pieces.

"What about the Tubers?" Commander Starling asked.

"We'll send fighters down to deal with them. I think they were left behind to guard something, perhaps," Brax suggested.

"Very well." The commander tapped her console. "Lieutenant Basker, contact *Shu* and send a team of fighters to the surface to end those Tubers. We don't want anything in the air."

"What about the city?" Brax asked.

"Ina claims the slaves are on the other side of the continent, so we bomb it," the commander said.

Ven was surprised by her orders. "Are you certain? Perhaps there's information down there..."

"The Prime was clear. We destroy the Statu cities. No questions asked," Starling said grimly.

Brax nodded. "Preparing suborbital cannons. Targets acquired. Dispatching now."

Ven watched as five detonations exploded in key sections of the city below, and when the plumes and dust settled, there was nothing left but rubble and craters.

"Ven, find the next city," the commander said.

———————

Brax wished he had *Cleo* to use on the surface, but the cruiser did the job just fine. It was larger than he liked, but it seated the few of them comfortably.

"Thanks for bringing me," Tarlen said. His sister was beside him, her big brown eyes staring out the viewer, and Doctor Nee was perched beside Brax.

"No problem, Tar. If Ina's correct, there might be some of the Bacal here," Brax told him, hoping he was right.

The region was rife with warship pieces, and Brax could tell this was where the majority of their manufacturing had happened. It was far less spread apart than the facility he'd been brought to on the other planet.

"There it is," he said, lowering toward the massive structure. It was at least a mile wide and tall enough to fit a cruise ship inside.

Basker and a couple of the Ugna fighters flanked him as they set to the ground. It was sandy here, a far cry from the forests of Casonu One, and the ship sank slightly as the landing gear pressed into the yellowy-brown surface.

Their group exited, Brax with an XRC-14 in his grip. Nee carried his handheld gun, and Tarlen left with one on his hip.

Basker and the others faced the building with their fighters, weapons aimed at the entrance. Brax felt lucky to have the support of the heavily-armed craft as he walked slowly toward the Statu building. The sun was hot, and he wiped his brow as they crossed the half-mile, his feet sinking with each step.

"I can't say I love the sand," Nee said from beside him.

"Neither do I." Belna struggled through it, and Brax slowed to allow the others to catch up.

The building was made of metal, the same kind of material the warship's hulls were created from. It appeared rough, choppy even, and Brax considered turning and leaving. His conscience wouldn't let him.

There were drones hovering overhead, and all sides of the structure were covered. Brax checked his tablet, but there was no indication of movement. He lifted his hand and reached toward the doors. They were tall, high enough to accommodate machinery going in and out, and he found a keypad beside them. He pressed the biggest button, assuming that would do the trick, and he jumped back as the doors pulled upward.

Brax activated a LightBot, sending it inside. Everyone with him remained silent, all curious as to what was in the building.

Brax stepped in behind the Bot, its bright rays shooting a spread of the beam over the foyer. He smelled the bodies, and almost thought they were dead. Then he noticed their eyes opening, some groaning, others crying out, and Tarlen rushed past him.

"They're Bacal!" Tarlen crouched at the front of the group, and Brax took stock. The room was packed with people: some standing in rows, their eyes bright white, others on the floor.

"We're here to help. We've come to bring you home," Brax said, hoping there was a way to make that happen.

TWENTY-THREE

Tarlen couldn't believe his eyes. Brax was giving orders to the bridge, relaying what they'd found, and Doctor Nee was scanning people, the worst of the ill. Tarlen guessed there were over two thousand of his people inside the building, along with countless others of different races.

The room was bright now, lights brought in, and they'd opened any windows and doors they'd found. They'd located none of the Statu, and the gathered prisoners claimed they hadn't seen any of them since they'd been sealed inside and the Statu had left in the warships.

"What of Greblok?" an old man asked Tarlen.

"It's doing well. We've joined the Concord, and Malin is being rebuilt." Tarlen was proud to pass this news.

"What of them?" a woman asked, her hair long and greasy. She pointed at the Bacal standing in lines, their eyes lacking pigment.

"Without the Statu to give them orders, they won't do much, but we have a way to fix them, isn't that right, Doctor Nee?" Tarlen peered at the doctor, who was administering a medispray to a young boy.

"The boy has it right. We'll have everyone here as fresh as a Polomian magic spa before you know it," Nee said, getting a smile from the kid he was working on.

Tarlen was at peace seeing his people being rescued.

He had no idea if anyone was going to come for them, or if Captain Baldwin had made it through the wormhole or not, but they'd managed to find the remainder of the Bacal, and that was enough for him.

Another fifty crew members were on the surface with them, spread out from the rest of their fleet, and he heard someone mention the Prime's name. Tarlen glanced to the doorway, where Prime Xune and Admiral Benitor walked in. Xune's face lit up as he saw the survivors, and Tarlen saw the honest man at that moment. The Concord was in good hands.

Nurse Kelli was wrapping a medicated bandage on someone's leg, and Tarlen left Belna with her. His sister had a knack for the medical bay, and he expected she'd ask to be trained in the field sooner rather than later. He hoped the two of them could stay on *Constantine* together, if they ever did return home.

"What's the word, Lieutenant Commander Daak?" Prime Xune asked Brax, and Tarlen came to stand with them.

"About forty injuries that we're tending to. Another one hundred or so are extremely malnourished, and almost all are dehydrated," Brax advised them.

Admiral Benitor scanned the room. "And a total head count?"

"Three thousand and twenty-four Bacal. The others number just under a thousand," Brax said.

Tarlen was shocked by the totals.

"And do we trust them all?" Benitor asked, implying there would be some like Ina and her companions, who'd brought lies and a virus to their ship.

"Nope. But I don't expect resistance now that the Statu are gone. There would be no point." Brax was optimistic about it, and so was Tarlen.

"Good work. Next we must decide on shelter." The Prime smiled as he looked at the people filing outside into the bright hot afternoon.

Tarlen followed Brax outside and was surprised by how quickly the drones were putting up temporary accommodations. They were going to remain on the surface until they knew what was happening with the wormhole.

"We'll stay in this location until we find a better spot: flatter land, no sand, and somewhere with a fresh water supply and an opportunity for growing food sources," Xune said.

"What if they never return?" Tarlen asked, his voice small.

Brax shook his head. "We'll make the trip ourselves. Leave everyone here like a colony and come back through the wormhole when we make it to Concord space."

"That'll take years." Tarlen hoped it didn't come to that, but being with his rescued people and the great crew of *Constantine*, he was fully aware the predicament could be a lot worse.

Someone called for assistance with a water station, and Tarlen jogged over, ready to help in any way he could.

Reeve walked through the grass, happy to feel the heat of the sun on her face. She'd spent so many years in the boiler rooms on starships and too few moments enjoying life like this. There was nothing left for her to do on *Constantine*, and she'd even moved from each Concord ship in their shrunken fleet to run diagnostics on each of their Star Drives.

When she was satisfied everything was in working order after the battles, she finally relented and took a shuttle to Casonu Two's new colony village. It was rough, still, but already they were beginning to plow fields, using modified tools from the retired ships' cargo holds. Some had been used as museums at one point and held strange devices Reeve didn't even understand the functions of.

Fires crackled around the village, people cooking meat from a fat six-legged animal. Even though it smelled good, she was heading for the lake, where her brother had said he'd be.

Four thousand plus their crews wasn't a lot of people, but spread out along the field's edge like this, it made their colony seem so much larger. Everyone appeared to be aligning, and tasks were being handled with efficiency. The Bacal were hard-working people, and even though the slaves with the white eyes weren't able to control their own bodies, they still took to commands, and the Prime justified their labor, saying they would want to help regardless. The only slave returned to her own mind was Tarlen's sister, Belna, and she agreed with the Prime.

Drones hovered in the air, watching over camp, and Reeve was confident they weren't going to encounter any resistance here on the planet. Basker had tracked down any remaining Tubers, and their fleet had handled the cities and any pieces of warships large enough to pose a future threat.

By all intents and purposes, this planet was theirs now. As far as homes went, they could have done worse. Tall trees hugged the lake's edge, and she smiled as she heard animals chittering away inside, upset by their interference.

"We don't want to be here either, friends," Reeve whispered to the hiding creatures as she walked through a newly-formed path leading to the water. It smelled damp, musky, and her boots found loose rocks as she closed in on the beach. Using her hand as a visor, she scanned the lake, spotting her brother a couple hundred yards to her left.

She took her time, enjoying the outside air, and eventually found Brax standing at the lake's edge, holding a wooden rod with a string attached to it.

"What's this all about?" she asked, grinning at him.

"It's fishing. Something an old Bacal man taught me. He made this himself." Brax held his arm out, showing her the woodwork.

"Very nice. What does it do?" she asked.

"On Greblok, they have something they call fish. Kind of like Nolix's ceephels, but with fins and no legs. We found a similar creature here, and it turns out they're almost as good as Cronski, if you can believe it." Brax wasn't in uniform, just the pants with a white shirt on, and he looked about as happy as she'd ever seen him.

"You want to stay, don't you?" she asked, taking a seat on an overturned log near the water.

Brax joined her but shrugged. "Would it be the worst thing?"

"I'd miss it all."

"So would I, but you know how I feel…"

"About space?" She laughed.

"Right. Being on the ground is kind of a nice change, and a simple existence where we hunt, catch, and grow our own food sounds kind of tantalizing," he told her.

"I can see doing this for a few days but, Brax, you'll grow bored. We all will. We're born for adventure, for the thrill of the chase, not sitting with a stick in our hands waiting for life to happen." Reeve spoke with passion and realized how much she meant the words.

"You're right, sister. But can I enjoy this for a little while longer?" he asked, and she nodded.

"You have another of those sticks?" she asked, and he passed her the one he was holding.

"You can use mine."

They sat there, chatting about nothing and everything for hours, and only moved when the sun began setting. As they neared camp, empty-handed, Reeve heard the content sounds of the villagers eating and talking.

They found Tarlen and his sister with Treena Starling, Admiral Benitor, and the Prime, who looked like everyone else as he sat around the fire, talking amiably with an older Bacal woman. Even Ven was smiling, the fire dancing in the reflection of his eyes.

Reeve would want to be tucked away in her boiler room eventually, but for now, there was no place she'd rather be.

---

*A*fter three weeks, Tom had grown very tired of walking the corridors of Earon Station. He'd decided to spend a few days on Earon, opting to visit a quaint seaside town along the north edge of Vanosh, but with each rotation of the planet, he was more anxious about their progress.

Tom checked his tablet, seeing no incoming messages from Zolin, and he dropped it to the couch, disappointed. Still no updates. He'd planned on coming to this place to cool his head and take a short break, but Tom couldn't bring himself to return to the station, where they waited on the processed Greblok ore shipment.

He sensed the engineers were annoyed with his persistent questions, and he took the hint. No, he'd stay here until they told him otherwise.

Tom walked through the rustic cabin, heading for the wide doors that slid open at his arrival, revealing the wavy sea beyond. This morning was rainy, a rare downpour for the time of the season along the northern coast, but he didn't mind. A good rainstorm cleared out debris and dust, and he wished it would also absolve his worried thoughts.

Were Zolin and Yephion keeping something from him? Admiral Molan had suggested they'd have the resources to power the wormhole generator in two weeks, and they were way past that now.

Tom glanced to the sky, as if he could see distant space beyond the clouds. A thunderclap boomed across the sea, lightning forking through the cool air. His balcony was wooden, as long as the cabin, and he walked along the wet surface in bare feet.

He missed his ship. He hadn't been captain very long, but he already yearned for his captain's quarters. He wanted the recycled air and overly simple cuisine that came with a cruise ship. He'd also begun to grow accustomed to the crew and their habits, and wished to be among them again.

Most of the anxiety he felt was related to the unknown. Had they all survived? Were they waiting there, or had they resolved to give up hope of a rescue? There were too many questions regarding his people, and he hated the fact that he was on this side, rather than with them.

The rain seemed about to slow, and Tom almost saw the sun peeking through the thinning clouds when they turned dark once again, matching his mood. They unleashed more precipitation, and Tom stood there, leaning over the thick wooden railing, getting soaked as he stared at the waves hitting the rocks only a handful of yards from his cabin.

A green creature he didn't know the name for bounded over the slippery rocks and into the water. Tom saw another following it into the sea, and smiled. If only life were so simple.

A beeping sound shook him from his reverie, and he sprinted inside, careful not to stumble on the wet deck. It was coming from his tablet, and he ran to the couch, dripping on the floor.

The message was from Zolin, and it said three words. *We are ready.*

He was back at Earon Station six hours later, jogging toward his ship, *Cleo*. A veritable fleet had been assembled to return through the wormhole, in case the Statu had won or brought reinforcements, but Tom hoped they wouldn't need any of them.

Zolin and Yephion were in the modified cruiser with the generator built in, and Tom sent them a message as he powered his expedition ship to life. *Is everything in order?*

The reply came promptly. *Waiting on your word.*

Tom grinned and strapped in, smoothing a hand over his uniform's chest. It felt good to be wearing his captain's red collar again after a few weeks without it. It was almost like he'd lost his identity wearing normal clothing.

He eased from the hangar, moving toward the location of the pending wormhole's arrival. The other Concord vessels were there, and he acknowledged the fleet through his viewer. "Hello, Captain Dannlo and our esteemed Ugna escorts. Thank you for the support." Dannlo was in a ten-year-old cruise ship, one of the newest models created before *Constantine* broke the mold.

"Good day, Baldwin. Glad to be of assistance. Is there anything we should know that the admiral may have left out?" Dannlo asked. He was a skinny Tekol, and his Zilph'i commander leaned in, whispering in his ear. "Commander Zyler tells me you think the Statu are gone."

"I'd put all the credits in your account on it," Baldwin said, winking at the captain.

He laughed in return. "Small wager, then. Let's hope you're right about this."

The image vanished, and Tom slowed *Cleo*, reaching out to Zolin. The engineer's face appeared on the viewer. "Okay, Zolin. Tell me, do you have enough ore to do this again?"

"Again? More than just the once?" Zolin looked petrified.

"Relax, we won't need that. Open the wormhole," Tom ordered, pressing his back into the pilot's seat in anticipation.

The colors spouted from the generator, shooting past *Cleo* in a kaleidoscope of bright hues. It wasn't long before the wormhole was open, and Yephion sent a message saying it was fully operational. Tom had been waiting for weeks for this moment, but something held him back. A growing worry for what might be on the other side filled his mind, and his hand froze on the throttle.

"Until we meet in the Vastness," he whispered, and sent *Cleo* inside the swirling entrance.

———

*T*reena Starling was bored. The executive crew was taking turns sitting on the bridge, and for now, it was only her and Lieutenant Darl filling out the seats. She thought she heard him breathing heavily and guessed the man was

dozing off. Any other time, that would be a fireable of-
fense, but since they'd done nothing but sit here, being
lulled by the constant chimes of the computer scanners
for hours, she'd cut the man some slack.

He was doing a good job replacing Zare, and she'd
told him as much before their shift began.

She'd been enjoying their little camp life below on
Casonu Two, but she was fully aware they'd have to leave
at some point. Brax seemed the most at home down
there, and she was considering ordering him to remain
behind to lead the colony during their mission to return
to Concord space.

It had been too long for the wormhole not to have
appeared again. It meant one thing. The Concord thought
them a lost cause and a danger, meaning they wouldn't be
reopening it any time soon. They'd speculated endlessly
about the fact that another fleet might be arriving to fend
off any Statu, but the Prime was clear on one thing: they
didn't have the resources. Not with the recent Border attacks and concerns with the Assembly.

Treena could only hope for the best, but she was
pragmatic. They'd have to do this themselves.

She checked the radars again, doing this process with
each passing hour, more as a device to keep her concentration, and she saw the nearest Ugna vessel out from the
planet in the direction of the wormhole's initial location.
There was another ship, *Andron,* a couple of hundred
thousand kilometers past the Ugna, in an effort to relay
messages should the rift return.

So far, it had all been quiet. Treena was about to
stand and walk the bridge for a moment, when the message came in from the Ugna.

The image of the pale female captain appeared, and
she spoke in a rush of excitement, rare for her race.

"Commander Starling. We have received word from *Andron*. The wormhole has returned, and a Concord fleet has arrived in-system."

Darl jumped in his seat as the voice carried through the bridge, and Treena watched him wipe a string of drool from his mouth with his sleeve. His eyes darted from the screen to her, and Treena stood, walking to the center of the viewer. "Is Captain Baldwin there?" she asked, listening as the question was dispatched.

"Yes. Captain Baldwin is among them."

Treena tapped the communicator and couldn't hide her elation as she reached out to the crew on the surface of Casonu Two. "Bridge to the executive crew."

"Brax here." Of course he was the first to reply.

"We have word that the captain is back."

"We're going home?" Reeve asked over the speaker.

"Yes, we are."

TWENTY-FOUR

*I*t felt right to be reunited with his ship. Constantine's AI walked alongside Tom as he strode through the corridors, moving with purpose for the meeting room, where the others awaited his arrival.

"Con, glad to see me?" Tom asked, not expecting an honest reply.

"Actually, I am, sir."

"Truthfully?" He stopped outside the entrance, facing the AI.

"Yes. As you know, I do have your grandfather's memories, and you've become somewhat of a routine…"

"I get it. I'm routine, so a computer program appreciates it," he said with a laugh.

Constantine smirked. "Something like that, sir."

Tom pressed the meeting room doors open and saw it was half full. Commander Starling stood as he entered, as did the others. Reeve was the first to arrive, and she threw her arms around him, pulling him into an embrace.

"It's good to see you, Captain," his chief engineer told him.

She broke away, and her twin patted Tom on the shoulder, giving it a squeeze. "Thank you for coming back."

The commander nodded to him, while Ven remained standing near the table. Nee walked over, saying he was happy to see the captain, and Tom mirrored the sentiment.

"I can't say it was fun waiting for the ore to be replaced, but here we are," Tom said, and Reeve's jaw dropped.

"That was the problem. We didn't calculate the energy drain to use the destabilizer and reboot the system. Zolin must have been kicking himself," Reeve said, running a hand over her face.

"No. He blamed you and took no responsibility," Tom joked.

"Really?"

"I'm kidding. It was fine. I was on pins and needles wondering what happened here, but I see you survived the last of the Statu. How many losses?" Tom asked, and Brax gave him the rundown of destroyed vessels and a total body count. It was too many. "I'm glad it's over. All were welcomed into the Vastness, of that I'm sure."

Prime Xune and the admiral greeted him, Benitor actually smiling at him. "Captain, you did well."

"Thank you. From what I could see, so did you. Haven't lost your touch?" he asked, and she shook her head.

"Fill me in," Tom said as they all took their seats. He sat beside Ven and patted the Ugna on the arm. "Ven, are you feeling okay?"

"I've been dreaming a lot lately," he said, his words slightly cryptic.

"About what?" Tom asked, glancing around the room. It didn't feel like the right time to be talking about his sleep patterns.

"The pattern of lights." Ven blinked a few times and turned to look Tom in the eyes. "But perhaps we can discuss this later."

"Very well. Are we prepared to bring the Bacal and

others onto our cruise ships?" Tom asked.

"Yes, we are. Captain, there's a group of them that have chosen to stay behind," Treena told him.

"Really?" He was a little surprised to hear this. "Why is that?"

Brax answered for them. "Mostly the older ones that have lived here for nearly all of their lives. They don't feel like there's a place for them back home any longer."

"Surely we'll help assimilate them into..." Tom peered at Admiral Benitor, whose lips were pursed.

"We've made the offer, but they've declined," she said.

"Okay. How many?"

"Three hundred in total, counting the ones from the warship we've held prisoner. We've asked the others, and they'll accept them into their community," Prime Xune said.

"And Ina?" Tom asked, knowing he'd offered her something else.

"She'll return to the surface," Xune said.

Tom shook his head. "I told her I'd bring her to Earon after it was over, if she helped me. She did."

"Tom, I don't think..." Benitor began, but Tom cut her off.

"I'm sorry. I'm a man of my word." He said this while staring her in the eyes. It had more than one meaning, and Benitor appeared to comprehend it.

"Fine. She can stay."

"Good. We'll bring the Bacal home, and escort Doctor DeLarose and the R-emergence team to Greblok immediately," Doctor Nee said.

"Then it's settled. Now, how about I see this little village before we leave?" Tom asked.

---

*I*na had been in her suite for days on end, weeks, but she was learning so much about the Concord in the meantime. A man named Constantine spent hours at a time with her, teaching her all about the Founders, the Code, and the many partners around Concord Space. It was the most exhilarating experience of her life.

She still didn't know what was to befall her, and the flickering computer program wouldn't answer her ceaseless inquiries about her eventual fate.

Ina showered, enamored at the wonderful technology, and dressed in a plain white jumpsuit. She dried her growing hair, using the brush afterwards. She stared in the mirror, barely recognizing her reflection. Her eyes were brighter, her cheeks not so hollow. The Adepts had lied about everything, and she was finally getting a chance to learn the truth about her people. Constantine was honest about it all, as far as she could tell, and humans didn't always do the honorable thing. But, truthfully, no one did.

If people could forgive the Concord's indiscretions, she hoped they'd forgive hers as well.

There was a chime, indicating someone was at the door, and she told the computer to let them in. None other than Captain Baldwin strode through, tall and handsome, looking much better than the last time they'd spoken. She supposed she did as well.

"Ina." The single word nearly brought tears to her eyes.

"Captain."

"We're leaving Casonu now," he told her, standing near the door. She peered over his shoulder, expecting an armed guard ready to escort her to a shuttle.

"I understand. I'll gather my…"

"Would you like to stay with us? I did tell you I'd bring you to Earon. I asked around while I was there, and used the surname you thought might have been your mother's. Turns out you have some cousins back home." The captain even smiled, his eyes growing bright as he delivered the news.

She stood speechless, but nodded, not trusting her voice.

"Then feel free to wander around." The captain called for Constantine, and the AI appeared. "Please escort our friend Ina if she wants to see the rest of our cruise ship."

"Yes, sir."

And with that, Captain Baldwin left Ina alone to contemplate her unknown future.

———

*T*homas Baldwin sat on the bridge of his cruise ship, *Constantine,* as they traveled out of the wormhole and into Earon's system. The trip had been uneventful, and Tom let out a sigh of relief as the other vessels trailed behind him.

The AI stood behind his chair, and Commander Starling appeared pleased with the entire venture. Ships lined a pathway for them to return to Earon Station, and Tom was shocked by how many of the Concord fleet, as well as private crafts, were in attendance.

"It looks like word spread," Treena said, and Tom laughed, thinking it was probably the loose lips from Gideon's Grill that told everyone the war with the Statu was finally over for good.

"A guy could get used to a return home like this,"

Brax said from his weapons station.

Prime Xune and the admiral were on *Shu*, and they remained behind *Constantine*, letting the now most-famous vessel in the Concord take the lead as they neared Earon Station. The wormhole collapsed behind them once they were sure all of their fleet had emerged, and Tom breathed a little easier after it was closed.

Instead of docking in their usual spot, Ven guided what remained of the retired fleet toward the archives, and they waited in anticipation as *Andron, Persi,* and the other few headed for the warehouse entrance.

Tom's attention drew to the viewer when Prime Xune's face appeared, Captain Rene Bouchard beside him, and Commander Kan Shu to his left. He spoke with a soft and caring tone, and drew everyone's attention. "We have been remiss in retiring some of these vessels prematurely. With recent discoveries, we realized that some of these moves were made without the best interest of our people at the heart of them. With that being said, I'm hereby bringing *Andron* and *Persi* out of retirement, along with a few other capable vessels. This will create some new opportunities for our hard-working Concord fleet crew members, but also a superior sense of peace along the Borders.

"The Statu have been vanquished, but we must focus on the positives, and deal with anyone from outside Concord Space trying to fight what we've just sacrificed many lives to uphold."

Tom leaned forward, aware this conversation would be heard around the Concord, and for years to come.

The Prime spoke again. "We have word that the Ugna home planet has been chosen, and they will be escorted to their new home in a few weeks. We've also heard the petition of five more worlds that would like to enter our fold, and we expect to have our decision shortly. The Concord has been through some tough times, but we're on the right track. Together, we'll ensure a bright future for all Concord members.

"*Without the past, there is no determining the outcome of the future.* We take this saying of the Code literally, and are confident that we can make our alliance stronger than ever."

The communication ended, and Tom's crew beamed at the Prime's words. With his grandfather's old command floating through space, no longer heading for the archives, Tom asked Ven to return them to Earon Station, where they would debrief with the rest of their fleet before being given another mission.

A few hours later, Tom was in his quarters, lying on his bed and wishing sleep would finally get hold of him. The events of the last few months kept circling around his mind, replaying in a constant loop. So much had happened...

Someone was at his door, and Tom sat up. "Enter."

"Captain Baldwin, I'm sorry for coming to your private quarters like this," Admiral Benitor said.

Tom quickly threw a shirt on and motioned for her to sit on the couch. "Think nothing of it. I was just staring at the ceiling anyway. Can I get you something to drink?"

"Sure. How about something strong?" she suggested.

Tom wondered what that meant for a seasoned Callalay admiral and went to the cupboards, pouring two liberal amounts of a brown liquid into clear glasses. He passed one to her and sat on the chair beside her. He lifted his glass, and they clinked them. He'd already done this again with Treena, his tradition after a successful mission. This didn't have the same feel to it. "What can I do for you, Admiral?"

"Call me Jalin, Tom."

"Okay… Jalin. What has you walking the corridors of *Constantine* at two in the morning?"

She met his gaze, her eyes pale and sad. "We have three more flagships in production. As you've suggested, one of them will be made to replace *Cecilia*, using the Link you returned for her. We've managed to improve the AI from the old model, and you'll be pleasantly surprised at the upgrades."

"That's good news. Surely that look on your face isn't because of this?" Tom took a sip, the drink strong, and it warmed his throat as it went down.

"We're short of good people, Tom. It's the price we pay. We fight a war, and executive teams are torn apart with promotions and new ships. It happens every time."

Tom had been so focused on this mission that he hadn't spent any time considering that his crew might be separated. "Who is it?" He leaned back and stared at her intensely while he waited for the reply.

"We want Commander Starling to captain *Cecilia*. We saw how she's handled her situation, and she continues to take charge, sticking her neck out and saving the day on each of your first three main missions." She paused, and Tom felt her hand settle on his knee. "Tom. Show me your support."

He did and gave her a small grin.

"This will be a good thing for the Concord. You know that." Jalin Benitor was an honorable woman and a great admiral, and Tom had no choice but to trust her.

"Fine. I see there's no way I can change your mind. I was getting used to things. With the Statu and Assembly behind us, I thought we could start to make a difference," Tom said quietly.

"You don't think you've made a difference so far?"

She laughed; the sound was pleasant, and she sank deeper into the couch as she finished her drink off, setting the glass on a side table next to her. "You really are a big dreamer, just like he was."

"Constantine?"

She nodded. "He was so much like you, but you have focus and drive for the missions that he never had."

"Because of his wife and my mother." Tom said it as a statement, not a question.

"That's right. Tom..." She paused again, reaching out her glass. He took it and went to refill it, while she continued, "There's more."

He stopped as he corked the decanter and turned to her, both hands full. "More?"

"We want you to escort the Elders to Driun F49," she said, taking the offered drink.

This was no surprise to him. "I thought we'd already discussed this."

"When you return, you'll no longer be the captain of *Constantine*." She took another sip, and Tom's arms felt like lead as they fell to his sides.

"What are you saying? I'm being let go? How can you do this?" The questions came fast and hard, his heart racing. He'd spent his entire life leading up to gaining a captaincy. "I know I've done some things with a little more... gusto than you might have liked, but the job..."

"Tom. Stop!" Her words were firm, and he obeyed, his expression somber. "We want to promote you to Admiral. We still have two openings, and the Prime and I agree that you're the best candidate to accompany me on the board. The Founders are all behind the decision, even Longshade, who you seemed to have agitated with your last visit."

Admiral? Tom slunk into his seat and grabbed the

liquor, taking a drink. "Are you serious?"

"I am."

"I'm too young…"

"You're not that young. You're older than your grandfather was…"

"Times were different. I…" So many emotions coursed through him, and he had no idea what to say.

"Say you'll do it."

Tom glanced up, meeting her gaze. The admiral was smiling, a rare sight, and he nodded. "Do I have a choice?"

"There's always a choice, Tom."

"Can I think about it?" he asked.

"You can have until you return from Driun F49. Is that fair?" Jalin asked.

He nodded and clenched his teeth, preparing for his next ask. "We never resolved Seda and Luci."

Jalin surprised him. "I've been meaning to discuss that with you. We've come to a decision."

TWENTY-FIVE

*T*he shuttle settled to the ground at the end of her mother's driveway. It was a gloomy day, rain dripping over the viewer. Tom was beside her, and he'd been abnormally quiet for the entire trip, as if he had something important on his mind.

Treena powered the shuttle down and turned to her captain. "Look... say it already."

He smiled at her, his perfect jawline and dimples making her wish for a moment that she wasn't wearing a robotic body. "Treena..."

Something was wrong, and she panicked for a moment. Was it about her mother? Luci? She'd spoken to her mom only yesterday.

"There's no easy way to tell you this, so I'll just do it. They want to offer you the newly improved *Cecilia*."

Treena sat motionless, letting the words wash over her like the rain that beat down on the hull of the shuttle. "Offer? As in..."

"Captain Starling. That has a nice ring to it, don't you think?" he asked.

She started to panic, the last couple years of recovery from her near-death experience threatening to envelop her. Tom seemed to notice, and he grabbed her hand. "This is a great opportunity for you, Treena."

"I know. But we were starting to be a real crew. A

great one too."

"You can start your own great crew," he said.

Treena tried to consider it, but it was too much at that moment. "I don't want to leave *Constantine*. I don't think I'm ready. I don't want to leave you, and Ven, and Reeve... even Brax." She laughed, trying to imagine working alongside anyone but that executive team. They'd accepted her in a way she'd never expected, and she honestly felt like they were as much her family as the woman in the house at the end of the driveway. She stared toward the home, where her mother would be sitting with Luci, waiting for their entrance, and contemplated her future.

"If you like, you can come with us to Driun F49 and decide after that. We've been offered some time," he said, and she caught his slip.

"We?"

His expression gave him away. "I haven't told anyone, but they want me to take a role as admiral."

If Thomas Baldwin was gone from *Constantine*, would that make her decision even easier? What if she stayed there as captain? Treena had too many questions and decided now wasn't the time for an answer.

"I'll come with you. Thank you for telling me. You really think I'd make it as a captain?" she asked.

"The best." He smiled again, and it reached his eyes.

Treena headed out the side of the shuttle, and they jogged through the rain, avoiding puddles the entire way. As they neared the entrance of the house, the doors flung open to reveal the small blonde girl, with Karen behind her, a hand settled on the girl's shoulder.

"Captain Baldwin!" Luci said, rushing to hug the man's leg. "Hi, Treena!" Treena received her own embrace, and she crouched, wrapping her arms around the small child.

Her mother waved them inside, where it was dry and warm; a fire crackled in the wood-burning fireplace across the living room.

"Thank you for watching her," Tom told Karen, and Treena's mom smiled.

"It's going to be tough letting her go. I forgot how much I enjoyed having a little girl around." Her gaze met Treena's, and tears formed around her eyes.

"Mom, always so dramatic. Luci will be heading to a village on Leria with her mother," Treena advised them.

Luci appeared torn. "My mom?"

"That's right," Tom said. "You'll be with your mom in a few days."

Luci cried now, and Karen held the girl as she let out two months' worth of pent-up emotions. "It'll be okay, Luci. Your mother misses you."

Treena knew the Prime hadn't wanted to change his original orders, but if there was anyone with the ability to change the Prime's mind, it was Thomas Baldwin. He held a strange power over those around him, and it was difficult to tell him no.

"What will I do?" Karen asked, leading them into the kitchen where a pot of tea was boiling.

"You'll figure it out, Mom. Maybe it's time you thought about yourself for a change. Didn't you always want to visit Kevis VII? Say the word, and you'll have the nicest beachside villa for a month," Treena said, and this seemed to brighten the gloomy mood emanating from her mother.

"That would be nice, dear."

"Then it's settled," Treena said, and they all took a seat around the table, letting her mom pour steaming tea for them.

Luci asked questions about where she was going, if

Karen was coming, if there would be trees and lakes and birds at their new home. Treena enjoyed the quiet afternoon, knowing there would be a lot of hard decisions coming up in the near future.

---

*I*t felt wonderful to be home on Greblok. Tarlen walked the streets of Malin, his home city, and Doctor Nee struggled to keep up. He was constantly gawking at the ancient structures, most of them being rebuilt with the assistance of the Concord's construction drones. The city was really coming together, and Tarlen almost couldn't tell that the entire place had been a pile of rubble a few months prior.

"What do you think?" he asked the doctor.

"I think the Bacal are a wonderful race of beings," Nee said, huffing from their long walk. "But they need some work on the public transportation. Do you really walk everywhere?"

"Sure."

"That explains why you're all so skinny," Nee said with a laugh, and Tarlen waved at Belna as he saw her outside their destination. "Thank you for the tour, son. It was enlightening."

The sun was beginning to set, and the air was already cooling. Tarlen noticed Penter beside Belna as they approached, and the two were deep in conversation.

"Penter," Tarlen said, nodding to the older man.

"Tarlen. I was just telling your sister about a great opportunity here in Malin," the former guard said.

Belna met his gaze, and it was clear she was excited about something. She'd been given contacts, coloring her irises again, and it was almost strange to see her with something other than white eyes now. "What is it?" Tarlen asked.

"They want me to work in the new R-emergence clinic that Doctor DeLarose is setting up here," she said.

"That's amazing," Tarlen told her, following his sister into the building.

There were a handful of Bacal inside, mostly family of the rescued slaves from the Statu world. At this point, half of them had been treated, with the rest being cared for while they waited their turn. Each of the surgeries had been successful, and they hoped that streak would continue.

Tarlen had searched through them on Casonu Two, trying to find his parents, but they weren't among the group, and he was confident now that they were lost into the Vastness forever.

"Why don't you stay too?" Belna asked, and he thought about the offer. "Come on, Tar. This is your home. These are your people. Plus, I don't want us to be far apart. We're all the family we have."

Tarlen glanced at Nee, who was pretending not to listen in on their conversation, and he smiled at Belna. "I'll think about it." Tarlen would miss *Constantine* if he stayed on Greblok. He'd miss all his new friends, and he'd hardly had any time with Kriss to see what that kiss had been about. But the idea of spending his days waking up in his old home and working to better Malin was awfully enticing as well.

"Good. Now, how about we see where we can help?"

"Ven Ittix, you look well." Elder Fayle's voice brought him out of his meditation, and he peered over the courtyard to see the Ugna leader walking toward him.

He stood in greeting as she arrived. "Elder Fayle, how do you like this space? The water reminds me of our meditation pools at home."

She glanced around the courtyard. "I think it's fine in a pinch. Where is the rest of the crew? The ship seems quiet."

"They're each attending to their own tasks, some personal, some for the good of the Concord," Ven told her.

He hadn't felt like himself recently, and he knew why. "Elder Hamesly told me some interesting information."

It was difficult to shock Fayle, but this did it. Her eyes squinted as she regained her composure. "What did he tell you?"

"That you're poison. That the Ugna seek power and are forcing children into drugs, and that it will only grow worse as you expand beyond the Zilph'i, bringing in other Founders." Ven studied her face, which remained stoic.

"Elder Hamesly is not well."

"He's no longer albino. He looks like any Zilph'i. He claims that you cannot only refrain from En'or, but also from the Talent, and that after some time, I could be as him. Free from the Ugna." Ven said the words without conviction, only fact.

"And is that what you seek, child?" she asked.

"No. But I wish to learn more. I don't think your motives are evil, but I don't understand them either," Ven admitted.

"It is time, then, Ven Ittix. Come to Driun F49 with us, and I will complete your training," she offered.

Ven had expected to confront her with the information and encounter some rebuttal, but not this. "I will consider the invitation."

"Very good. Now, how have you been feeling?"

"I see a pattern. My senses are stronger than ever, and I no longer have need of En'or," he said.

"You have brought a piece of the Vastness with you. Close your eyes and let me teach you something." She sat beside him on the bench and took his hand.

Elder Fayle began to hum, repeating her mantra. He joined, and soon he felt them lift off the bench, growing weightless. He saw the lights, the pattern dancing in his eyelids, and she spoke, explaining so much, yet so little.

———————

*A*fter a couple of weeks away from the bridge, Tom felt like he'd returned home. Everyone was here, and he wondered if this would be his last mission as captain of the flagship. He smiled at Constantine's AI, and the man only tilted his head in a knowing nod.

Brax Daak looked rested, and his sister was on the opposite end of the bridge: a rare occurrence, since she preferred the comfort of her boiler room. Commander Starling was beside Tom, and seeing all of the executive crew in one place felt... right.

Tarlen was still on Greblok, helping his people recover. Tom knew the boy would have a bright future in whatever endeavors he sought out.

Luci had departed aboard an unmarked freighter a few days ago, and she was likely reunited with Seda by now. He hoped the woman, who'd been an enemy of the Concord, understood and appreciated the bending of the rules for her. Tom hadn't made the bargain for her benefit, but a child shouldn't grow up without a parent. He could attest to that.

Tom checked the radar, seeing the twenty or so Ugna vessels that were coming with them to Driun F49. The system was far from the Founders, twice the distance as Earon was from Nolix, and that was where the Concord had decided was the best fit for their newest member. Never before had a race that was technically part of one of the Founders been granted recognition as their own Concord partner, and now Thomas Baldwin was bringing them there. His resume was filling up quickly.

"Captain, the Ugna are prepared for departure," Ven advised, and Tom remained seated. From here, Earon Station hung to their right, a giant structure with many purposes. He'd been glad to spend some time studying it, but didn't plan on returning any time soon. He thought about being planetside, perhaps in Nolix with the other admirals, and a shiver shot through his veins.

Thomas Baldwin wasn't meant to sit in an office, high above the ground in a skyscraper, stuck in the middle of a city with millions of bodies around him.

He was meant to be among the stars.

It was in his blood.

"Bring us out," he told Ven, and *Constantine* led the way, moving from Earon Station, then the human home world.

Soon the Star Drive kicked in, and Tom smiled as they began their escort mission.

EPILOGUE

Elder Fayle checked over her shoulder, knowing no one was there. It was a habit when she traveled away from her village on Leria. She'd never trusted anyone but her own people.

Her console displayed a messaging system, and she sat motionless, using her mind to press the keypad. Re-routing the security on *Constantine* was simpler than she'd expected, and a minute later, she was confident the communication would be secure. There would be no record of the transmission, and she peered one last time to the locked door before beginning the call.

She cleared her throat, her mouth dry from hours of meditation.

His face appeared, the room he occupied dim and dank. "High Elder Wylen. I apologize for the delay in our interaction."

"No need to apologize, Elder Fayle. I understand you've been busy. I heard the news. You have done well to secure the planet. How much do they know?" His voice was like gravel, his eyes red as lava.

"Only what we agreed upon," she advised, proud of the fact she'd managed to join the Concord so easily. They'd speculated the timing could have been worse, but strings had been pulled in order for them to achieve their goals.

"They don't suspect anything?" he asked.

"They are unaware of our contact with the Statu, or the fact that we funded the Assembly." Everything had been performed with timely precision, placing the Concord in a state of desperation. At their lowest, it had been easy to swoop in and save the day.

"And your recruit? This Ven Ittix?"

"He knows nothing, but he's curious. I'll keep an eye on him," Elder Fayle said.

"If he's too inquisitive, you know what to do," her superior rasped.

She nodded but felt in her heart that killing Ven wasn't an option. He was like a son to her. "Anything else you would like from me?" she asked, scared of what he might suggest.

"Secure our home. We'll move to stage two when it's time."

"And when will that be?" she asked.

"Await the signal." The image of the bald pale man shrouded in shadows vanished, leaving her screen blank. Her own reflection stared back at her, and she shuddered, knowing she must live with the dire things she'd carried out.

She peered to the viewscreen on the wall, seeing that they'd departed Earon space, moving toward her final destination. Elder Fayle closed her eyes, hoping she'd find forgiveness in the Vastness one day.

The End

ABOUT THE AUTHOR

Nathan Hystad is an author from Sherwood Park, Alberta, Canada. Follow him at www.nathanhytad.com for news on releases and special deals.

CPSIA information can be obtained
at www.ICGtesting.com
Printed in the USA
BVHW052023070622
639130BV00003B/39